The Federal Case

Also by J.B. Manheim:

FICTION

The Deadball Files

Book 1: This Never Happened:
The Mystery Behind the Death of Christy Mathewson

Book 2: TheGameKeepers:
Whitewash, Blackmail, and Baseball's Darkest Secrets

Book 3: Doubleday Doubletake:
One Ball, Three Strikes, One Man Out

SELECTED NONFICTION

Strategy in Information and Influence Campaigns:
How Policy Advocates, Social Movements, Insurgent Groups,
Corporations, Governments and Others Get What They Want

Strategic Public Diplomacy and American Foreign Policy

All of the People, All the Time:
Strategic Communication and American Politics

The Federal Case

BOOK FOUR of The Deadball Files

a novel by
J. B. Manheim

MILFORD
HOUSE
an imprint of Sunbury Press, Inc.
Mechanicsburg, PA USA

MILFORD HOUSE

an imprint of Sunbury Press, Inc.
Mechanicsburg, PA USA

FIRST MILFORD HOUSE PRESS EDITION: July 2023

Set in Adobe Garamond Pro | Interior design by Crystal Devine | Cover by Lawrence Knorr | Edited by Sarah Peachey.

The Gambler: Words and Music by Don Schlitz. Copyright @1977 Sony Music Publishing (US) LLC. Copyright Renewed. All Rights Administered by Sony Music Publishing (US) LLC, 424 Church Street, Suite 1200, Nashville, TN 37219. International Copyright Secured All Rights Reserved. Reprinted by Permission of Hal Leonard LLC.

Publisher's Cataloging-in-Publication Data
Names: Manheim, J.B., author.
Title: The federal case / J.B. Manheim.
Description: First trade paperback edition. | Mechanicsburg, PA : Milford House Press, 2023.
Summary: A century-old legal battle between Major League Baseball and the upstart Federal League. An old legal document, once lost, now found. Young night-schooled lawyer Andy Dennum takes on the baseball establishment, the law firm that fired him, and a mystery from his own past. At stake? The viability of Major League Baseball's business model, and Andy's future as a lawyer. You win some, you lose some. Some get rained out.
Identifiers: ISBN : 979-8-88819-126-2 (paperback) | ISBN : 979-8-88819-127-9 (ePub).
Subjects: FICTION / Sports | FICTION / Thrillers / Legal | SPORTS & RECREATION / Baseball / General.

Product of the United States of America
0 1 1 2 3 5 8 13 21 34 55

For the Love of Books!

For My Sister Leslie
Always On The Ball, Never Off Base

The Lineup Card

The Box Score

Author's Note

Readers of earlier books in this series may be surprised to discover that the Commissioner has remained a free man. All will become clear. And readers who are just beginning to explore *The Deadball Files* need only know at the outset that the Commissioner is, to put it gently, not a very nice man. Not a very nice man at all.

The Federal Case revolves around subtleties in the law and legal practice. Andy Dennum, the protagonist of this particular tale, is a fictional lawyer, and a young and inexperienced one at that. I am not a lawyer, and I have not even played one on television. Together, Andy and I have made a good faith effort to capture the issues and procedures in question here. For those more knowledgeable in such matters, we hope you will find the product of our efforts to be plausible. We throw ourselves upon the mercy of the reader.

As this book was going to press, the Oakland Athletics baseball team announced its plans for moving to Las Vegas. Just one more wrinkle in *The Federal Case*.

Any thoughts, statements, or actions of actual historical figures portrayed here that go beyond the known and documented historical record should be assumed to be fictitious. Specifically, any thoughts, statements, or actions attributed to Major League Baseball or to any of its affiliated teams or executives, past or present, for the purpose of advancing the storyline exist only in the author's imagination. As for the undertakings of the fictional characters portrayed here, I leave it to the reader to figure out what might be real and what not. It is, as always, a fine line. But wherever that line may fall, the sum of this work lies on the side of fiction.

Making (of) a Federal Case

The structure of professional baseball at the highest level has always been fluid. Major League franchises move from one city to another, the leagues expand and contract and reconfigure themselves, divisions are formed, and divisional boundaries shift in a constant evolution driven by greed, convenience, politics, demographic changes, real estate values, divergent regulatory and tax burdens, and even the weather. The loyalties of fans are less fluid, but only so long as it takes for one generation to pass and another to replace it. But as for the players . . . Ah, the players. They are, as a group, a bundle of emerging and declining skills playing a child's game to support themselves, their families, and their hangers-on, all the while knowing that their shelf-life in that game is limited and disappearing day by day. They are in it for the love of what they do, but they are also primarily in it for the money—sometimes quite a lot of money. It is the clash of these three prevailing forces that defines the history of Major League Baseball and always has.

Professionalism—pay for play—eased its way into the sport through club games in the mid to late nineteenth century, and as it did, a winnowing occurred. Not all teams were good enough to draw followers willing to part with their money for the enjoyment of spectating, and not all players were worthy of being compensated for their play. By 1876, enough cream had risen to the top to permit the churning of butter. The National League of Professional Baseball Clubs, the first to declare itself a "major" league, was formed. The first teams were located in Chicago, Philadelphia, Boston, Hartford, New York, St. Louis, Cincinnati, and

Louisville. By 1880, six of these teams had dropped out and were replaced by the likes of Detroit, Cleveland, Buffalo, and Providence. Other changes followed.

So, too, did other leagues—the American Association, the Union League, the Players League—only to drop back within a year or so. But in the process, these challengers set in motion forces that are still evident in the game today—salary caps, the reserve clause that prevented players from jumping from team to team, and even a players' strike. The National League absorbed some of the cities represented in these leagues, expanding to twelve teams in 1883, and many of their players. Then, in 1900, a lower-level group of teams, called the Western League, rechristened itself as the American League and granted franchises to major cities that had been abandoned by the National League as it underwent its various transformations. In 1901, the American League declared itself a "major" league, offering the same level of play as its older rival. After two years of competing for money and talent, the two organizations reached an accord in 1903, the so-called National Agreement, under which they agreed, in effect, to divide the spoils. This was to be the definitive establishment of Major League Baseball.

Alas, while the National and American Leagues may have agreed to divide the spoils, that did not mean there were no longer spoilers. After all, at the highest level, only the sixteen teams of the two combined leagues had agreed to their arrangement, which created a multi-state, bipartite monopoly. Was that enough to keep the history of foment, jealousy, greed, and opportunism at bay? It was not.

In 1913, the Federal League of Base Ball Clubs began play with teams in six cities. That number expanded to eight, half of which overlapped those of the two established leagues, the following year when the Federal League declared itself the third "major" league. With backing from industrialists like oil baron Harry Sinclair and ice magnate Phil Ball, the Federal League trod a familiar path to growth and legitimacy—pirating players from the established leagues. Known as "kangaroos" for their action, a number of major league players—among them five future inductees to the Baseball Hall of Fame—followed the money and jumped to the Federal League. Battles over contracts made and broken, fan loyalties, faltering attendance, and the like ensued, much as they had in earlier rounds of reorganization.

Then lightning struck. During the 1914–1915 off-season, Federal League owners filed a lawsuit against their American and National League counterparts, claiming that the older leagues were restraining trade in violation of the nation's new antitrust laws. The litigation landed in the court of Federal District Judge Kenesaw Mountain Landis, who encouraged the parties to negotiate but otherwise left the matter to wither away on his docket. As the litigation languished during the 1915 season, the finances of the Federal League deteriorated to the point where it could no longer operate. An informal arrangement was reached under which owners of the American and National League teams bought out four of the Federal League franchises, while two Federal League owners were permitted to purchase a pair of struggling teams in the established leagues.

Left out of the arrangement were two teams, those in Kansas City and Baltimore, the first having been forced by that time to declare bankruptcy and the second having rejected an offer to participate. The Baltimore franchise, the Terrapins, later sued Major League Baseball under the Sherman Anti-Trust Act. In 1922, the Supreme Court decided that case, *Federal Baseball Club v. National League*, in a ruling that exempted baseball from the antitrust laws on the basis that its activities did not amount to traditional interstate commerce. The financial house of Baseball has been built on the foundation of that ruling, and on the resultant shared interests of its franchise holders, for the century and more ever since. Now, that foundation may be about to crumble.

You've go to know when to hold 'em
Know when to fold 'em
Know when to walk away
And know when to run.

—"The Gambler"
Written by Don Schlitz, Performed by Kenny Rogers

Climbing Mount Landis

Kenny, as he was known to friends, sat behind the ornate mahogany desk in his sixth-floor office, but anyone, friend or foe, who had the temerity to call him by that name in *this* place and time would quickly find his goose cooked and his potatoes roasting over an open fire. For this sixth floor was in the Federal Court Building in Chicago, and Kenny happened to be the Honorable Judge of the Northern District of Illinois. It was January 1914, and the Hawk Wind, not yet named, blew hard off the lake and straight down East Adams, swirling around the building's recently completed facade. It was a good thing his beloved Cubs were not playing today.

Kenny loved the trappings of power and knew how to use them to maximum effect. From the bench in Room 627, his marbled courtroom, he looked out on two murals, one of King John accepting the Magna Carta, the other of Moses just before he smashed the first set of tablets bearing the Ten Commandments. The justice Kenny dispensed fell somewhere between the two models. He had the stern countenance of a jurist, the dramatic flare of a thespian, and a name that connoted power: Kenesaw Mountain Landis.

Today's business, however, was best conducted outside public purview, in the confines of his richly paneled office with its mementos of past glories and its framed Cubs pennant, a gift from the club's president, Jim Hart, in whose box at the West Side Grounds he was often sighted. It was matched, in the interests of justice no doubt, with a White Stockings banner, though it was never clear to visitors whether that one represented the Cubs by their original name or their now-crosstown American League rivals who took on the White Stockings moniker once it had been abandoned. Seated across the desk from him were two teams of lawyers, one representing the National and American Leagues, the other the upstart Federal League. The issue was antitrust; specifically the Bill of Complaint that had been filed on January 5 on behalf of the Federal League alleging that the National and American Leagues, their respective presidents, and the team owners, operated as a monopoly to the detriment of the Federal League and its member clubs, and the complainants were hopeful. Landis was the hero of the newly powerful forces of trust-busting, having issued the first major ruling under the Sherman Anti-Trust Act, in which he levied a fine of $29 million on the Standard Oil Company. In the course of that litigation, he had successfully tracked down and summoned to his courtroom none other than John D. Rockefeller himself, then held him to account. The Federals, to their credit, had done a bit of venue shopping, filing in the Northern District of Illinois precisely so that Judge Landis would receive the case.

Edward Gates, managing partner of the Myers and Gates law firm and general counsel for the Federal League, was the first to speak. But, "Your Honor" was as far as he got. Landis held up his hand.

"Gentlemen," he said, addressing both Gates and his colleagues George Pepper and George Miller, representing the National and the American Leagues, respectively, on the defense team. "I have read this complaint, and I await a timely filing from the respondents. I have asked my clerk to schedule a preliminary hearing on the matter for later this month. Let me see . . . yes, Tuesday the twentieth. We'll expect the matter to be concluded that week and no later. See that it is. And let me caution you." He drew his five-foot-seven frame to its full seated height. "Both sides must understand that any blows at the thing called baseball would be regarded by this court as a blow to a national institution. And it is the court's strong preference that this matter be resolved by the parties themselves, preferably in the near term. Have I made myself clear?"

Almost in unison, Gates, Pepper, and Miller all responded, "Yes, Your Honor."

"Then we have no further business today. We'll convene here one hour before the hearing to work out any procedural matters."

And with that, Landis picked up an unrelated brief that had been sitting on his desk and began reading. The assembled attorneys took their cue and quietly filed out of his office. Neither side, however, made any move to open negotiations. Indeed, Gates and the two Georges barely exchanged a word, choosing instead to descend to the street in separate elevators.

<hr>

This was the kind of job that God had created just for first-year associates. Oh, and She was a vengeful God.

Andy Dennum knew he wasn't regarded as the brightest light in the firm's legal candelabra. But he had worked hard at becoming a solid lawyer, spending his days as an insurance investigator for the state to pay for his nights at Madison-Jefferson School of Law, or Mad Jeff's House of Torts as his new colleagues had coined it. If they only knew what the M-J students themselves called the place: The Emergency Room—a richly deserved sobriquet reflecting the number of literal ambulance chasers it produced each year.

Okay, so he wasn't Harvard or Yale or Columbia or Chicago. He knew that. But after a grueling six years of part-time study in the trenches of legal education, he also knew the law. He knew it at a granular level, something those self-righteous twits on seventeen, his fellow associates with their gold-embossed, leatherbound personal legal libraries and their years clerking for this or that Supreme, never would. He told himself that was the reason he'd managed to land a position at Stetson, Varney, and Handelmann, a white-shoe Wall Street firm if ever there was one. But a few days on this, his very first assignment, told a different story. He was nothing more than a stable boy, hired to muck out the detritus of the mergers long past that had eventually birthed this legal powerhouse. And after just over a week spent in the deepest recesses of the firm's basement archive, he was coming to realize just how far down the pecking order he truly was.

"You know you're going to start at the very bottom," his supervising partner, Joey Coy, had told him in what was, perhaps, the greatest understatement of his still-young life. "If you're going to prosper at Stetson, Varney," Joey said, employing the shorthand name everyone used for the firm, "a good place to start is by learning our history. And you're going to have to do some things the Ivy League associates we brought in this year are simply not prepared to do."

Never were truer words spoken, Andy thought. *Because I can't imagine one of those dilettantes being willing to do this crap.* Here he was in the lower bowels of the building and tasked with a purge. As Coy had explained it, the firm was about to celebrate its hundred and fiftieth anniversary, tracing all the way back to Manzetta Law, a firm that had served Italian immigrants in New York City toward the end of the nineteenth century. Manzetta had merged with Brian and Ives of Chicago and Kansas City, which begat Manzetta and Brian, which had merged with Varney and Smyth, which begat Varney and Brian, which begat, which begat, which begat. The last partner named on the actual masthead, Handelmann, had died twenty years ago, but the SVH brand was so powerful by then that the consensus within the firm at the time had been to retain it. Nothing had changed since.

The thing about law firms, though, as Andy was coming to realize, was that they had a hard time throwing anything away. A lot of the time, they couldn't, because some case or client might come up again in the legal lottery. But as the files piled up and aged, eventually they had no purpose beyond consuming valuable storage space and gathering dust. In fact, since no one was alive who remembered what was in them, they came to pose a hazard much greater than fire. There might be something in those files that would embarrass a client or, worse yet, the firm itself. And there was Andy, alone in the basement, the one-man hazmat team.

Coy had been, well, coy about it all. "Listen," he had said, "I want you to go down there and figure out what's in those boxes. Do not make an inventory. Nothing in writing. Just make a basic assessment. See if there are any ticking time bombs, and if you find one, let me know right away. You're a good lawyer, Andy, or we wouldn't have hired you. You'll know it if you see it."

Janine, Coy's senior associate, which made her Andy's other boss, was less kind. "You know," she told him over coffee in the breakroom the next morning, "we hire a night school grunt like you every year and stick them down in the basement. That's why you're starting with the files from 1914 and not 1880-something. That project has been going on for years. Joey didn't hire you for your legal chops. He hired you because you worked all those years as an investigator. He figured you were savvy enough that your nose might twitch if you came across something other than just the dust."

If Andy's hopes had been inflated at all by having landed at Stetson, Varney, that brief conversation had certainly let the air out. But the money was good, better than the state paid, and he was coming to terms with what was looking like a less-structured future than he had thought. He turned to the next box and the next.

⚫⚫⚫

The new electrical intercom on Ban Johnson's desk buzzed, followed by the voice of his secretary. "Sir, Mr. McParland is here."

"Send him in, Greta."

"Jim, nice to see you again," he said as he rose from his desk to shake his visitor's hand. "How long has it been?"

"Mornin', Mr. J.," came the reply. "I believe the last time we spoke was right after Homestead when you was still reportin' for the Cinci paper. And with all respect, sir, we wasn't on the best of terms back then."

"Well, no, I guess we weren't, were we. But hell, Jim, times change, and I think you and your little firm can be of some service to me. Still, I do have one concern. I must be able to rely on your discretion. The very last thing I need is some publicity hound bragging in the papers or even talking to them."

"Sir, it's true that the Pinkertons do get a good bit of publicity. But you have to understand that it's because some of our clients want that, benefit from it. You take Homestead. Now, Mr. Frick, he wanted to make a point with those steel unionists, and to make that point, well, they needed to know what he was willing to do—what *we* were willing to do. So we did what we said we would, and he wanted us to have that credit, mainly, I suspect, because we had our own reputation at the time and it was useful to him. Same with Mr. Rockefeller out in Colorado, if you recall that one. But we have a lot of clients, especially over on the investigation side of the business rather than the security guard side, that don't want anyone to know we're at work, and the fact you don't know that will tell you just how discrete we can be.

"Plus, of course, and I think this was just a little before you got involved with baseball, so you maybe don't know about it, but back a few years before that Homestead business, we even did some work for your people. Old Mr. Spalding, he hired us to keep an eye on his players here in Chicago—make sure they weren't drinking and carousing and such, and then he got it to where the whole league was having us report on their players' habits to the board of directors themselves."

"Actually, Jim, I do know that. If I hadn't talked with some of those men already, well, you wouldn't be here this morning. But I raise it to make a point. The task I want to discuss with you is extremely sensitive, not just for me but for a large number of very important men who would be greatly dismayed if your activities ever came to light. That must never happen, or the consequences would be as serious for you as for . . . as for anyone. Do I make myself clear?"

"As a church bell on Sunday, sir."

Ban Johnson paused to organize his thoughts, then proceeded.

"Jim, I don't know if you follow baseball much. But a few years ago, I led a bit of a rebellion against the old National League. Took control of the Western League out in the Midwest, which was a pretty good minor league. We had teams in Detroit and Chicago and Milwaukee and Indy and KC and so on, and we were part of an agreement with the Nationals and a bunch of other leagues. But then the Nationals made a mistake. In 1899, they went from twelve teams to eight—dropped Baltimore, Cleveland, Louisville, and Washington. Me and Charley Comiskey, we saw our chance, and we changed our own mix of teams, moved some of them into those markets and dropped and added some others, and we renamed it the American League. After the 1900 season, well, we dropped out of the arrangement of sorts that there was among all the leagues, and we declared ourselves a major league, just like the Nationals. I can't say they appreciated that, and things got real nasty once we made our point by hiring away a bunch of their players and such. Went on like that for a couple of years, it did, but finally, about ten years ago, we all signed a big peace treaty and set up something called the National Commission to run the game from the majors on down. Now, what you need to know is that I sit on that commission and, in point of fact, I can pretty much get it to do whatever I want."

"Yes, sir. I didn't really know much of that history, but I do know about the commission, and I know you are a very influential man these days."

"All right, let me come to the point. Comiskey and I, we set a pattern when we took on the Nationals and beat them at their own game, so to speak. And now, there's an upstart league called the Federals, and they're trying to do the same thing to us. They even have teams in a bunch of the same cities we used. But we see them coming, and we know how to stop them. That's where you come in.

"Here's what I want you to do. . . ."

As the weeks went by, Andy found that some of the really early cases were pretty strange, at least to a contemporary eye. There was *Dortmund v. Ingleside*, for example, where some poor fellow had lost control of his dog, and the dog had run into a butcher shop and sampled the goods. Dortmund, of course, was the butcher and figured he had a sure winner. But Ingleside, who, Andy guessed, must have been politically connected, and who, needless to say, was represented by one of the Stetson, Varney predecessor firms, got a state health inspector to visit the butcher shop and declare the entire inventory a hazard because of infestations of mice and flies. The inspector then testified as a witness for Ingleside, describing in detail his observations. The court found that any damage the respondent's dog might have caused was therefore inconsequential and was not grounds for compensation.

Then there was *Eagle Feather Cleaners v. Charleston Chemical*. Charleston was a manufacturer of the chemicals used in dry cleaning, which it supplied to Eagle Feather. Apparently, one batch of chemicals was not properly constituted, and when Eagle Feather used them for a day's cleaning, every garment in the batch was stained with random blue marks and pock-marked with myriad small holes. The garments also gave off a rancid odor. The company had to replace every garment it had laundered that day or face the loss of many customers. By stepping up on its own and replacing the ruined clothing, Eagle Feather limited the total damage to its business, something lawyers call mitigation. Andy knew that demonstrating mitigation of that sort was usually a strong argument supporting a litigant's case. It made them look like reasonable folks and added to the credibility of their position. But in this case, the respondent, the chemical company, demanded a jury trial, in the course of which its attorneys, from another predecessor firm, brought in evidence that the owner of Eagle Feather was an inveterate gambler who was deeply in debt. The implication was that he had fabricated the incident so as to defraud Charleston of sufficient funds to let him pay off his creditors, who, it was suggested, were not upstanding members of the local community. So far as Andy could tell, no actual evidence of such a link was ever provided, but the doubt sown was enough to lead the jurors to find for the respondent. The day following the verdict, Charleston filed suit against Eagle Feather for defamation, claiming that the cleaner's false allegations had damaged *its* reputation and caused *it* to lose sales. No doubt aided by the company itself and its attorneys, that countersuit, *Charleston Chemical v. Eagle Feather Cleaners,* received extensive publicity in the newspapers of the day, which seemed to have been the point of the exercise. A few weeks later, once the entire incident had faded from view, the defamation action was quietly dropped. As far as Andy could tell, the files made no reference to any change in its manufacturing process or quality control efforts on the part of Charleston.

After reading his way through the first couple of dozen boxes, Andy was left with the clear impression that Stetson, Varney's reputation as a hard-nosed, take-it-to-the-line legal advocate was built into the firm's DNA. It seemed to him that every one of the firms that had merged into this budding colossus, at least the ones in the files he was reading from the 1910s, had been of a similar character. Perhaps that had been the rationale for the entire series of mergers themselves, and in its way, it made sense. When it came to tactics like intimidation, obfuscation, and straight-out power plays, size could be a major advantage. And the bigger the firm, the bigger, richer, and more powerful and influential the clients it was likely to attract. In these century-old case files, Andy came to feel, he was watching the emergence of the modern-day legal profession, or at least the emergence of big-firm law. As the boxes passed in review and time passed by, that impression only grew stronger. He was working for a firm that placed a great value on sharp elbows and always had. On a whim, he pulled out his phone and took a selfie standing in front of the five-high rows of boxes. *I'll frame that and put it on my wall when I make partner*, he mused to himself.

He turned to the next box, an unusually lightweight one bearing the label "In re: Parker T. Grissom" with the date February 14, 1918. *At least*, Andy thought as he surveyed the seemingly endless ranks of shelving, *I am up to year four*. He moved down the aisle and placed the box on the table he had been using as a workspace.

◆━◆

"So, Jim, it's been, what, three weeks since I asked you to track down the ownership of each of these clubs. What have you got for me?"

"Yes sir. As you know, we have field offices in several of those cities, which made things a little easier. A couple of the others, though, required that we dispatch detectives to search out the records, newspaper stories, and what have you. I apologize that all of that has taken so long, but I think we have a pretty complete list." With that, he passed a single typed page across the desk to Johnson.

"Okay," his client mused. "Let's see what we've got here. . . . the Brooklyn Tip-Tops, that's Bob and George Ward, the bread guys. Those two are slick operators, but they know which side of the toast gets the butter. Excellent. Now, Buffalo. . . . It looks like they sold shares to the general public, but if I'm reading this right, only as some kind of marketing ploy. And these four guys—Mullen, Enos, Cabana, Robertson—they held onto control. Walter Mullen is clearly the man to deal with there. I think Charley might have done some real estate deals with him. Have to check that out. Now, Weeghman here in Chicago, of course we know him very well. Thinks he's going to eat our lunch, outdo the White Stockings *and* the Cubs. Well, Sir Charles may be in for a rude surprise. There are some things about his partner Walker that he may not know. In the end, we may have to share the market here, but if so, it's going to be on our terms. Let's see. . . . Ed Krause in Indy is rumored to be losing his shirt, even though the team's been winning. There's lots of ways to pressure guys who are in that much trouble. I'm sure we'll think of something. Hell, even left on its own, that team may not be there by next season. Pittsburgh . . . that's Eddie Gwinner. We know him, too. Finance guy. If there's money in it, Eddie will be there. That's a piece of cake. Now, in St. Louis, you've got Ed Steininger as the big cheese. But I know that Ed's really just the front man. The real powers out there are Phil Ball and Otto Stifel. Those guys may be dangerous. Beer money and cold storage, so it's a natural partnership. And they're not afraid to throw around some cash. I heard they just stole Joe Tinker from the Cubs, and they hired Three-Finger Brown to run the show on the field. Couple of smart moves. That pair are businessmen first, not baseball men. That's where we'll find a way to sort them out. But I've heard that Phil is the driving force behind the new league, and he had to have been one of the guys that just pushed out the old Federal's president, John Powers, and put Jim Gilmore on the throne this year. Gilmore's no baseball man, either, so he has to be somebody's stooge. My money's on Philip De Catesby Ball as the puppet master.

"That leaves Baltimore. . . . Is Ned Hanlon really the head guy there?"

"That's what we determined. He was just running the club, but then he bought it, or at least enough of it to control things."

"Well, that's not good. He's going to be a pain. . . . My problem, not yours. And let's see. . . . Kansas City . . . you don't have a name? What's the story there?"

"Sir, as far as we have been able to ascertain, there is no controlling owner in Kansas City. The president of the club is a guy by the name of C.C. Madison. There's a vice president, Conrad Mann, and at least one outspoken board member by the name of Haff. But the fact is, they have a whole bunch of shareholders, and it's not clear anybody can make a deal of any sort without their support. It's almost like people there view the team as a community asset, which makes it all very political."

"Damn," responded Johnson. "All right. Forget about most of these teams. Now that we have the names of their top men, we can figure out how to deal with them. And Baltimore . . . well, if Hanlon's really the guy, that is a bag of shit. He doesn't like me or Charley, and he's damn sticky to deal with. But again, not a problem for you. For the moment at least, let's just focus on KC.

"Here's what I'd like you to do. I had some dealings with the guys out there back in the day. But since Big Jim Pendergast died a few years ago, nothing moves in that town without the blessing of his little brother, Tom. They call him TJ. Don't know him well, but I've heard that TJ is not above a little fast dealing. I need you to arrange a 'chance' meeting between TJ and me, if you know what I mean. We have quite a number of teams that train every year down in Hot Springs, in Arkansas, and the locals have been doing some building down there, ballparks and such. But they just had a terrible fire last year. Burned through a lot of the town. I'm thinking I need to go and take a good look at the facilities down there, see how good they are for us going forward. And see what's left of the town. Now, Hot Springs isn't all that far from Kansas City, and I'm sure there's a train. I'll bet TJ goes down there from time to time to take the waters. I want you, personally, to go out to KC and find out from TJ exactly when he might be down there for a getaway. See where he likes to stay. Oh, and take him a box of Upmanns— with my compliments. Tell him you and I ran into one another at the opening of that new River Roast restaurant over on the Chicago River and you had mentioned you might be heading out west on some projects. Don't be any more specific than that. Just make sure he gets the message."

"I know how to get to Mr. Pendergast," McParland replied. "It'll take me a day or so to make the arrangements at the other end. But I'll be on my way out there within the week."

"Excellent. Make sure you keep me posted, so I can clear my schedule."

⸎

Andy blew the dust off the Grissom box, popped the lid, and peeked inside, surprised by what he saw. For inside was only a single, thin file folder tied off with a red ribbon, suggesting that it was the complete file. He reached in, pulled out the folder, undid the ribbon, and opened the file. It contained three pieces of paper held together by a large metal paperclip.

On top of the "stack" was a handwritten note which had been prepared by one of the firm's then-attorneys. It appeared to have been inserted in the file when it was opened in January 1918. That was only a month or so before the February 14 date on the box itself, suggesting that the matter in question, whatever it was, had been short-lived. Andy read the note:

Law Firm of Brian and Ives

Memorandum to the File
January 5, 1918

The sole document in this file is held in trust for the Client, Mr. Parker T. Grissom. Mr. Grissom has been represented by John M. Zane, Esq., of Chicago, and is in the process of changing his legal representation. The Client has instructed specifically that, in any communication or exchange of information with Mr. Zane, the Firm is to make NO REFERENCE to the enclosed document. Once the transfer of documents, including all extant Powers of Attorney, has been effected, work is to commence on redrafting all of Mr. Grissom's estate documents to clarify the standing of his respective beneficiaries and to incorporate explicit reference to the aforementioned document, which has heretofore been held in a safety-deposit box at the First National Bank of Kansas City.

Orren C. Davis
Partner

That got Andy's attention. A secret document, or at least one that this Mr. Grissom had kept secret from his attorney in Chicago. He made a mental note to see if he could find out who this John Zane was. Maybe he could figure out why Grissom had kept the document from him. That, at least, would be more interesting than simply pawing through papers hour after hour. And, he thought, he could justify the effort under Coy's instruction to keep an eye out for anything out of the ordinary and potentially threatening to Stetson, Varney. An instruction like this was not what he or any attorney would regard as commonplace.

Clearly, there were no estate documents in the thin folder he held in his hand. Though he knew the result, he nevertheless took one more look into the file box to be sure he had not missed what would surely be a thicker sheaf of papers than this. Of course, it was not there. Then, it occurred to him that he should revisit the spot where he had pulled out the box itself, making sure it was in the correct chronological location, and survey the surrounding boxes in case there was a second related file. He retraced his steps, found everything to be in order, and came up empty. So he returned to the table, and set the Davis memorandum aside so that he could focus his attention on the document itself.

———◆❮❯◆———

As was their practice, Garry Herrmann called the meeting to order, then the three men, all of whom had known one another for years, shed the cloak of formality. Herrmann had chaired the National Commission since its inception in 1903 when the peace treaty between the National League and the upstart American League established the structure of Major League Baseball and the terms of the armistice. Ban Johnson, the driving force behind the American League's rise and effectively its permanent emissary, had served as long. The newest member was National League President John Tener, a former pitcher and outfielder for Baltimore in the American Association, for the National League version of the Chicago White Stockings, and for Pittsburgh's entry in the short-lived Players League, an early effort to redress the imbalance of power between club owners and the players by organizing the latter group as a sort of de facto workers cooperative. He'd been around the game for many years and was well known to Johnson and Herrmann. He was also a former member of Congress and, at the time of the meeting, the sitting governor of Pennsylvania.

Tener was not without serious baseball chops—he had even organized the first of what became annual baseball matches between the Republicans and Democrats on Capitol Hill—but of the three, he was most distracted by his other responsibilities. For his part, Herrmann had been serving as president of the Cincinnati Reds since 1902, but he did not have solid roots in the game, having honed his managerial skills in the public sector as he rose through the ranks of George Cox's political machine. Together, these two facts left a power vacuum at the National Commission that Johnson was only too eager to fill. As importantly in the present context, Johnson had experience as one who had jumpstarted an insurgency against the previous governing structure of the game, Tener had the experience of one who had himself jumped to an "outlaw" league and seen it fail, and Herrmann had a political finger well trained to sense the slightest breeze.

"Ban, this is your meeting," Herrmann said. "What's on your mind?"

"Garry, Governor. Thanks for agreeing to get together on such short notice. When I tell you what I have been hearing, I think you'll understand. We all know that, until the grand deal was struck in 1903 and this group was created to oversee the game, baseball, and especially major league level baseball, had a history of chaos and instability. Teams came and went, players jumped across leagues—like you, John," he said with a wink. "And as a result, the whole enterprise was far less stable and less profitable for all than it could have been. We are here charged specifically with maintaining order and putting an end to the uncertainty so we and everyone else can make money.

"As I have mentioned before, a few months ago, I started hearing rumors that a small group of men would like to start the chaos all over again by forming what they will claim to be yet another major league and by raiding our leagues for players and other talent. As I am sure you will appreciate, that can only lead to trouble. We need to stop this effort in its tracks. That will probably all be somewhat abstract to you, Garry, but the governor and I have been through it—hell, to be honest, each of us in our own way has *instigated* it—and we know well the dynamics of the thing. John's Players League experience will have taught him the pitfalls. Teach you to get hooked up with that John Montgomery Ward fellow," he said, giving the National League president a sharp look, then flashed a wry smile as he added, "but my own effort was rather more successful. It's the reason we are sitting here sipping coffee this morning. And I am uniquely attuned, I think, to the signs and the dangers.

"So what do we do about this so-called Federal League? Of course, they did not sign on to the National Agreement and have been operating out west as an outlaw league, but they have some serious money. Harry-Sinclair-type money—enough money to do some consequential raiding. I'm not sure you fellows are aware of this, but not long ago the Federals pushed out John Powers as their president, the guy who put the damned league together, and put in Jim Gilmore. Gilmore's no baseball man, and my own assessment is that he's there as a figurehead. I think the real power in all of this is Phil Ball out in St. Louis. If you look at the St. Louis Federal team itself, it's set up just that way, with a figurehead president and Phil and Otto Stifel running the show behind the scenes."

"The Ice King is behind this?" The query came from Tener.

"Governor, I'm not sure at this point, but that's my best guess. Gilmore is Ball's man. And Phil Ball is one ambitious fellow.

"Now, before I asked for this meeting today, I wanted to nail down as much information about the Federals as I could. So I asked Jim McParland to look into the matter. I'm not sure if you know Jim—Governor, you very well might, what with all the labor issues in Pennsylvania—but he's the fellow who took over running the Pinkerton Agency after Allen's sons died. . . ."

Tener interrupted. "*The* Jim McParland? The one who infiltrated the Molly McGuire's back in the seventies and then broke up the strike at Carnegie Steel? He's running Pinkerton these days?"

"Indeed he is," Johnson continued. "And as you just suggested, he's pretty good at infiltrating organizations and such. Of course, he doesn't do that work himself these days—he's getting old just like the rest of us—but he knows what he's doing, and he seems to have the right people working for him.

"In any event, I asked Jim to figure out for me the ownership of all of these Federal League clubs. I know from my own experience that information like that can be critical to building up a strategy against them. And I wanted to use this meeting to share with you both what he learned, and also so that we can start to formulate a plan for cutting the knees out from under this threat."

Slowly and carefully, so as not to damage the pages, Andy removed the large metal paperclip from the pages before him. As he did so, the backmost page fluttered to the table. When he focused his attention on it, he immediately realized why. For this was not a full sheet of paper at all but rather a news clipping that had been appended to the file. It was now yellowed and a bit stiff, though the climate-controlled circumstances of its storage had held its deterioration to a minimum. Setting the other two pages aside, he picked it up and saw that it was part of a page from the *Kansas City Star* dated February 10, 1918.

Local Industrialist Among Latest Victims of Kansas Fever

Local business leader Parker T. Grissom, 57, of Overland Park, departed this life at his home yesterday. The family reports that he had been stricken with a cough and fever only a few days before and had declined rapidly.

According to his family, Mr. Grissom was born in 1861 in Chicago, where his father was an executive with the Union Stockyards Company. A graduate of North Western University, Mr. Grissom was among the youngest managers employed by the Armour Meatpacking Company in Chicago, and he moved to Kansas City in 1890 to oversee a local expansion of the company's operations. It was in connection with these responsibilities that Mr. Grissom is reported to have traveled to Haskell County, Kansas, in January, at the very time that the unusual influenza that has since spread throughout the region, now referred to as the Kansas Fever, first appeared among the population of that county. His illness struck just days after his return.

Mr. Grissom was active in many local business and philanthropic endeavors, playing roles of leadership in the Kansas City Convention Bureau and the Associated Charities of Kansas City. He was also among the most active shareholders of the short-lived Kansas City Packers base ball team in the Federal League, though he apparently escaped the devastating effects that the team's bankruptcy in 1915 imposed on certain investors.

Ever the pioneer, Mr. Grissom was among the first area residents to build a home and move across the state line to the new "suburb" of Overland Park, where the family resides on Merriam Lane. Mr. Grissom is survived by his wife of 32 years, Annette, a daughter, Mrs. Arlene Colbert, of Kansas City, and a son, Raymond, of St. Louis. Major Raymond Grissom is currently serving in France.

A celebration of life will be held Sunday, February 17, at 2 P.M., at the Davis Funeral Chapel, 531 Shawnee Street, Leavenworth. Burial will be private.

Well, thought Andy. *That explains why the file is so small.* This Grissom fellow had obviously written his will or whatever the estate documents were when he lived in Chicago years before and probably never thought much more about it. For whatever reason, quite possibly the spread of the Spanish flu or maybe some family event, he must have suddenly discovered his mortality and decided he needed a lawyer closer to home to update his papers. Of course, it could have been something else altogether. But whatever it was, Andy realized, the planning came too late. A month after he started the process, and most likely before he ever had a chance to begin drafting a new will, he was dead. File closed.

Then Andy realized that, even if true and more or less accurate, this explanation did not address the one underlying mystery raised by the Davis cover memo. Why had Mr. Grissom been so determined that . . . what was that name . . . John Zane should not learn about the remaining document in the file? With that, he turned his attention to the third sheet of paper.

"Look at this list, Garry," Johnson noted as the two met a few weeks later. "The Federals are trying to buy their way to the top by stealing some of our best players. Allen, Austin, Bedient, Berghammer, Bender, Birdwell, Caldwell, Chase, Crandall, Fischer, Ford, Hendrix, Johnson, Konetchy, Magee, Marsans, Marquard—well, that guy's crazy; they can have him—McKechnie, Myers, O'Connor, Perritt, Plank, Quinn, Seaton, Wingo. We outflanked them when they signed up Walter Johnson. Thank goodness Clark was able to talk some sense into that guy. So I guess they decided to try to overwhelm us with numbers, drive our costs through the roof, and force us to come to terms with them.

"The weak spot here, it seems to me, is the players themselves. It's the old complaint about pay. Now, we could do it Clark's way with Johnson and just outbid these damn outlaws. But I have a better idea. If they're so concerned about money, rather than offer them more, maybe we should sue the lot of them for breach of contract or violation of the reserve rule or whatever fits and basically threaten to take away the money they're getting to jump. Maybe imply, or just say outright, that they are putting their careers at risk. I think George Pepper is in the office this week. Let's get him in here and see what he says."

"I hear what you're saying, Ban. I'm a little nervous about suing so many of our players . . . well, former players. Still, it might make sense if we can figure out a way to do it."

Johnson reached for the telephone on his desk and dialed a number.

"Counsel's office," said a female voice at the other end of the line.

"Doris, this is Ban Johnson. Is George in the office this week? Or is he back in Pennsylvania?"

"Yes, Mr. Johnson. He's here. Would you like me to put him on the line?"

"No. Just please tell him that Mr. Herrmann and I are meeting and that we'd like him to join us as soon as possible." Hanging up, he shouted to his secretary, "Greta! Please get Governor Tener on the long distance as quickly as you can."

Four minutes later there was a knock on the door. George Pepper pushed it open and walked in. His bearing was that of a handsome man by the standards of the times, and an accomplished one. He had taught law at the University of Pennsylvania for two decades before being named a trustee of the university, headed the Pennsylvania Bar Association, and published extensively in legal journals, all the while conducting a private practice that showed him to be a clever and sophisticated high-profile litigator. It was this latter experience and skillset that had brought him to the attention of the National Commission, for whom he provided counsel when major issues arose. At Johnson's urging, Pepper had been focused on the Federal League matter for some weeks now.

"George," said Johnson, "Good to see you."

Garry Herrmann echoed the sentiment, and the three settled into the leather chairs around Johnson's conference table. Johnson laid out his thinking on seizing the initiative by suing the players.

"Well," said Pepper after giving the suggestion some thought, "My advice would be yes and no. Yes, I think it's a clever idea to sue some players. The Federal owners have deep pockets, and they'd probably welcome being sued. But the players are vulnerable. The best evidence of that is how cheaply some of them jumped."

Tener, listening in from Harrisburg, blew a whistle of some sort into his telephone set to get the attention of the others and insert himself into the conversation. "Speaking from bitter experience," he said loudly enough that all could hear, "I can tell you that anything legal scares the crap out of a lot of the players who'd otherwise jump. When we did the Players League thing, that really cut down our numbers."

"That said," Pepper resumed, "I don't think a massive wave of lawsuits is wise. First, it would spread our legal resources thin and would be very expensive. Remember that you need to sue in relevant venues, and that might mean chasing players all over the country and ending up in courts that were predisposed to be friendly to them. It's much more complicated than suing a single league or a small number of teams. Second, you'd have to make the same or similar arguments in many different courtrooms, and the results would almost surely be mixed. There's simply no telling how that would eventually be resolved at the appellate level. And finally, if you sue all of the players on this list of yours, you will look greedy and heavy-handed. Remember, you have customers, and your customers couldn't care less about you. They follow the players, and that's where their natural sympathies will lie, especially if you seem to be flailing about against every one of them.

"But . . . suppose that instead, you picked out three or four of these players, players for whom you could define egregious violations of contracts and the like, and you made examples of them, spun out a story around them. The rest of those boys, well, they'd get the idea real quick. Then, you make it look like you are spreading out the effort. Send them some demand letters, that sort of thing. I'm guessing one of two things would happen. One, they'd start coming home to mama, begging to be let back into the league on whatever terms you're willing to offer. Or two, they'd start pressuring the owners of their new teams for protection and more money. That bumps up *their* costs—exactly what they're trying to do to you. From what I've been able to ascertain, there is some serious money in that league, but it's not evenly spread around. There are some real weak operators over there, and they will feel that pressure. Between the threat of losing their marquee players and seeing their legal and other costs rise, well, that may just be enough to push them out. And without enough viable teams, there *is* no Federal League.

"I've been looking at that list, and I have some candidates to suggest. One is George Johnson over in Kansas City. Tossed a game for Cincinnati one day, five days later he's pitching for the Packers against Chicago. He was obviously under contract to the Reds, and he obviously violated it.

"Hal Chase is another."

"That son-of-a-bitch!" Johnson exclaimed. "I saved his ass when he was throwing games in 1910 and Stallings wanted to can him. And how does he reward that? He comes out to Chicago, makes a royal spectacle of himself, lazy as hell, and then sticks it in Charley's nose by going across town and starting to play for the Buffalo Federal team against the Cubs. Let's go after Chase for damn sure."

"Let me add that legally it's important to note that this is not the first time he's jumped to an outlaw league. Back in '07 he jumped to the California League, too. It's true he has a following, but it should be easy to paint the guy as a total mercenary with no loyalties except to himself. Good target.

"Third, I like Armando Marsans. He—"

"That one's mine!" shouted Herrmann. "We did everything for that guy at Cincinnati—even got some paperwork saying he was white as the driven snow so he could play in the majors. But what a temper. He was always at war with Buck Herzog about some thing or other, and he really lost it in one game just before he walked out. Sent me a damn letter full of demands. I showed the letter to Buck, and Buck told him to go screw himself. Next thing we know, he's signed up with the Federals in St. Louis. They'd been after him for months, and I wouldn't be surprised if the whole thing was a setup. You look at that letter, and you just know some Cuban immigrant didn't write it. That was a lawyer at work, and we got the same exact letter, word for word, from Davenport, but we kept him."

"Precisely," Pepper continued. "The interesting twist for Marsans is the suggestion of a conspiracy by the Federal League to interfere with our existing contracts.

"The fourth name, and the last one on my list, is Lee Magee."

"Magee?" queried Johnson. "Why Magee?"

"Morals. The guy's a drunk and a womanizer. Now that in itself, as I need not tell you, is not so unusual in a player. But Magee has the added baggage of having been named in a divorce suit there in St. Louis. Some poor sap practically found the guy in bed with his wife. There's nothing special about Magee as a player or his jump to the Federals. But if we include him as one of three or four players we sue, it lets us leverage his reputation, and that will undercut the popularity of the other players that jumped.

"So, that's my recommendation, fellows. We sue on the grounds of contract violations, disloyalty, anti-competitive conspiracy, and morals. Now whether it's the Commission that sues, or the leagues, or the teams, we can talk about the pros and cons once we decide on an overall legal strategy."

"George," said Johnson, "I'm convinced. That's brilliant, and it's sure to generate pressure *and* publicity."

"John," the American League president said into the telephone. "Did you get all that? What do you think?"

There was no response. The connection had apparently been broken while Pepper had been speaking.

"Well," said Johnson after a pause, "we'll count John as a 'yes.' Garry?"

"I concur," added Garry Herrmann. "How do we get started?"

<hr>

Andy glanced at his watch and was surprised to see how little of the workday was left. His mind was filling with questions about Grissom, Zane, and the whole matter, small as it seemed. He wanted to dig into it but thought that, in the circumstances, he'd best not use the resources of Stetson, Varney—at least not until he had something more solid to bring to Joey Coy. But on his own time. Who could object to that? So he took the elevator up to his office, a seldom-visited space on a seldom-consulted floor, punched in his code and the task code for the inventory of old case files, and photocopied the three documents. He placed the copies in his briefcase. Next, he carried the file bearing the originals back to the archives, replaced it in its box, and set the box back in its space on the shelf. Then he ascended once more, grabbed his briefcase, and headed home. A little Napa Valley red and a little Silicon Valley algorithmic search would make for an evening that at least held the potential for turning out interesting.

It was hard to miss the Arlington Hotel. It was the biggest and grandest building in all of Hot Springs, and perhaps even the entire country. At least that was the way it was described by travel writer Charles Cutter, whose 1892 Guide Book, *Cutter's Guide to the Hot Springs of Arkansas*, characterized it as "the most elegant and complete hotel in America." The hotel had been brand new then, built on the site of an earlier structure with the same name, and featured three hundred rooms on five levels, with a rotunda and glass dome, a grand ornamental oak stairway, a full-length veranda with arcades, and the other posh amenities a wealthy traveler would expect, all wrapped in an impressive Spanish Renaissance exterior. Ban Johnson had visited Hot Springs a couple of times before and knew the hotel well. It came as no surprise to him that it was also the favored destination of Tom Pendergast.

Johnson walked through the well-appointed lobby, past the entrance to the Pink Parlor, or ladies' lounge, and on to the elegant dining room. Rather than waiting to be seated, he walked into the space and looked around. He knew he wouldn't recognize Pendergast himself among the well-heeled men in the room. But he also knew that men like Pendergast invariably traveled with muscle, muscle that was easy to spot. And there it was, over in the far righthand corner of the restaurant, in the form of a large man with close-cropped hair and a thick neck who looked distinctly uncomfortable in his suit and tie. Sure enough, as Johnson approached the table occupied by a heavyset but rather genteel-looking man in a dark three-piece suit, muscle moved to intersect his path. At a word from the man at the table, he stepped back, allowing the interloper to approach.

"Councilman," Johnson said, using the man's political title as a show of respect.

"Mr. Johnson. How nice to meet you. And what a pleasant surprise that you should happen to be here for breakfast on this fine morning. Please call me TJ."

"My friends—and I hope that will include you—call me Ban. It is very nice to meet you, TJ. You know, it is a delightful coincidence to find you here today, because I actually have a couple of things I've been wanting to talk with you about. Shall we order?"

It was at this moment that a waiter appeared, offering fresh coffee and juice. Both men placed breakfast orders indicative of hearty appetites.

"Okay," said TJ, turning to his more natural persona. "Let's cut the bullshit. Thanks for the smokes. What is it you wanted to see me about?"

"Right to the point. I like that. I had some business dealings with your late brother years ago, and he was the same way. And by the way, please do accept my belated condolences. I liked Jim very much."

The younger Pendergast nodded.

"As I'm sure you know, TJ, Kansas City pictures itself as something of a baseball town. There've been teams there from various leagues ever since the professional game got its act together years ago. And you have one now, the Packers."

Pendergast nodded slightly in acknowledgment. He was obviously, Johnson observed, a cards-close-to-the-chest kind of guy.

"The Packers are headed up by a couple of local guys—Madison and Mann—plus there's some loudmouth on their board by the name of Haff. TJ, if these are close friends of yours, please tell me now."

Johnson paused, but Pendergast was either not interested in the men he had named or he was, as suspected, a good poker player. So Johnson took a chance and continued.

"They run the team, but it doesn't appear that they own enough of it to actually be in control. In fact, from what we can figure out, nobody really controls that team. It has way too many shareholders and seems to operate more like an old club team than a real professional organization. Anyway, the Packers play in one of the new minor leagues called the Federal League. And that's what we in baseball call an outlaw league.

"See, there's this contract of sorts called the National Agreement that was settled on about ten or so years ago. It set up the two major leagues, the American and the National, and a bunch of minor leagues in other cities, and it laid down some rules about things like the standard terms of player contracts. Things that add to the stability of the game. But the outlaw leagues, well, they play by a different set of rules. That is to say, they refuse to follow the terms of the National Agreement, and from time to time they try to steal players away from the regular teams by paying them wages nobody can really afford or other kinds of inducements. And baseball players, well, most of them aren't smart enough to understand what they're giving up if they chase that money. It makes for a difficult situation, but most of the time we can keep it well in hand."

"Come now, Ban. I thought we were cutting through the crap. You think I don't know you ran an outlaw league yourself, the Western League, and you had a team in my town, the Blues, that you took away when you decided to go big-time?"

"That's true, TJ. And I meant no disrespect. But you are actually making my point for me. The reason we took the Blues franchise and moved it to Washington was that we were building something bigger—that was the start of the move to establish the American as a major league—and to be honest, Kansas City was a minor league town, and as far as baseball is concerned, it always will be. That's just how it is. There's nothing wrong with that, and it's not a knock on the city. There just aren't enough people, and there isn't enough money, to support a major league team. Plus, you aren't on the way to any other cities in the league, so the cost for a team to come out there to play is very high. Economically, it just doesn't make sense to have a major league team in KC.

"And that's just what the Federals want to do. They want to take their little outlaw league and declare that it's really a major league. There's a lot of money behind that—Chicago money, St. Louis money. And they're using it to steal players away from the existing majors so they can try to look like what they claim. But there is no Kansas City money to speak of. So if they succeed—and I sincerely hope they will not—but even if they do, well, TJ, Kansas City's going to get screwed again. It's a dead-level certainty. And for the same reasons as before. Don't get me wrong. Kansas City is a great place and a great baseball town. People support your teams. But Kansas City will never be a Major League Baseball town. Not in our lifetimes, or our kids', or their kids'. I'm just trying to be honest here. And that's why I wanted to talk with you.

"That operation in your town is weak, and it is certain to fail. There's nothing you or I or any of us can do to stop that. So the question is, are there ways we can use that failure to our mutual advantage? I think there are."

Andy pulled the cork from a bottle of blended red, not great but imminently drinkable, and half-filled one of the glasses he'd picked up recently from the nearby Williams Sonoma. He swirled the liquid, placed his nose over the lip of the glass, and inhaled deeply. Meh. But then, he already knew that. He took the glass into the other room and settled into the desk chair. It was time to do a little research on the day's find.

He started with Parker T. Grissom. It was not a common name, but it nevertheless required a bit of sorting to get past the various listings promising to find everything from Grissom's address and phone number to his arrest record—in every state and territory—for a small subscription fee. Wikipedia had no listing for the man, which was hardly surprising considering that he had labored in obscurity and died a hundred years before the service was created. They have some sort of notability filter, he figured, and Grissom obviously did not pass through it, even on the unlikely chance he was ever put to the test. Finally, on the second page of Andy's search results, he found a link to a newspaper obituary, which turned out to be the very one he had found in the Stetson, Varney file. It was only when he added a second element to the search, one he had gleaned from the third, and primary, document in the file, that he found something of potential interest. Parker T. Grissom, it seems, had been a shareholder of the local baseball team, the Kansas City Packers, in something called the Federal League. Andy was a baseball fan of sorts, but he'd never heard of either the team or the league. Again, of course, this was Kansas City and a hundred years ago. Still, Grissom, as Andy now knew but Wikipedia apparently did not, was a bit more than an average shareholder. Time to file that one away for the moment.

Andy started a list. He'd need to do a little research on this Kansas City team and on the Federal League. Later. But first, there was this Chicago lawyer, John M. Zane.

John Maxcy Zane. He was alive and in Chicago at the right time, so that was almost surely the guy, but not much in the man's basic biography pointed to any obvious problem. At first glance, he seemed to have had a rather pedestrian career. He was about twenty-five when he was admitted to the bar and did mainly commercial work and some on patents and trademarks. Taught for a while at Northwestern and Chicago Universities, but that didn't last. His claim to fame seemed to be some nasty review he'd published in the *Michigan Law Review* of some kind of book about Richard II, as in the fourteenth-century English king. Andy had no idea what that was all about but decided that it was not germane to his current interest and would have to wait. Probably forever. He did not add it to the list.

Further down the search results, though, he did find a reference to a book Zane had authored called *The Story of Law*. Apparently he was deep into the history of law from Roman times onward. That might explain the bit about Richard II. Following up, Andy came to a longer and richer profile of the man. It turned out his father, Charles, had been a lawyer as well, in Springfield, Illinois, and active in Republican politics. Charles, it seems, was the lawyer who replaced Abraham Lincoln in the Lincoln and Herndon law firm when Lincoln went off to Washington as president. And Charles's wife, John's mother, was a niece of William Herndon, the other half of the firm. Zane completed his studies at the University of Michigan in 1884, at which point he moved to Utah, where his father had just been appointed chief justice of the Federal Territorial Court. *Nothing like connections*, thought Andy, ruing for a moment his own lack thereof. John read law with his father and was admitted to the Utah Bar four years later. Over the next decade, he made a name for himself, mainly as an appellate advocate, before moving from Utah to Chicago, where he joined a legal partnership and continued his writing. He handled cases on patents and commercial matters, but also some involving antitrust issues, eminent domain, and constitutional challenges to the emerging regulatory authority of the government. Between 1912 and 1924, he argued half a dozen cases before the US Supreme Court.

Okay, thought Andy. *So this guy was more important than it seemed at first.* And since Zane handled a lot of commercial cases for Chicago companies, he could see ways in which he might have connected with some junior executive from Armour. Or maybe he was a neighbor or family friend. Or—Andy's memory kicked in—that obit said Grissom studied at Northwestern. Maybe they connected somehow when Zane taught there. It wasn't at all clear what any of that had to do with Grissom's estate, though that was probably just work that Zane referred to one of his other partners or even to some fellow who was reading law at the firm during that time. Zane would have still been Grissom's point of contact, especially if he saw that as important to his business relationships for some reason. But it said nothing at all about why Grissom would have wanted to keep his latest business venture from Zane. In his head, Andy marked that as still to be determined.

⋅⊰⊱⋅

"What did you have in mind?" asked Pendergast, his growing interest beginning to show on his face.

"Simply this. I want to make sure that the Federal League is never in a position to make a legit claim to be a major league, and I want to use the league's greatest vulnerability to bring that about. I believe the KC club, the Packers, is that vulnerability. They have very little money, surely not enough to meet the demands they will face, and they have no real leadership. I want to exploit that, and I need your help to do it. I know that's a tough place to put you in with regard to civic pride, but, TJ, I think we can find a way to make that worth your while."

"I'm listening."

"I need to find some guy who has shares of the stock in that club— the more, the better, but at least some—and who, for want of a more delicate term, can be reached. Maybe he's short on cash, maybe he hates the other fellows with shares, maybe he has ambitions of his own, maybe somebody's got something on him. It doesn't matter what, but I need to find the right guy, and I need to find some serious leverage. Depending on what his weakness is, I'll make him an offer that he'll find attractive. And in exchange, all he has to do is find some way to take the Kansas City club off the table and hopefully the Federal League with it. We'll help with that, too."

"Just for the sake of argument here, Johnson," TJ responded, "let's say that I do know such a fellow or how to find one like him. I'm taking a risk here. I mean, I'm a member of the City Council, and you're asking me to take my city out of the running for a major league baseball team. If that ever got out, I'd be cooked. Why would I want to take that risk? What's in that deal for me?"

"Fair enough. Tell me what it would take. I know that KC will never be a major league town, but it's a great town for a good minor league team in a good league. I could guarantee that would happen, and if you want, I can promise you as much of an ownership stake as you want. And if we do this right, no one will ever be the wiser about your own role. In fact, if the current team folds and there's a good new franchise in town, you could be a big hero."

"Yeah. Wishes and promises like that are horseshit, and you know it. But there are a couple of things I want if I help you on this, and I think you can make them happen. First, I don't give two winks, myself, about baseball in Kansas City or anywhere else. But I have some friends who do. They ain't owners or managers or anything like that, but they have ways of making good money off the game. Do I need to spell that out for you?"

"No. I think I know what you mean."

"Well, sometimes guys like you like to show how goody-two-shoes you and your game are by making trouble for guys like them. There won't be none of that crap as long as I'm alive, and I hope that's a long time. I don't care what you do in New York or Chicago or anywhere, but you keep the hell out of Kansas City, and you stay away from my friends in KC if you should happen across them somewhere else. You'll know who they are. Can you do that?"

"Yes, we can do that," Johnson replied without hesitation. In truth, he was not surprised by the terms.

"One more thing. And this is important, because this is how I'm going to keep the stink of this thing off me. I don't know how much you know about Kansas City politics, and I'm thinking probably not much. Now, you say you knew Jim way back, and you two were able to do whatever it was that needed doing. Things have gotten more complicated since then. We still run the south side of town, and not much happens that we don't know about or have a hand in. But there's this other guy, Joe Shannon, and he runs things on the north side. And the two of us, well, let's just say we're not the best of friends. And at least one of those names you mentioned before from that ball club, well, I know that guy lives or works over on the north side, and he does business with that prick. When this thing, whatever it is, happens, and the baseball club folds, I want you to do or say something that makes it look like you and Shannon were in it together and pulled it off. You don't need to give a speech or anything like that, but just drop a word or two about how you and Shannon are friends, or ran into each other, or something. In fact, maybe you could make a point of running into that guy just by chance somewhere in Kansas City and having a drink, kind of like the two of us, only without the actual discussion part. Just social. I can tell you where. Then, if anybody was to look, they'd find a witness or two who saw you together. Maybe even snap a photograph. Let people decide it's Shannon who cooked this thing up with you and cost the town its team. You can deny it, and he sure will. But the eyes, well, they don't deceive, do they?"

Ban Johnson pushed his plate away, sat back in his chair, and just smiled. "Get me that name," was all he said.

⬤⬤⬤

Andy's research continued deeper into the wine and deeper into the night. He felt as if he were missing something obvious, and if it was something obvious, he was certainly missing it. Why did Grissom want to isolate himself from John Zane. . . . Who were Zane's other clients? Maybe that's where he'd find the answer. Or perhaps in one of his writings.

Andy hesitated but then logged into Westlaw's Legal Resource Index using his Stetson, Varney credential. This was, after all, legitimate research for the firm, not just idle curiosity. Or so he told himself. Zane was, in his day, a legal scholar of sorts, and this was the place to find obscure references in legal publications. Once connected to the index, he meant to take the fast lane first and key in "John Zane" in the author search but entered it instead in the keyword search box. He had hit return before realizing his mistake. And the stars aligned. Zane was apparently mentioned in a fairly recent—well, within the last ten years recent—law review article by someone named Nathaniel Grow. Interestingly, the article was about professional sports teams that went bankrupt. This rang a bell somewhere in Andy's brain, but he couldn't quite think why. Then he began reading the article. *Of course*, he thought. *That has to be the connection!*

John Zane, as it turned out, was the lawyer for the Kansas City Packers baseball team. At least he was the lawyer during the trial when the team was in bankruptcy and was suing the Federal League—still had to check that out—for having driven the team out of business so the league could move the franchise elsewhere. Apparently, or so the Packers argued, there was some skullduggery relating to a loan the league had made to the team to give it time to recapitalize itself. Then the league had basically seized the team without giving them a chance to pay off the loan. That left the league free to move the franchise, which they must have wanted to do for some still-to-be-determined reason.

Zane was the lawyer for the Kansas City ball club. Grissom was a part owner of the club. Zane had prepared or overseen the preparation of Grissom's estate or knew him some other way back in his Chicago days. And for all Andy knew, Grissom might have been the fellow who connected Zane to the team in the first place. *We need a good lawyer, and I know this fellow from Chicago.* . . . That sort of thing.

But Andy had one more piece of information, and now it made perfect sense. Andy had the document Grissom wanted to make sure Zane never saw.

The document arrived in Ban Johnson's morning mail—a large brown envelope with a hand-stamped Kansas City postmark but no return address. Inside was a photograph of a single piece of paper. It had the appearance of a legal document. Ban Johnson reached for his reading glasses and was richly rewarded for the effort.

"Greta, would you get me Mr. McParland on the phone, please?"

State of Illinois
County of Cook
Circuit Court, First Municipal District

Record of Negotiated Resolution

Case Number: *CC900216-14627*

It is hereby recorded that *Armour & Company* (hereafter Party One) will hold in abeyance the charges of *fraud and felony theft* against *Parker Thomas Grissom* (hereafter Party Two) that were brought before this Court on *17 February 1890*.

Party Two undertakes the following:

1. To acknowledge his error in improperly accounting for certain business expenses and to refrain from engaging in such activity in the future while in the employ of Party One.

2. To provide full restitution to Party One in the amount of $5,127.64 through payroll deductions over a period of five calendar years from this date.

3. To accept demotion to the position of branch manager and reassignment from Chicago Headquarters to Kansas City, Missouri, until such time as Party One shall deem him fit for additional responsibilities.

4. To accept a reduction in gross salary commensurate with his new position.

5. To hold harmless Party One and any and all of its agents and employees from any claim for recompense or release from this Agreement.

This document represents an indefinite suspension of proceedings in this case. The failure by Party Two to abide by the terms of this Agreement will result in the immediate reimposition of the aforementioned charges. By signing below, Party Two hereby waives any claim of expiration of any statute of limitations that might otherwise apply.

Done This Date: *1 March 1890*

Party One: Philip D. Armour for Armour & Company

Party Two: *Parker Thomas Grissom*

Attested for the Court: *John H. Zane, Esq., Special Mediator*

Andy took the next day, a Friday, and the weekend to organize his thoughts. First thing Monday morning, he called Joey Coy's secretary to request an appointment. Coy, she told him, was at a partners' meeting in Denver for the next three days but was expected back in the office on Thursday morning. Andy could have fifteen minutes at 2:30 that afternoon.

He had best be prompt.

The sharp elbows here at Stetson, Varney, he mused, *are apparent at many levels.*

⎯⎯⎯⎯⎯⎯⎯⎯⎯⎯⎯⎯

"Jim, thanks for coming in. You remember our little Kansas City project, right?"

"Of course I do, Mr. Johnson. Is there some additional way we can help you with that?"

"Actually, there is. I'm afraid this is another one where I have to ask you for the personal touch. I need to be confident it is done with just the right message and tone.

"By coincidence, not long after you and I last met, I was down in Hot Springs to assess the situation after the fire and I chanced to run into Tom Pendergast." Johnson paused and a wordless smile passed between the two men. "I happened to mention to him the little problem we were having in his home town, and he allowed as how he might be able to suggest someone I could talk with and, perhaps, find a way to sort it out. Have a look at this. It arrived in the mail yesterday with no indication who might have sent it." With that, he passed to the Pinkerton man the document he had received in the mail.

McParland perused the brief court record and looked up.

"This Mr. Grissom," Johnson continued, "is one of the owners of the Kansas City Packers baseball club. This is a good start, but I want to know everything you can find out about him. Okay to use the troops for that; it's pretty standard. Then I'm going to want you to go out there and pay Mr. Grissom a visit.

"My best guess is you're going to find out that our Mr. Grissom is perceived as a paragon of the community. Some kind of businessman or do-gooder. After all, the men who run the ball club have taken him on as a member of their group, and such men usually avoid associating in that way with a genuine blackguard or a man of known low morality. Show him the document. That should get his attention. Make sure he knows you're with Pinkertons. And drop a mention that your client is a friend of Tom Pendergast *and* Joe Shannon and some of *their* friends. Be especially sure to mention Shannon. That should loosen him up pretty good.

"When you're ready, I'll be sure you have a train ticket for him and a reservation at the Palmer House. Tell him I want to see him in Chicago the very next day. And tell him he is not to mention your visit, where he will be for the next day or two, or whom he is to see, or he can expect to have a very rough ride. Don't give him time to think about it. And when you leave him, I want you to stick around and tail him. See if he goes anywhere else and talks to anyone before the train station. If he does that, let me know by telephone so I can brace him with the knowledge when he shows up here. You see any problems with that?"

"No, sir, no problems at all. Let me get an operative in KC to track down that information. Then I'll check in with you, get the travel papers, and head out there. You can probably expect to have him sitting right here by this time next week."

"Excellent. As always, Jim, a pleasure."

⚬⚬⚬

Coy glanced up from his desk with an annoyed expression that indicated this particular interruption had better be important. "Mr. Dennum, what brings you here? How are things down in The Catacombs?"

"That's actually what I wanted to talk with you about. Thank you for seeing me. I know you're busy, so I'll try to be succinct."

Coy nodded approvingly.

"I've been making good progress down there, I think. I started with 1914, and I was just getting into the files from early 1918 when I came across an odd situation. I remember you told me to be on the lookout for anything out of the ordinary that might somehow bite us in the rear. Honestly, Mr. Coy, I'm not sure this is one of those things, but I'm also not sure it's not. So I thought I'd best run it by you and see what you thought."

With that, Andy took out an exceptionally thin file. Opening it, he placed three sheets of paper on Coy's desk.

"These three pieces of paper were the only things in one entire file box. I looked around in the other nearby files, but there was no indication this had been misfiled or that there were any other associated papers."

He pointed to Orren Davis's cover memo. "There was no Stetson, Varney back then, of course, but this Orren Davis fellow was a partner in one of our predecessor firms, so for all intents and purposes, he was one of us. As you can see, this was simply meant as a temporary note to the file that seemed to have two purposes. The first was to establish a client relationship with this particular client, a man named Parker T. Grissom. And the second appears to have been a reminder to anyone else at the firm who might happen across the file that the main document there was not to be shared in any way with a Chicago lawyer by the name of Zane. It's that last part that made me curious. Zane appears to have done some sort of legal work for Grissom—probably estate work, but it's impossible to know for sure. In any event, Grissom did not want Zane to know about this other document.

"The next thing I looked at was this newspaper clipping," Andy said, pointing to the browned-out partial page. "It's an obituary for Parker Grissom, who seems to have died shortly after visiting with Mr. Davis, and apparently before there was any transfer of documents to the firm from Chicago. Indeed, it's not clear they—well, we—ever got any such documents. The file itself was ribboned, suggesting it was complete, and the box was dated in February 1918, which means the matter was closed as far as the firm was concerned almost as soon as it was opened. The paper says this guy died of something they called Kansas Fever, which I'd never heard of. But it turns out, which I never knew, that the so-called Spanish flu in 1918—the influenza pandemic—may have started in a county out in southwest Kansas, the very same one Grissom visited. The guy was one of the very first victims of that pandemic."

Andy could see that Coy was losing his patience, so he hurried on before his boss could end the meeting.

"That," he said, pushing forward the third document, "gets us to this, which is really the reason I'm here. As you'll see, this is an agreement of sorts between Mr. Grissom and Mr. Byron Bancroft Johnson of Chicago along with two other men. As you can see from the obit, Grissom was a shareholder in the Kansas City baseball team of that era. Byron Bancroft Johnson is Ban Johnson. At the time all of this was happening, Johnson was the president of the American League and a member of something called the National Commission, which was the governing body of Major League Baseball. From what I've been able to glean in my research, Ban Johnson was the single most powerful man in professional baseball, and if anybody put this arrangement together, it had to have been him. This seems to have been some sort of personal service contract dating back to 1914.

"In 1914, the Kansas City baseball team was part of something called the Federal League, and that league was in the process of buying off players from the two established major leagues—the ones we know today—to bolster a claim that it constituted a third major league. The National and American Leagues were fighting tooth and nail to keep that from happening—and to hold on to their players and some restrictive contract terms that made major league ball pretty profitable. The Federal League was apparently a real threat.

"Now, looking at this document, it's not clear what sort of service this Mr. Grissom did for Johnson and his colleagues, but as you can see from the rest of the document, it must have had some significant value. That's not a bad payoff for whatever it was. And the thing to keep in mind is that there was a huge amount of litigation surrounding all of this activity.

"The Federal League sued the National Commission, each of the two major leagues, and all or most of their member teams for violating the antitrust laws. That case ended up in the court of Kenesaw Mountain Landis in Chicago, and it just kind of died there over a year or so. Eventually, there was a settlement. I haven't had a chance to research the terms of that yet. But Landis himself was hired on just a few years later as the very first Commissioner of Baseball. That was not long after the 1919 Black Sox Scandal broke. Maybe that was a payoff, but who can say.

"And while that was going on, the Federal League had legal problems of its own. It looks like the team in Kansas City was a pretty weak franchise financially, and at one point, they had to borrow money from the league just to make payroll. That was right around the time of this big push to be a major league. And apparently, the guy running the league, name of Gilmore, I think, played fast and loose and called in the loan, which the league had agreed not to do, and then up and moved the franchise to Washington, DC. Well, that sent the Kansas City club into bankruptcy, and they sued the league and I'm not sure who else for breach of contract.

"So, in brief, all of this shit's going down all at once, and the Kansas City team is right in the middle of it. And here is our Mr. Grissom working for Ban Johnson and friends on the side and later on doing his level best to make sure that this Chicago lawyer, John Zane, doesn't find out about it. Ever.

"That struck me as odd, so I did a little research on Zane, and it turned out he was also right in the middle of this legal mess. Whatever else he was doing, he was the attorney for the Kansas City team in its lawsuit against the Federal League. Now, what the earlier connection between Grissom and Zane was, I don't know. Haven't found any obvious connection yet, though I do have two or three ideas to pursue. But the whole dynamic of the thing makes me think there was something improper going on. And, Mr. Coy, I don't think anybody at the firm ever found out what it was. Earlier this week, I was able to track down some information on our would-have-been colleague Orren Davis. It turns out that he died of the flu, too. He was stricken shortly after he opened this file for Grissom. Hell, maybe that's how he caught it. Draw your own conclusion. But that meant it was somebody else who closed the file, and the firm never pursued any related matters. Chances are, after the file was closed, no one would ever have opened it again until I did last week."

Joey Coy was a sharp lawyer, and what he saw in the document set his mind racing. "So what you're telling me is that we had a client whose heirs and their successors may have a valid claim to the benefits spelled out in this personal service contract, and there is no reason to believe that they or anyone else is aware of the contract itself, let alone its contents. Have I got that right?"

"Yes, sir. That's what I'm telling you."

"They're *suing* us? Those lying, thieving bastards are suing *us*?" Johnson was livid when the legal service arrived and he had a chance to look it over. He had Garry Herrmann in his office and John Tener on the telephone. "They're encouraging our players to break their contracts with us—legally valid contracts—to go play in their second-rate league, and they're ignoring the rules that all of baseball lives by to keep the peace, and they're pushing salaries to the damn moon, and they're suing *us*?"

Herrmann, who had also been served that morning, was equally irate, if less demonstrative. Tener had not yet seen the litigation but expected that he would receive his own copy by day's end.

"This is war," Johnson continued. "And we're not going to take it lying down." He paused. "Here's what I think we need to do. John, would you take charge of marshaling our forces? Contact all the teams and tell them what's coming and to keep their damn mouths shut tight until we come up with a unified response to this bullshit."

"I'm on it, Ban."

"Thanks. And Garry, could I suggest that you get Pepper involved right away and also our American League counsel, George Miller? Make sure they've seen these papers, get them thinking about how we can best defend against this conspiracy and antitrust stuff, and arrange a meeting for all of us, and of course John, as soon as everyone can get to town here. Light a fire under them if you need to."

"Right."

"While you two are doing that, I'm going to do a little digging into the Federals and some of these ball clubs, see what I can find beyond what we already know. I have a couple of lines in the water, but you two would be better off not knowing the details if that's agreeable."

The conversation continued for a few minutes more, then Tener, who was in New York at the time, hung up and Herrmann returned to his own office. Johnson picked up his phone once more.

"Greta, Jim McParland. Yesterday!"

⚾

Coy had his feet propped up on the desk when Andy was ushered into his office. "Take a load off," he said, gesturing to one of the visitor chairs. "I don't suppose you've come up with anything else in the last few days—any other files related to the Grissom matter in the other boxes from that time period." It was a statement, not a question.

"No. There's nothing else. I'm almost certain of that."

"Good. Good. I took the file to the conflicts committee along with a summary of the other research you did. And nice job on that, by the way. And I also had a chat with Chet."

Andy knew that Chet referred to Chester Kinnalley, the firm's managing partner.

"See, this is not an uncommon kind of situation. We had a client whose interests we are still obligated to protect. And we have to decide what those interests are, or were. On the one hand, you have the assets mentioned in the agreement as accruing to Mr. Grissom. Of course, they had zero value at the time of the transfer. Whether that's still the case is a legal matter, and a potentially complex one. On the other hand, you have the client's clear and strong instruction to maintain confidentiality and his apparent but never accomplished intention to alert his heirs to the arrangement into which he had entered so that they might accrue any possible future benefits.

"Set against that is the hundred years of history since that agreement was reached. That history has included numerous changes and realignments of parties who may or may not be bound by the terms of the arrangement. And it also includes the fact that, over time, some of those parties or interests closely associated with them have become clients of this firm. Important clients of this firm.

"Put another way, we are conflicted. We have clients, or at least client interests, on both sides of the issue. And in a situation like this, we must choose sides. We can represent the interests of Mr. Grissom and his heirs, or we can represent the successors, if that they are, to the other party to the agreement. And honestly, Andy, it's not a close call. In the unlikely circumstance that this matter ever came to be litigated, we would have to side with the firm's newer and larger clients.

"Chet and I also discussed the question of whether, having discovered this document, Stetson, Varney is obligated to disclose its existence to an interested party. The thing is, so far as we know, there is no such party.

We don't know the terms of Grissom's will, the one Orren Davis was planning to revise, and we don't know if he has any living heirs all these years later. If there were such heirs and they had any legal entitlement to the assets, both of which, again, are undetermined, we do know that no such party has stepped forward to assert a claim. So even if we had an ethical or legal obligation to disclose, there is no one to whom to do so.

"So here's what I want you to do. Take this file and put it back to sleep in its proper place in the archives. Then take the box—the whole box—and put it in the burn bag. Move everything else around a bit to make it look right. And then forget you ever saw that box. You got that?"

With that, Coy handed the file across the desk to Andy and gestured toward the door.

<hr>

A nervous Parker Grissom was seated at the table in Ban Johnson's Chicago office waiting for his host to conclude an earlier meeting elsewhere in the building. He was a slim, bespectacled man with a stylish mustache, looking every bit the mid-level corporate bureaucrat that he was. On a different occasion, the Major League memorabilia scattered around the room—the photographs, the autographed baseballs, the detailed architectural model of the recently opened Comiskey Park, the personal awards and certificates of recognition—would have fascinated him. Today, they merely added to the intimidation of his having been summoned to this place and this moment.

Johnson entered the room and immediately made a point of acknowledging Grissom's presence and offering a greeting that gave every appearance of being pleasant. *No need*, he thought to himself, *to be heavy-handed with this fellow. At least not now.* Grissom knew he was the weaker party in this meeting, knew it very well, and Johnson had decided to ease the burden a bit, even as the pressure remained securely in play.

"Mr. Grissom. Thank you so much for coming up here to visit with me. I do apologize for the inconvenience and for the short notice. I trust you have found the hotel accommodations to your liking?"

"Yes, sir, Mr. Johnson. I mean, the Palmer House. That's the best, sir. And thank you. But I must confess to you, I'm a little confused. I'm just a meat guy from Kansas City. How can I be of any assistance to you? I mean, look around this office. With all respect, sir, you and I, well, we're just in different leagues."

"Please, Parker. May I call you Parker? And I'm just Ban. What you've just said is exactly why you are here. We are in different leagues. And the one you are in—the Federal League, to be clear—is causing the one I am in a great deal of trouble these days. I want you to help me with that. I'm hoping that you and I can come to some sort of mutually beneficial arrangement."

"I'm sorry, sir . . . ah, Ban, but I'm still confused. As I'm sure you know, I am here under . . . somewhat trying circumstances. And yet, you speak of making an arrangement that is mutually beneficial. I'm not sure I understand."

Johnson smiled. This was going to be easy.

"Look," he said. "I did ask Mr. McParland to come out to KC to meet you and invite you up to Chicago. And again, I apologize for the short notice. I asked him to be sure you would come. Beyond that, I'm not sure just what he might have said to you. And if that was somehow inappropriate, I apologize. I'm not sure how much you know about our Mr. McParland, but he is actually the man running the whole of the Pinkerton Agency—I'm sure you know who they are—and I went to him because I always try to solve problems from the top down. Saves time, and it usually brings the most capable people into the game from the outset. Now, I acknowledge that Mr. McParland has a personal history that is, shall we say, colorful. It was he who infiltrated the Molly McGuires years ago and he who led the Pinkertons more recently in dealing with the steelworkers up in Pennsylvania. You probably read about that. And I'm sure there's much more. But in all of those instances, he was simply following the instructions of his superiors at the agency. Nothing more. Personally, I have found him to be an honorable man, and I assume that he will have adjusted easily to the more, ah, genteel role that he now occupies. So if he should give the appearance of retaining something of a hard edge, well, perhaps you can overlook that as I do."

The hook was set. McParland, well, he might do anything. But a gentleman like Ban Johnson could hardly be held responsible for the man's methods.

"So, if we have settled that, here's the thing. And I am speaking now as a member of the National Commission. This little outlaw league of yours is beginning to annoy us. They . . . you . . . are stealing our players by overpaying them and encouraging them to ignore legally binding contracts that they have signed. In the process, you are undermining the key element of all of those contracts, the reserve rule. And it won't surprise me if, before too long, you start moving into our existing markets. As you may or may not know, your league has just brought suit against all of Major League Baseball. We're not stupid, Parker. In fact, I invented all of these tactics myself when I took over the Western League back in the day, called it the American League, and went after the National League, which was the only major league at the time. There is nothing your league can do that I cannot anticipate and counter."

"But, sir . . . Ban . . . I'm, well, a nobody. It might be that what you say is happening. I don't know. But if it is, I assure you, sir, that I have no part in it."

"Ah, Parker, but you do. You see, I know that you hold voting shares in the Kansas City ball club, what is it . . . the Packers. And I know, perhaps better than you do, that your ball club is in deep financial trouble. It will not surprise me in the least if the organization faces ruin in a very short time."

"And you want to help us through that, and I am to play some role?" inserted Grissom.

"Half right. I want that club to fail. I want it to fail hard, and I want it to fail fast. And yes, I want you to play a role in that demise. And, when the club fails, I want you to help me set up the entire damn Federal League to follow it down the drain. I want you to push the Packers club toward the brink. Demand information from Madison and Mann. Make them disclose the dangerous state of the club's finances. Undermine them where and when you can. Be the burr under their saddle. Dissension among the shareholders, distrust of the leaders—that's what I want. And I want you to understand clearly . . . they truly do deserve this. They have failed, and they are about to take the club, you, and your fellow shareholders with them.

"Then, once the club is bankrupt, once the failure has set in, I want you to poison the air around the league itself. It is the league's fault that your organization has failed, and they must be made to pay. Sue them on as many grounds as possible. Breach of contract, fraudulent activities . . . whatever you can cook up. Sue them in court, attack them in the press, and soak up as much of their attention and their resources as you can. That's what I want."

Grissom started to speak but stopped when Johnson held up his hand.

"I know what you are about to say. You are a small fish in a large pond. But that is exactly why I have chosen you, and it is exactly why this will work. You are not one of the swells at the top of the organization. You are one of the people who put your faith in them. Unlike all of the other clubs in that league—unlike most professional ball clubs anywhere—your Kansas City operation is bottom-up in a way. No one seems to hold a controlling interest. The club has sold itself as a representation of the city and cemented that by selling shares far and wide. That is probably how you got your shares, and it makes you a perfect spokesperson, not only for the large group of owners but for the entire city. It is precisely because you are an everyman that you will have great influence if you do this right. And you will."

Time to twist the knife.

"All of that is true. But we both know, and I readily acknowledge, that as one among the many, the best you can be is an effective provocateur. And much of what must be done will require the work of a skilled attorney. As it happens, I know just such a man here in Chicago. His name is John Maxcy Zane." Johnson paused to allow the name to sink in and was rewarded with a flash of recognition and a small shudder. "He's a prominent and respected attorney here and around the country. He specializes in commercial litigation, so this will be right down his alley. I will make sure that Mr. Zane makes himself available, and you will be the local hero who successfully recruits such a valuable advocate to your cause."

At this point, Grissom felt queasy, felt his head spinning, felt his legs grow weak. Zane! Why did it have to be Zane? And then, of course, he knew exactly why it had to be Zane. Grissom was really in a fix now. He lost focus momentarily but regained it when Johnson started to speak once more.

"Now, Parker, I know this is a lot to take in. And I really think you will come out of this as a local hero. Maybe even have a political career. In fact, I might be able to help you with that, perhaps connect you with Tom Pendergast or Joe Shannon and so forth. But I confess to you I know there is a risk that things could go the other way, that you could end up getting blamed for things over which, in truth, you have no control. And risk ought to be accompanied by suitable rewards."

He pushed a document across the table toward Grissom.

"Here's a little document I have asked our lawyers to prepare. I know by the simple fact that you have purchased shares in your local team that you have an interest in baseball and are willing to step up and put your money behind that interest. And I know, and in your heart of hearts, you realize, that the current club, the Kansas City Packers, is going nowhere but into the tank. Kansas City today is a minor league town. It's too small and too remote to support a major league team. Even if the Federal League succeeds in this ridiculous effort to be accepted as on par with the American and the National, Kansas City will not be there when it happens. I understand the dream. Believe me, I do. But it will not be coming true for you and your fellow Kansas Citians.

"But that's now. Look at what's happened to this country, to your state, and to your city. Millions of new immigrants finding their places across the land, new industries making products you and I never dreamed of, railroads crisscrossing the land, automobiles. Aeroplanes, for God's sake. This country is all about growth and change. Why, I predict the day is coming when these United States will become a real world power. Not today, maybe not next year, but soon. And when that happens, I'm sure Kansas City will be swept along in the excitement. And what I want to offer you and your loved ones in return for this modest assistance I have requested is the chance to share in that when the inevitable happens. It is all set forth here in this document. Please, take a moment to read the terms of our offer."

Memorandum of Agreement

I, Parker T. Grissom, undersigned, do hereby agree to render such personal services to the National Commission as I may be assigned for the purpose of strengthening the organization and standing of the game of baseball at the professional level. The referenced services will be provided for a period commencing upon the date below and continuing for not more than two years therefrom.

In compensation for the services to be rendered, the National Commission, represented by the undersigned officers, duly authorized, which organization is the governing body of organized professional baseball, affirms that Parker T. Grissom, his heirs and legal successors, will be entitled in perpetuity, or until disposed of, to ownership of ten percent of any affiliated Major League Baseball franchise that may, at some future and undetermined date, be awarded to the city of Kansas City, Missouri, or the surrounding metropolitan area to a radius of 25 miles from the city center, by this Commission, by the American or National Baseball Leagues, or by any of their successor organizations, and to any revenues and ancillary benefits that may attend to such ownership.

Nothing in this Memorandum of Agreement constitutes a commitment by the National Commission, nor by the American or National Leagues, to award a Major League Baseball franchise to Kansas City or to any other locality in the State of Missouri, the State of Kansas, or elsewhere, nor is any such commitment or award anticipated at this time.

This document constitutes in its entirety the agreement between the parties, and is made under and subject to the laws of the State of Illinois.

Done this Seventh Day of January, in the Year of Our Lord 1914, By:

Greta Peabody James
Witness

August Herrmann
Chairman, National Commission

Byron Bancroft Johnson
President, American League of Professional Baseball Clubs

John K. Tener
President, National League of Professional Baseball Clubs

"Here's a pen," Johnson said, holding one out toward Grissom. "Sign it."

Grissom again looked confused, this time by his seeming good fortune. "You're giving me ten percent of a major league baseball team?" he said, somewhat incredulously.

"Yes," said Johnson. "But, of course, only if there is one. And if it falls within the jurisdiction of the National Commission and the existing leagues.

To be clear, we are not talking here about this outlaw Federal League fantasy, and we are not making any commitment of any kind to place a team in Kansas City now or in the future. So what we are offering you in exchange for some very modest assistance to facilitate an outcome that will occur one way or another regardless—and you will see that all of us who matter have already signed the document before a witness, my secretary, whom you have met—is a piece of the dream of Major League Baseball in Kansas City, should that dream ever become reality. Do you dare to dream, Parker?"

———

Andy took the Grissom file from Joey, left his office, and headed straight for the elevator and down to the basement archives, his mind in some degree of disarray. He'd been sure Coy would share his excitement over what he had uncovered so far over the document and what it portended. It had not occurred to him that the firm would want to ignore this document, or even worse, take the other side if it ever came to light. But he had his instructions, and Coy was the boss.

Andy did exactly as he had been instructed. He went into the archive area and angrily dropped the folder into its chronological resting place, then took the box labeled "Parker T. Grissom" from the shelf, carried it over to the "burn bag," or in this case, the area of the archive set aside for documents set to be destroyed, and dropped it onto the pile. He then returned to the shelves and pushed the remaining boxes in the immediate area around so as to obscure the fact that one of their number was missing. *No one*, he thought, *will be looking around here anyway, at least not for another hundred years.*

———

"Who's representing the Federals?" The question, from George Williams, counsel to the American League, was directed to his colleague and National League counterpart, George Pepper. At least in the extant matter, Pepper also represented the National Commission.

"Ed Gates from Myers and Gates. You know him?" came the reply.

"I do," answered Williams. "Sharp advocate, good on details. But I think we can best him here on the bigger picture. You see who the judge is?"

"It's Landis," said Pepper. "They filed in the Northern District, and they must think that gives them an advantage."

"Why is that?" This from Garry Herrmann, who, along with Johnson and Tener, filled out the dance card.

"Kenesaw Mountain Landis," offered Williams. "The guy's a real stickler for procedure, and he's a showboat when it comes to judicial authority. Well, most judges at that level are like that. But what makes Landis different is that he's really signed on to this new wave of breaking up the trusts and fighting against business interests. You remember that judge that hauled John D. Rockefeller across the country and into court? That was Landis, and that is vintage Landis behavior."

"I agree," injected Pepper. "But let's remember, too, that Landis really does value adherence to the rules. And the Federal League is nothing if not a blatant violator of the rules agreed on by virtually the entire baseball industry. *And* they are encouraging players under valid contracts to ignore the obligations they have agreed to. If we have an angle that can offset a claim of anticompetitive behavior, I think it lies somewhere on that ground."

"Does the lawsuit name all of the clubs in both leagues as respondents?" asked Johnson, who had sat quietly through the initial stage of the discussion.

"Yes, Ban, it does," Pepper responded. "So we will have one hell of a job getting all of the clubs and whatever legal counsel they retain to coordinate a response."

"No," replied Johnson, breaking into a smile, "that won't be a problem. And we've got this case won."

"Beg pardon?" said Pepper. "Why is that?"

"It's just this. The Federals have overlooked something. Landis may be a trustbuster and play to the papers, but the good judge is also—and I would wager more fundamentally—a baseball fan and, more specifically, a diehard Cubs fan. On the nights we don't see him at Comiskey, he's usually in the owner's box watching the Cubs. He even lets his court out early so he can get to the games. And now the Federals have sued the Cubs. The judge's beloved Cubs. I'd bet dollars to doughnuts he'll find a way to make this case come out right for us. We just have to stand back and let him.

"I have also heard, by the way, that there may be some unhappiness brewing within the Federal League itself. Unhappy teams, relocations, financial problems, maybe even some slick dealing among themselves. I can't say where I heard that, and I can't vouch for it, either. But let's just say that it wouldn't surprise me if that turned out to be the case. And if it does, well, it might be that all we need to do is sit back and wait for the whole thing to collapse under its own weight."

Both of the Georges looked closely at Johnson, knowing that he had perhaps the best intelligence network in all of baseball and that he seldom spoke without reason. Williams broke the brief silence.

"Be that as it may, Ban, and I do hope you are right, we have a meeting in chambers with Judge Landis tomorrow and we need to be prepared. We can easily ask for some time to read and digest the complaint, which we've only just seen. In addition, as of the last time I asked, there are some clubs named in there as respondents who have yet to receive service. Knowing Landis, he will want to schedule an evidentiary hearing in the near future. Look how quickly he called for the meeting in chambers. In the same week as the filing, which is extraordinary. But he is certain to give us at least a week or two to prepare. And we'd best do that."

Garry Herrmann reasserted himself as chairman of the National Commission and, accordingly, as the principal at this meeting. "We have a conference room set up for you gentlemen down the hall. You can work there, store your papers, and so forth. We'll be sure it's all secure."

And with that, the meeting broke up. The attorneys headed down the hallway to begin their preparations while the three baseball executives lingered.

"John," said Johnson, "you have obviously done your part well. That was a good first session, and I think we have the proper representation here. Garry, how are arrangements coming with the clubs?"

"I sent out telegrams to all of them the other day alerting them to expect legal service and instructing them to reply when they had seen the papers. So far, I have heard from eleven of the sixteen. I also advised them that the commission and the leagues were preparing a unified response and that, even as they might feel compelled to contact their own attorneys, it was essential that they not speak or act independently, especially in the papers, once they get hold of this."

"Excellent," said Johnson. "You will both be interested to know that our friend Mr. Grissom was easily persuaded to sign the document. We all know that Kansas City will *never* be a Major League Baseball town. So our offer is of no value whatsoever. But I convinced Grissom that he was part of the dream of owning a club and that was enough. Well, that plus reminding him that the Pinkertons can be a nasty bunch, that Jim McParland can sometimes lose control of himself, and that either of the local bosses out in KC, Pendergast and Shannon and the thugs they both associate with, might take an interest as well. I even had a brainstorm right in the middle of the discussion, and I told him we'd arrange it so John Zane himself—the lawyer who wrote up his confidential agreement with Armour years ago—would come down from Chicago to help him out on the legal end."

"Bravo, Ban!" shouted Herrmann. "What a great touch."

Tener smiled at the audacity of the play and thought how glad he was that Ban and he were on the same side this time. "You know, Ban," he offered, "if you ever decide to retire from baseball, with that set of skills and Flagler's new railroad, you could have a whole new career selling ocean-view swamp land in Florida." It was meant as a compliment.

All three men took it precisely so and shared a hearty guffaw.

Free Agency

Andy continued in his labors in the archive, but his mood, sullen since the meeting with Joey Coy, was not lightened by immersing himself in work. There were some additional interesting case files, to be sure. In 1918, a rash of defense industry cases found the firm advocating for expansion and monopoly in the name of national defense. The year 1919 put the firm itself in the crosshairs as a wave of anarchist bombs dispatched through the postal system exploded outside the homes of numerous judges and other prominent public officials, taking the lives, among others, of two jurists who had built their careers in Stetson, Varney predecessor practices. Not only did the firm handle both estates, but it also represented the insurance industry in a series of cases that determined whether liability for compensating the victims rested with their respective insurers since all were targeted in their private homes, or with the government since all were targeted by virtue of their positions. It was, of course, the government that ended up covering the firm's fees. The next year, on September 16, 1920, the attacks moved even closer to home when a horse cart filled with explosives was detonated on Wall Street, claiming thirty-eight lives, including that of a named partner at an early predecessor firm, a death that apparently precipitated the merger of his firm into this one. There was a seemingly deliberate ambiguity in the estate file in this instance, but Andy took from it the suggestion that the young lady who was injured while accompanying the partner in question was not a member of his family.

Through it all, the future Stetson, Varney grew and prospered as the defender of American industrial management and might. Its client list came to include most of the leading companies of the era, and the firm itself rose rapidly through the ranks of the legal profession.

For a historian, it was a fascinating period. But for a lawyer like Andy, tasked as he was simply with danger-proofing century-old case files, it became increasingly tedious. Still, he valued the job and needed the money to survive. And as the end of his first year approached, he hoped that the anniversary would occasion his release from this bondage. In the event, it did.

As was the custom at law firms large and small, first-year associates were routinely scheduled for evaluation after one year of work. So it came as no surprise when Andy received an email from his supervisor, Joey Coy, telling him to arrange an appointment through Coy's secretary for sometime during the week after next. Andy scheduled the appointment, then set about preparing himself for the review. As instructed at the outset, and seemingly reasonably given the nature of his tasking, he had not maintained any notes on what he discovered in the myriad boxes he was to review. So he thought it wise to take a day and prepare, at least, a summary report on the amount of work he had accomplished. To that end, he went back to the first case file he had reviewed, a matter that was closed out in 1914, and counted the number of boxes between that point on the archive shelves and the last box he had processed. He was surprised to find that he had worked his way through 626 boxes of files covering a period of nearly seven years as well as three record system transitions as the mergers followed one upon the other. Then he realized he had overlooked something and bumped the count up to 627 boxes of files. He had all but forgotten the one box he had been instructed to burn. How could Joey fail to recognize that he, Andy Dennum, had paid his dues?

As it turned out, Joey had no difficulty whatsoever in failing to recognize so obvious a fact. That became clear at the outset as Andy entered Joey's office and headed for a chair across the desk from his boss.

"Andy, don't bother sitting down. I have the unenviable task today of informing you that your services are no longer required at Stetson, Varney. You've done good work, and I will be happy to write you a glowing letter of recommendation. But I'm afraid we were a trifle optimistic in our first-year hiring last year, and we seem to have more soldiers on the staff than we can place on the battlefield. You've been on the firm's in-house project for the last year, which, by our accounting, makes you a cost center rather than a revenue driver, and that cannot continue forever. Had you used some of your time to bring in new business for the firm or to assist some of the partners on other matters, things might be different. But that's water under the bridge. So we are letting you go. Your final paycheck will include two weeks of severance pay. You'll find a security officer with a box waiting for you at your cubicle downstairs. You'll have fifteen minutes to gather your personal items and turn in your badge and keys. Then you'll be escorted from the building. I'm very sorry things have turned out this way. You are a good lawyer, and I wish you the best."

Twenty minutes later, standing on the street outside the Stetson, Varney building holding his boxed life, Andy paused to catch his breath. It was only then that he recalled Janine's words nearly a year earlier. "We hire a night school grunt like you every year and stick them down in the basement," she had said, all but predicting that his employment had a fixed shelf life. At the time, he'd thought she was being deliberately cruel. But perhaps she had been the only honest person in the building.

⚓

Suddenly, and, if he were honest with himself, unexpectedly—he had always known at some level that this might happen, but he had managed to pile a great deal of dirt atop that level—Andy faced some potentially life-changing decisions. How badly did he want to be a lawyer? How badly did he want to be a lawyer at one of the big New York firms? How likely did he think that was now that he'd been let go by one of the biggest and most influential of them all? And more to the point, should he or should he not renew the lease on his apartment? The renewal notice, with its five percent rent increase, had been waiting for him in the day's mail when he returned home with his Stetson, Varney box. Altogether, the epitome of a terrible, no good, very bad day.

Andy needed time and space to think, and both seemed to be in short supply. The walls of his modest apartment in the city might not literally be closing in, but they, like the rest of his world, gave a good imitation of doing so. He needed to breathe. He needed to gather himself. He needed . . . New Jersey.

The lines of John Gorka's old paean to the state flashed through his mind.

"I'm from New Jersey, I don't expect too much / If the world ended today, I would adjust."

Gorka was an acquired taste Andy had come to only lately, an accident of curiosity that had been aroused by another singer's cover of a different tune in a performance at one of the neighborhood bars. A casual search, a brief sampling, and twenty-some downloads later, he was quite a fan. And even though they came from two very different places—Gorka from Woodbridge Township, across from Staten Island, and Andy from Mendham, in the "wilds" of north central Jersey, attested by the fact that the houses had side yards—he felt that the two were kindred Jersey spirits. At the very least, he heard the essence of his own angst in the songwriter's lyrics. And on that day, that angst was running away with him.

So, when Andy awoke the next morning and had showered, dressed, and sucked down some coffee, he packed a small bag with some clothes and essentials and headed for the North Fork Express bus stop at Third Avenue and Forty-second. There, he knew, the northbound Ronkonkema-Cornell buses left every half hour for the Hilton Garden Inn in Rockaway, north of Mendham, where he could grab a taxi for the last dozen or so miles. Once back home, he could reclaim his old clunker of a Ford Escape, which might or might not turn over by the usual fifth try.

For Andy, though, home wasn't exactly home anymore. His parents—actually his adoptive parents, but the only ones he had ever known—had moved to Florida the first chance they had after his grandmother had passed away a couple of years ago. So the house was still there, but these days it was little more than a waypoint, well maintained by a contract crew and always at the ready when Mom and Dad felt the need to escape the summer heat or take in a few New York museums. Andy himself had moved away when he had taken the Stetson, Varney job.

The ride out to the Hilton was slower than usual. Something about the traffic, he guessed, though he was lost in thought and barely attending to the scenery, let alone the road. But eventually they reached the cookie-cutter hotel on Mount Hope Avenue. He grabbed his bag, stepped down from the bus, and walked into the lobby to ask the clerk to call him a cab. Between the hotels and the mall just across the road, the area was attractive to the drivers, and a cab pulled up under the front portico almost before he could walk back outside. The driver wanted to talk; Andy did not. So he barely heard the heavily accented monologue about the annual decline of the New York Mets and how it could all be laid at the feet of the governor of New Jersey.

Finally, mercifully, the familiar outline of the house came into view, and the cabbie pulled over at the front walk.

"Dis de right place?" he queried.

"It is. Thanks very much," Andy replied, tapping his credit card on the small terminal attached to the back of the front seat, adding a nice tip.

After seeing the tip, the cabbie turned around and handed Andy a business card. "If yuz ever need a cab, yuz can just call me direct. No need ta go tru da company."

Everyone's an entrepreneur, thought Andy. But what he said was, "Thanks very much. I'll do that." Taking the card, he stepped out of the cab, closed the door, and walked to the front porch steps. Taking a quick look around to reset his sense of place, he climbed the steps, took out his key, and turned the lock. As he opened the door, the alarm sounded inside. After just a moment's panic because he had forgotten about the alarm system, he remembered the code and punched it in. To his immense relief, the noise stopped.

The house had a musty smell from having been closed up for so long, but the maintenance people seemed to be doing a decent job. Everything was clean and orderly, and the thermostat, set to keep the house warm enough in winter not to freeze the pipes and cool enough in summer to prevent mold and mildew, seemed to be working as well. He climbed the stairs to his old room, tossed his bag on the floor near the closet, and threw himself onto the bed. There he lay for an hour or more as he tried to come up with his Plan B for life.

To his amazement, the old Ford Escape turned over on the second try. The maintenance crew must have been charged with keeping the battery fresh, something his parents had neglected to mention. *Excellent,* he thought, *one burden lifted without a struggle.* He decided to drive around town for a while just to get his bearings.

In the old days, at least days that were old to Andy, wags used to describe Mendham as a giant Italian restaurant with a residential subsidiary. The town boasted five such eateries. And that was about it. But now, some of those old places were gone, replaced by a Greek restaurant and some sort of diner. That was change, Mendham style. His old high school, West Morris Mendham—Go Minutemen!—was still there. Dante's was still there, thank goodness, practically across the street from the school, looking smaller than he remembered and a little further away. There had been times when he'd relied on those pies for all the basic food groups. And the Black Horse. And, of course, Bailey's funeral parlor, just around the corner, where they had held the remembrance for his grandmother. In fact, when you came down to it, he realized, it was still kind of home. The anxiety began to lift, and he felt grounded once again.

Parked on Hilltop in front of the funeral home, Andy happened to glance across the street and had to stifle a laugh. There was the sign commemorating the town's one real claim to fame. It was where Abner Doubleday, the guy who invented baseball, had come to die. Well, technically, as Andy knew, he had come to retire in the town, but eventually, as these things go, he died there. His old house, like old Abner himself, was gone, but there was a nice historical marker on the spot where it had sat. Of course, that was back in the 1890s or so, and Andy didn't know of any local history that had merited a big metal sign in the intervening years.

Part of Andy's purpose in driving around the town was to do some scouting. After all, he needed to make a living, and he had only two trades—lawyer and investigator. Which would it be? And whichever it was, he needed to find a niche. There did not seem to be any private investigation firms in the town itself, but a quick online search had shown there were some larger operations in nearby Morristown, and he had realized at once he had no interest in them. That pointed toward the law.

He knew there were literally dozens of lawyers in Morris County, which included Mendham, but thought there might be fewer in Mendham itself, or at least in the Borough that lay at its heart. On his quick and disorganized tour, he spotted three or four shingles, all for solo or small legal practices. *That*, he thought, *might be promising*.

Andy resolved that he would try to visit with a few local attorneys, but he held out little hope of joining one of these firms. It was, after all, a small market, and among them, they had surely divided what business there was. In addition, even those that had more than one practitioner associated with them tended to be family firms in one form or another. Unless he happened across an elderly lawyer interested in selling his practice, he would be seen as nothing other than what he was—a prospective new competitor in a closed market.

It was in the second week of Andy's tour of the local legal landscape that his luck changed. He was sitting in the office of one of the solo practices and going through his customary queries when the attorney, Lou D'Antonio, stood up, closed the door to his outer office, and came around his desk to sit in the second of the two brown leather client chairs.

"Andrew," he said. "You would have no reason to know this, but many years ago I was the attorney who assisted your parents when they adopted you." Andy's eyes widened at this revelation, but the gesture eluded D'Antonio, who simply continued making his point. Andy made a mental note to revisit this conversation at an early opportunity.

"There was a lot of paperwork," D'Antonio was saying, "because . . . well, there just was. And I used to run into your dad at the country club from time to time, though I must confess I haven't seen him now for quite some time. Are your folks doing all right?"

"They are, sir. I don't know if you knew my grandmother, but she passed away a couple of years ago, and I guess that was like a burden being lifted or something. Because just a couple of months later, Mom and Dad moved down to Florida. So that's why you haven't seen them. But they're doing just fine. Might be up here for a time this summer just to get away from the gators down there."

"Well, that's very reassuring. Please give them my regards. But here's the thing. I'm afraid I am not doing so well. Ticker's going on the fritz, and my fancy doctor over in the city tells me I just have to step back from working so hard. Well, to be honest, from working altogether. I haven't told Betty yet," he was clearly referring to his receptionist-secretary-legal assistant in the outer office, "let alone any of my clients or anyone else. But I have to stop working, and I have to do it yesterday. So your being here today might just be a godsend for both of us. And the fact that I have, in a sense, known you almost your whole life, well, that's just the frosting on the cake. What say you and me go over to the diner for some lunch and see what we can see."

So it was that over a pair of salads and a shared piece of cherry pie, a deal was struck. D'Antonio Law was to become D'Antonio and Dennum, and on the most generous of terms. Lou said that he had managed to save up a good deal of money over the years and didn't really have anyone to leave it to. All that he asked for was a declining percentage of ownership and of Andy's net income from the practice, a place he could come and keep his hand in when he got bored with golf and fishing and reading all the old sci-fi novels he'd not had time for over the years and his name on the firm until he passed. For his part, Andy would take on all of D'Antonio's existing clients, or at least do his level best, with Lou's help, to keep them, and he would keep Betty on in some capacity for as long as she wanted to do the work. That would provide a core clientele in commercial law, real estate, family law, and estate planning—the meat and potatoes of small-firm law. Beyond that, Andy was free to take the practice in any direction he liked. Andy would start with sixty percent of the firm and be the managing partner. *Big ship*, thought Andy, *small pond*. It was perfect!

Once the basics were agreed upon, Lou sat back for a moment, pensive, then he offered this. "Andrew, if you don't mind, I'd like to give you some advice. You be good to my clients, and they'll be good to you. Most of them, they've been with me for a long time. They're steady, and there's not much fancy about what they need. You just do right by them, and you will make a go of this. And you know, there's a lot of people here who will remember your parents, and they'll remember you, some of them, through their kids, so unless you were a real troublemaker back in high school, that'll give you a head start, too. But all those people, well, like me, they're getting older, so you can't ever just sit back. You have got to put yourself out there in the town and meet the younger crowd, get that business so you can grow with it. I haven't had the energy to do that for some years now, because I figured I'd just wind down the practice when I wound down myself. But now that's not an option for me, and to be totally honest, it leaves you with a challenge. You have some time. Use it well. Get to know folks. Do good things around town. If you do that, well, you can have a really good life around here."

Andy and Lou returned to Lou's office, where together they broke the news to Betty. Then they set about drafting the papers to make their new arrangement a reality.

⚊⚊⚊ ⬥ ⚊⚊⚊

Andy had a step up since, having attended law school in the state, New Jersey had been the first place he had sat for the bar exam. And he had not been away so long afterward that his license even needed a renewal.

On the other hand, convincing Betty that he cared about the town and knew what he was doing would take a bit longer. And Betty, he came quickly to realize, was the key to this practice. Lou, as he'd said, had been slowing down for several years. Betty, by contrast, was picking up the pace year by year. Not only had she been taking on more and more responsibility around the office, but it was Betty who had been out in the community, joining the clubs, serving on the committees, and working at the volunteer jobs that were so essential to maintaining the flow of business into the firm. Everybody, he sensed, loved Betty, and where Betty went, they would follow.

While the papers were being drafted and processed, Andy took a day to drive into the city and clear out his apartment. The furniture was all rented from the landlord, so it was just his clothes, his computer, a few law books and papers, his dishes and silverware, and a few other items that he had to move. It was tight, but everything fit into the Escape. The last item into the Ford was the Stetson, Varney box, the contents of which he had not touched since hurriedly placing them there. He

57

emailed the landlord, declining the new lease, dropped the keys with the super, and headed west to his new life.

Once everything was signed, notarized, photocopied, and Martinized, whatever that was, Lou set aside a room with a desk and some chairs and Andy moved in, lock, stock, and box. Betty watched the process out of the corner of her eye, all the while giving off an air of . . . Andy couldn't decide if it was suspicion, disgust, or just plain old curiosity. Whatever it was, he knew he had to deal with it right away.

On Andy's third day in the office, Lou called in to say he'd be delayed until around noon. Andy used the opportunity to plop himself into the chair beside Betty's desk. She looked up slowly and turned toward him with a sort of crusty amused smile. "Yes, Andy?" she said.

"Betty, look. I know you and Lou go back a long way, and I know this change has come up all of a sudden. I can only imagine how you must be feeling. But Lou really is having problems. I'm sure you know that, even if you didn't guess how bad it was getting. And I know I showed up out of the blue and that all this change is happening really fast.

"But, Betty, I can't do this without you. Even an idiot could see that you're the one who makes this place run these days, that you keep Lou on the straight and narrow. He couldn't have done it without you, and neither can I. I really want you to stay here, and I want to do whatever I can to make sure that you do. So I need you to feel like you can say anything to me. I don't care if it's good or bad, if you need to say it, then just say it. If I need to wear a different tie because some client doesn't like the color red, then tell me. If you think I am overlooking some legal point—and I know after so many years working here that you know more law than you're supposed to let on—you tell me. If I bring you some flowers or some chocolates and you'd rather have licorice sticks, you tell me. Can we do that?"

Andy held his breath.

"Did I hear mention of chocolates?" came Betty's reply, accompanied by what passed on her face for a big smile. And suddenly Andy knew everything would be just fine.

"Chocolates it is," he said, returning the smile. "And I could actually use some of your help right now. I grew up here, but I've been away for years and I've never lived here as an adult. I need to find some ways of getting involved in the community where I can meet some new people and make some good contacts for the business. Have you got any suggestions for places I could start?"

"Actually, I do have one idea," Betty said.

—⟐⟐—

The Village at Hacklebarney would not have been Andy's first pick of a place to make friends and generate business. He'd never heard of the place. He knew that Hacklebarney State Park was west of town a few miles, out along the line between Morris and Chester Counties. He remembered hiking some trails out there, maybe along some rocky creek, back in middle school. Apparently, a development company had bought up a lot of adjacent land and had built one of those life care communities that were becoming so popular with the Boomers as they got older. Called it the Village at Hacklebarney, maybe on the theory that anyone who couldn't pronounce the name was too far gone to move in. Anyway, there it was, and Betty had a contact on the program committee. They were, she said, always looking for speakers who would interest their residents, and a lawyer who did estate planning, well, that was just the ticket.

So it was that Andy found himself taking a surprisingly pleasant twenty-minute drive out to the *real* wilds of New Jersey. Just before he reached the park proper, he saw the Village looming through the trees off to one side of the road. He turned into the drive where a countrified modern sign indicated, followed along for a half mile or so, and parked in the visitors' lot a short walk from the main entrance. Once inside the building, he presented himself at the front desk and asked for Anne Wiltgies, the program director. The receptionist directed him down a hallway to the right.

"You must be Mr. Dennum," said the thin, fiftyish woman in the programs office, rising from her desk as Andy tapped on the open door.

"Andy, please."

"And I am Anne. It's very nice to meet you. I'm sure I speak for everyone here at the Village when I tell you how much we appreciate your taking time from your busy schedule to participate in our little program here."

"Not at all. It's my pleasure."

"Things will get going in about fifteen minutes," she said. "Let me show you to the events space, and you can have a look at the setup. We usually have forty or fifty of our residents at these sessions, plus some of our staff and, of course, the other speakers. We are going to ask you to speak first, but I do hope you'll be able to stay the entire hour and a half to hear the others."

With that, the two of them walked back down the hallway to reception, then turned to the right, passed a bank of mailboxes used by the residents and through a lobby of sorts, then turned right again into a large meeting room. Rows of chairs were arranged in the room theater style, with an aisle down the middle, and there was a grand piano off in one corner at the front. Center front was a modest lectern with a microphone affixed to its top surface. Andy did not see a wire running from the microphone to an amplifier and concluded that whatever wiring was required was handled through outlets in the floor, which struck him as a good idea in a setting populated by older folks.

"Feel free to check out the podium there, and just grab any seat that you like," suggested Anne. "Excuse me for a moment, but I see someone I need to speak with." And off she went.

The room was already filling with a mixture of residents and, perhaps, some of their friends or family members from outside the community, as well as a few staff members with metallic Village name badges on their tunics. He took a seat at the near end of the front row, close to the entrance, in case he felt the need to escape quietly after his talk. As the room continued to fill, a custodian began adding chairs at the rear.

Shortly after Andy had settled himself, and as he was reviewing the notes for his talk, Anne Wiltgies was back with a bearded man in his thirties and an attractive woman in what Andy guessed to be her late twenties, whom Anne introduced as the other two speakers for the day. The man sat down beside Andy and the woman in the chair just to his left. The pair either already knew each other or had just met in Anne's office.

"Jeff McKenzie-Boyd," said the man, holding out his hand to Andy. "I'm with the Chester Township Senior Resource Center."

"Andy Dennum," he replied. "I'm an attorney over in Mendham."

The young woman leaned forward at that point and offered her own hand. "Keiley Barefoot," was all she said.

"I'm Andy. Andy Dennum," he said, nodding and smiling.

It was at that point that Anne Wiltgies walked to the podium and turned on the microphone.

"I am delighted to see so many of you could be with us this morning. We have a wonderful program on tap with three terrific guest speakers, so please make them all feel welcome."

The room filled with polite applause as she gestured toward the threesome seated in the front row at stage left.

"Our first speaker today is an attorney from Mendham Borough, Andrew Dennum. Andy, as you may have heard, has just become the new partner of Lou D'Antonio, someone I am sure many of you know. Andy has graciously agreed to speak with us today about wills and estate planning, something I know many in this room have an interest in. As is our custom, we've asked our speakers to talk for about fifteen or twenty minutes, then to take questions for a few minutes afterward. Andy, the floor is yours."

Andy rose from his chair and walked to the microphone. "Anne, thank you so much for the invitation. I am so pleased to be here today." And with that, he launched into an extremely boring discussion of why everyone needed to have a will, why one had to be especially careful regarding what was in the will, some things to think about before contacting an attorney to help in drafting a will (to save time and money), and why it was important in most circumstances to share with one's family members what was in the will. The time flew by, and more hands were raised in the audience than he had time to select for questions.

"I see by the way that Anne is tapping her toe," he concluded to laughter, "that my time is up. I will try to stay a few minutes after the program to answer some of the questions I couldn't get to. All I will say here at the end is this: Don't think you don't need a will, and don't try to write one by yourself. For this, you need a lawyer, and there are many in the nearby communities who can give you the help you need. Thank you very much for your attention."

This time, as he walked to his chair and sat down, the applause was more sustained and enthusiastic. *Man*, he thought to himself. *Betty was certainly right about this place. I think I can make this work.*

Next up was Jeff McKenzie-Boyd, the bearded fellow from the Senior Resource Center. Andy got the sense that Jeff was a regular here at the Village, not least because Anne rose only to say that he needed no introduction. He had an easy manner about him and seemed to be sharing inside jokes with some in the audience. His presentation touched on the role of the Center as a kind of information source and clearing house for services available to seniors in the western end of the county but centered more on specific upcoming events and activities such as storytelling, oral histories, and exercise classes. He took a few questions about the times and dates of specific coming events and one or two about other staff members at the Center, then sat down, having used less than his full allotted time.

It was then Ms. Barefoot's turn. Anne took the podium first.

"Last on our program for the day is Ms. Keiley Barefoot. Keiley is here to talk about a topic I know many of you are keenly interested in: genealogy, and specifically, some of the resources you can use to trace your ancestors and find out that you were all royalty in a past life." That got a laugh. "All of you except for Todd Grantham, who's trying to hide back there in the corner. We all know that Todd was a toad in a past life." That got a collective belly laugh, including from Todd, who was obviously the target of a running inside joke. It was a joke Anne then shared with the uninitiated. "Before I get hauled up before Social Services," she said, "I should explain to the newcomers in our midst that last year Todd played a toad in our little production of 'Alice Through the Looking Glass,' and he absolutely stole the show." Todd beamed at the back while others around the room smiled at the memory and nodded their assent.

Keiley Barefoot then walked to the podium and began to talk about family trees, online ancestor-tracing services, various sources of records like vital statistics and immigration files that held valuable data, and the value of oral histories that folks in the room might record for the benefit of their own posterity. *She really is quite lovely*, mused Andy, lost in his thoughts for a few moments before tuning back in to her presentation. *And she seems pretty smart, too*, he added as she continued. After offering the audience a checklist of ways to start tracing their respective roots, she answered a few of the questions indicated by raised hands and, like Andy, promised to stick around a while to answer some more.

When Keiley reached her seat, Anne Wiltgies returned to the microphone. "Just one reminder," she said. "Next month we'll be having our annual 'Ask the Undertaker' program featuring . . ." She was interrupted by a round of applause and a room full of smiles. She continued, "featuring our regular expert Morgan Montgomery. This year's topic will be: Cremation, The Burning Question on Everyone's Mind." More applause and some titters. "I guess I should let our visitors today in on that joke as well."

She then turned to the threesome seated in the front row. "Morgan comes every year. He really is a funeral director, and he plays the part to the hilt. He always arrives driving a big old black 1960s-style Cadillac hearse, one of those with the big fins in the back. Dresses and sounds like . . . Lurch from *The Addams Family*. Makes a big show of it, he's always very informative, and he's always got some new undertaker jokes. You won't understand until you're older, but a lot of people here enjoy laughing about it. After all, what's the alternative?"

Then, to the audience, "How about a big round of applause for our speakers today!"

With that, the program concluded, and the room began to empty.

Jeff made a quick exit, but Andy and Keiley were both in demand. At Anne's suggestion, they positioned themselves in opposite corners of the room, each surrounded by enquiring minds that wanted to know. Whether Andy's crowd was larger or whether their questions were simply more detailed, he did not know. But by the time he came up for air and looked across the room, to his disappointment he saw that Keiley had already left.

It was with a sense of both surprise and pleasure, then, that, as he walked out of the room and into the small lobby area, he saw she was actually waiting for him.

"Andy, hi. We didn't get much chance to talk in there, but I thought your presentation was interesting. I have never thought about wills and estates and things, and I guess everyone should. It's just so . . . morbid.

Oops!" she exclaimed, worried that she'd just committed a major faux pas. "I'm sorry! I shouldn't have said that."

Andy laughed. "No, no. Not at all. When people are our age, that's exactly how it seems. Morbid. Good word. If I'm being truthful with you, I don't even have one yet myself. Same reason."

"Really?" she asked.

"Yep. Until recently, I was doing mostly other kinds of law, and I never really thought about doing a will. But estates are a big part of this practice I just joined, and I guess I shouldn't be telling people they should do something I haven't even done yet myself.

"But I was interested in your talk, because that family tree thing is kind of weird for me. I was adopted when I was young, so my adoptive parents are the only ones I know. And no one ever talked much about where I was born or who my real parents were. Except for this one weird coincidence. When I was interviewing for this job, my new partner, who's been around here forever, let slip that he had had something to do with my adoption papers way back when. I guess my adoptive parents—I just think of them as my parents, period—were clients and friends of his. I've been meaning to press him a bit about that, see if I can find out anything. But like I said, the whole idea of a family tree is sort of alien to me. Sometime maybe you can tell me more about it."

Keiley smiled broadly. "Got lunch plans?"

⁕

Since they had arrived separately at the Village center, Andy and Keiley agreed to meet back up in half an hour at the Black Horse in Mendham. They turned off their cell phones because it seemed the thing to do, then got to know a bit about each other over two mugs of local lager and some sandwiches—a Pub Burger for him and a Crispy Eggplant for her.

"Can you actually drink beer with an eggplant sandwich?" he asked with a degree of genuine amazement.

"Guess we'll find out," was her faux testy reply.

"I really was interested in your talk," Andy continued. "Honestly, it's a topic I have never thought about. I don't think my mom and dad ever knew anything about my birth parents, or if they did, they never said a word about it."

"But you said your new law partner . . ."

"Lou."

"Yes, Lou. You said he told you he'd done some of the paperwork for the adoption? He might know who they were."

"Right. It's been hectic since that conversation. There were all the partnership papers to complete, and moving into the office, and then getting started trying to build up some clients . . . doing things like today just to meet people since I've been away for so long. And Lou has been spending less and less time in the office. He's got some health issues, which is why he was so open to my joining. But I do plan to revisit that with him as soon as I get a chance. At this point, I have no idea what he knows or what he'd tell me."

"Well, if you can get a name or something, maybe where they lived, I might be able to help you trace your family connections back in time. That's if you're interested in that sort of thing."

"Thanks for that. You know, it's like I said. I've just never really given that much thought. I want to mull on that for a while. So . . . how'd you get to be a professional genealogist? Can you really make a living at that?"

"Oh, no, I'm not a professional. I just do it on the side. I enjoy history. I like to read about it. And this genealogy stuff is just a hobby. In real life, I'm a cartographer."

"You're a heart doctor?" asked Andy with some emphasis.

Keiley laughed. "No. That's a cardiologist. I'm a cartographer. I design maps for a living."

"Wow. I don't think I have ever met a cartographer before. What kind of maps? You mean like city maps and highway maps and so forth? How does that work?"

"Well, when I was starting out, that's exactly what I was working on. Road maps, city planning maps, and so forth. I was working for a big mapmaker in New York, just doing whatever basic work they assigned me. After a while, it got pretty boring, so I started looking around for a way to go off on my own and do something more interesting. I got a contract out here doing specialty maps of some of the parkland in the area, and I liked it so much I decided to stay. So I have my own little studio just this side of Morristown, and so far, I've been able to keep busy and fed doing all kinds of small-project specialty maps. None of the big companies want that work, so it's been a pleasant little niche in the market. What about you? How did you end up in Mendham? Was that always the plan, to come back home?"

"Not exactly," Andy replied. He then proceeded to tell her about his insurance work, his six years of night school, and his crack at the big time that ended up being something completely different. "I guess you could say," he concluded, "that I reached for the top and ended up in the basement. Not," he hastened to add, "that I don't like where I am right now. This morning was my first real immersion in this kind of practice, and I have to confess, I rather enjoyed it. And I like the thought of having real people as clients."

Keiley picked up the thread. "It sounds like we're both, in our own ways, refugees from big firms and life in the city. We ought to keep in touch. You never know when some law client will need a good map."

He smiled. "You never know. And I like that idea. But while you've got me thinking about it, I want to head back to the office and see if I can catch up with Lou."

When Andy got back to the office, Betty was beside herself. He had come to think of her as unflappable, but suddenly she was nothing but flap.

"Where have you been?" she wanted to know. "I thought you were due back here hours ago."

"Well I'm here now. That was a great idea you had. I found that I enjoyed doing that talk at the Village program, and then there were lots of questions. And afterward, I went and had lunch with one of the other speakers. What's got you so stirred up?"

"Lou's in the hospital over in Morristown."

"Oh my god, what happened?"

"They think he had a stroke. A couple of his neighbors stopped by for a visit this morning, and when he didn't answer the door, one of them went and got his spare key and went in. Found him there lying on the floor. He might have also hit his head on the way down. Anyway, they called an ambulance, then they called me. I went over quick as I could, but there wasn't much I could do except close up the house. I came back here and called the hospital, but they either didn't know anything or wouldn't say. You know how it is now with the privacy laws. If you're not joined at the hip to a patient, they won't tell you a thing. But apparently, it didn't look good."

"Does he have a doctor over there? Somebody we can check in with?"

"He has a woman here in town, Madge Carter. I'm not sure what kind of medicine she does. I mean, I knew Lou was having some serious problems, but he would never tell me just what they were. Heart, cancer. You always assume the worst."

"He told me his ticker was giving him problems," Andy inserted, surprised that on this aspect of Lou's life, he might have better information than Betty. "So maybe that's her area. We can look her up easily enough and find out."

"I don't even know if she knows about this," Betty realized. "Let me track her down and make sure she knows to go see him at the hospital. I just might be able to find out a little bit more, too, just woman to woman."

"Betty, keep me posted. I'll stay here for a while, then maybe you and I will close up and head over to Morristown together."

It seemed to Andy that half the town had turned out for Lou's funeral, which consisted only of a brief graveside ceremony. Lou had lived in the Borough his entire professional life and had clearly helped many of his neighbors in that time. He and Betty were the closest thing to family his partner had, and Andy felt himself an imposter in that role. But Betty needed his support, and he was happy to give it. It took a good twenty minutes for the line of well-wishers to pass by and extend their condolences to the pair, and toward the end, Andy was both surprised and pleased to see that Keiley was among them.

"I didn't expect to see you here," he said as he took her hand.

"I saw the notice in the paper," Keiley replied, "and I thought you might need a little bit of moral support. I hope you don't mind."

"Are you kidding? I'm glad you're here." Then, turning to his side, he said, "Betty, this is a new friend of mine, Keiley Barefoot. She was one of the other speakers at that Village program last week." To Keiley he added, "Betty is the person in charge of our office, and I think she's been Lou's closest friend for a very long time."

"Betty, it's very nice to meet you. I'm so sorry for your loss. I only knew Lou from what Andy told me over lunch last week, but he sounds like he must have been a terrific fellow."

"So this is the 'other speaker' you had lunch with that day?" Betty said to Andy with a smile. "You've been holding out on me, young man. And she came here today for someone she doesn't even know? I like her." Then to Keiley, "Thank you so much for coming, dear. I hope I get to see some more of you. Maybe help keep this rookie in line."

All three had a good laugh. Keiley moved on, allowing the few stragglers to connect with Betty. But she lingered for a while and caught Andy's eye.

"You must have had a hard day. Why don't you come over to my place later and let me fix you dinner?"

"You cook?" he said in mock shock. "Actually, that sounds terrific. Not sure I'll be very good company, but I promise to try."

"Good. Bring some red wine." Keiley proceeded to give him the address and some minimal directions. "I'll look for you around seven."

Keiley lived in a smallish two-story brick house on a tree-lined street just west of Morristown. It might almost have seemed to have a rural character had it not been for the several commercial strips he had passed through to reach it. Beside the front door was a small brass plaque that read "Barefoot Mapping." He rang the bell and was rewarded with a prompt click of the door lock.

"Right on time," she said, opening the brightly painted door. "I like that."

"On time and bearing gifts," Andy replied, holding out a bottle of Provenance Rutherford cab.

"Ooooh," she cooed. "Why don't you bring that in here? If you're nice, I might share it with you."

A few minutes later the two sat, wine glasses in hand, in a pair of old but still comfortable chairs in the small living room. Andy glanced around and was left with the impression that comfortable was actually the best way of describing the entire room, which combined soft seating and soft lighting with a carved coffee table of a wood he could not identify. On the wall were three pieces of art that might best be characterized as exercises in geometric design. It occurred to him that they might be just that.

"Did you do the drawings on the wall?" he asked her.

"Actually, I did. Back when I was working in the city, I did them as a form of relaxation. I was doing some studies of graphic forms, and the chance to play around with the seeming regularity of geometry was too tempting to pass up. What do you think?"

"I really like them. They're almost three-dimensional."

At the latter comment, she brightened. "I love that you saw that in them. It's just what I was after. Thank you."

"So, tell me all about your maps. By the way, I love the name of the company, Barefoot Mapping. It conjures up a wonderful image. Is Barefoot a Native American name of some sort?"

She laughed. "No, nothing like that. It's an old English name from maybe a thousand years ago. Pretty much describes the people who had it. It's been spelled about twenty different ways over the centuries, but in the end, it all comes back to people walking around without shoes. In my case, I've been able to trace it back to a pair of brothers, James and John Barefoot, who landed down in Maryland and Virginia in 1634. But I'm afraid I'm not related to anyone famous. I guess if you start out barefoot, you end up that way." She smiled, as did Andy. "Would you like to see the family tree I made for myself? I did it a few years ago when I was just getting started with the business. I use it as kind of a work sample."

"Absolutely."

She stood up and began walking toward the other side of the house. Andy rose from his chair and followed. "Over there," she was saying, pointing toward the rear of the house, "is the bedroom. And this," indicating the room they were entering, "is my humble office."

Inside the smallish room was an antique desk with a contemporary ergonomic desk chair, two old but sturdy wooden chairs for clients, and a bookshelf. A small street-facing window illuminated the room, aided by several cans suspended from lighting tracks in the ceiling. The walls were painted a muted blue color of some sort. On the wall directly behind the desk, well lit and with obvious pride of place, was a drawing of an ancient tree—an oak, he guessed—on which were growing a great many vines, rising from the surrounding soil, winding around the trunk, intersecting with one another here and there, and eventually narrowing to a single unified shoot. Every few inches, vine leaves dotted the network of stems. As he moved closer, Andy could see that each leaf had, artfully imbedded within its veins, the name of a person who was, he gathered, one of Keiley's ancestors. In the single leaf at the top of the vinal network, he could see a miniaturized portrait of a young girl of perhaps six or eight years.

"You?" he asked.

"Yes. It's from a photo I found one day in an old box in the family attic. I always liked that picture, so I decided to use it here."

"This . . . map? This is just amazing. You're not just a mapmaker. You're a genuine artist. I mean, the whole concept and the way you've done this. It's just incredible."

"Thank you, kind sir," Keiley replied with a little curtsy. "Like I told you the other day, I like to think that maps can show up in unexpected ways and places. This is really just a standard map of what we've come to call a family tree, but instead of boxes and arrows, I decided to map it out quite literally. Not that original, I'm afraid. After all, it *is* called a family tree. So I decided that, instead of tree branches for the generations, I would use a climber. Of course, in nature, the vines would start out with a single stem and branch out, going upward, so it's backward—many branches leading to just one leaf. When you think about it, I suppose it is just the littlest bit egocentric. But I just said, so what. Besides, if the vine really was spreading out, why, it would eventually kill the tree! Anyway, this little mapping exercise was how I got into my hobby, genealogy. Plus, it's a good way to engage the imaginations of the people who come here looking for maps that are a little out of the ordinary. Would you like to see my studio?"

"Of course," he responded.

"We'll have to go upstairs for that. I warn you, though, there might be wet paint around, so watch what you touch."

On the upper floor of the house, Keiley had removed the interior walls where she could. All of the windows around the perimeter were uncovered, and Andy assumed they provided ample light for working during the day. They were supplemented with large recessed cans that eliminated any and all shadows when switched on as they were now. The room was cluttered with work tables, an easel, and multiple bunches of tubes and small bottles filled with paints of many colors. Projects at various stages of completion stood like open files in the sections of a wooden rack that looked purpose-built. One corner of the space, however, stood apart. It comprised a small desk with notepaper and some colored pencils on top, another bookshelf similar to the one in the office downstairs, and another oldish and comfortable-looking chair.

"This is all very impressive," he said. Then, pointing toward the area that looked more like a study carrel than a studio, he asked, "What's this?"

"I call that my Inspiration Corner," she said. "When I start a project, I can sit there and page through those books, and something usually comes to me. Sometimes it's from an architect, like Frank Lloyd Wright, or from designers, like the Cartier family, who did some interesting jewelry based in geometries, or some of the old mapmakers, and . . . Did you ever hear of Edward Tufte?" She pronounced it "tuff-tee."

"Tufte? That's a strange name. No, can't say that I have. One of the old mapmakers?"

"No, he is, or was—I'm not sure at this point if he's still around—a statistician at Yale. He was really into telling statistical and other stories, even historical events, through graphic design. I don't know how much of it he just collected and how much he came up with himself. But he used to go around the country doing these seminars on what you might call narrative graphic design. And he published several books full of examples. If you look on the second shelf there, you'll see that I have them all."

Andy did as instructed and worked his way down the shelf. There was a family history of the Cartiers by one of their descendants; a book called *The Wright Style*, which he assumed meant Frank; one titled *Maps: Finding Our Place in the World*, which, he guessed, must have a lot of maps in it; and one that looked like it must be a textbook or some such. It was called *Information Graphics: A Comprehensive Illustrated Reference*. Then he came to a set of four books authored by this fellow Tufte. The collection of idea generators continued down the shelf from there.

Keiley walked over to the corner and pulled one of the Tufte books, *Visual Explanations*, from its resting place. She opened the book to a two-page graphic near the center. Andy had the sense that the book somehow knew of its own volition to open to that very place. The drawing resembled nothing so much as a complex relief map of a hillside that showed the smallest variations in altitude.

"I'm spending a lot of time thinking about this one," she was saying, "especially when someone comes in and wants some kind of genealogy chart. It comes from an old study of the history of rock and roll somebody did back in the 1970s. If you look, it tells the story of the growth of rock music starting from a half dozen or so points of origin, like Bill Haley and Fats Domino and Johnny Mathis, and it tracks the influence of each one through the musicians who came later. It's very complex and captures a huge amount of information, but you can tell at a glance what's happening on the page.

"The basic dimension it's capturing is the passage of time, and I keep thinking it must have some application in my generation mapping. But the trouble is, it all goes in the wrong direction. People want to look backward, like the vines downstairs, and find their roots. They might want to look generations into the future and see what becomes of their own descendants, but the problem there is obvious. So I keep looking at it, but I'm about to give up."

Andy was staring at the diagram in the book and listening to Keiley, but his mind was elsewhere at the same time. Something was nagging at him. And then he realized what it was.

"I may have a way you can do that," he said. "And who knows? There might be some other ideas in Tufte you can use as well."

"I'm all ears," she replied. "But tell me downstairs. If I let dinner burn, you'll never trust me to cook again. Besides," she added, holding up an empty glass, "that's where the rest of the wine is."

Once they were settled at her small dining table just off the living room, Keiley disappeared into the kitchen. She reemerged a moment later using two bakers gloves to carry a steaming hot pie, which she set down on a trivet in the middle of the table. Taking a pie cutter, she cut and removed a large slice, about a quarter of the pie, and put it on a plate that she then passed to Andy. His eyes widened and his mouth began to water just from the look and smell of it. As she finished serving herself, also generously, she told him, "It's Irish stew pie. Barefoot might be an old English name, but Keiley is totally Irish. Comes from an old Gaelic word. I don't know what my parents were thinking when they set up this little culture clash in my head. But I long ago decided to embrace it." She flashed that same, now familiar little smile.

"What does it mean? Do you know?"

"I do know, but it's a little embarrassing to say. It means 'graceful.'" Andy thought he saw a slight blush as she said it.

"Well, Colleen," he offered, surprised at himself for knowing, let alone recalling, the Irish term for a young lady, "I believe you are well named."

"Enough!" he said. "Tell me about your genealogy problem. Were you able to get anything from Lou before he passed? I remember you were going to ask him about your adoption."

"No. That didn't work out. That same day we met out at the Village is when he had his stroke. Betty was frantic by the time I got back to the office. And far as I know, he never spoke another word to anyone. There might be something in the files, and I guess at some point, I'll take a look and see if I can find anything. But no. I was thinking about something different. It hit me when you were talking upstairs about that Tufte chart being backward for the kind of tracing people want you to do."

"Okay . . ."

"I told you a little the other day about my stint of big law and how that didn't work out. What I didn't tell you then was that I spent my entire year at that firm down in their catacombs unearthing dead cases and reburying them. In various incarnations—and that would be an interesting exercise in genealogy in itself. Stetson, Varney—that was the firm—goes back through generations of other law firms that merged into one another over the years." Andy paused, noticing a flicker of some sort in her eyes. "What?"

"Oh, nothing. You just gave me an idea for a whole new kind of mapping client. But I don't want to interrupt. We can talk about that later. Go on."

"Well," he continued, "people like us, and companies, we have to keep certain records for a fixed number of years, like for tax audits and the like. But law firms, they have to keep things forever, or at least they're smart if they do. Because you never know when some piece of litigation will raise issues or demand evidence that goes way back. So they have these really deep archives. And as time passes and more firms, with their own archives, merge into one another, it doesn't take too long before nobody has any idea what's in those old files.

"Apparently, at Stetson, Varney, which has a very long history, the way they deal with that problem is to hire some poor schlub to spend a year working through those old files from whatever point it was where the previous year's schlub left off. I didn't realize it at the time, but last year's schlub was me. I started sometime in 1914, and I made it into the early twenties before they declined to renew me for a second year, which is to say, they fired me. Nothing to do with my work. It's just what those bastards do every year.

"Anyway, part way through, I came across this strange file." Andy went on to describe the three-page Grissom file, careful not to reveal any particulars that might violate any issues of ethics or confidentiality. "My boss, one of the senior partners at the firm, basically told me to deep-six the whole thing. He told me to stick the file back in its place, then destroy the box I had found it in. And that is what I did, and I basically forgot all about it until a moment ago up in your studio when we were looking at that chart.

"What I am wondering is this. You do all of this research, starting with living people and figuring out who their ancestors were. But can you do it the other way around? Can you take the name of somebody, say somebody who might have left behind something of value—for now, let's just say a treasure map—that no one knew about, and trace his heirs forward to see who today might have a claim on that map if it turned up?"

"Absolutely," she said without hesitation. "In some ways, it would even be easier, because you know the actual starting point. So it *is* like that chart in Tufte. But then you run into another problem, don't you? Because it's not really the later family tree you want to find, but only the part that would have some legal claim to the property. I have no idea how you'd do that."

"You're right, of course. But if you could identify the people in each generation, I could play legal researcher and find the relevant probate records."

"What's that?"

"Whenever somebody dies, at least these days, their will is filed with a court in their state of residence or the state where their will was drafted. That's called probate, and the records are pretty localized, usually by county. And a lawyer, or really anyone, can go into those records— they're public—and follow the money, so to speak. You can read the will. Now it's a little fuzzier than that in reality. Some wills never get probated, some states have different rules than others, some filing systems are more accessible than others. But with some luck, if you know where somebody lived when they died, you can often find documentation of who their heirs were and what they inherited. In a case like this one I'm describing, you'd be looking for whoever got what's called the residuary assets, or the leftovers after any specific bequests, because an undiscovered asset would necessarily be residuary in nature. Since no one knows specifically that they own it, whatever it is, they couldn't possibly bequeath it directly to someone else."

"So let me get this straight. You're thinking that I might start from the death of a particular person and track their descendants forward to the present day. And each time I mapped a given generation, you'd go into the probate records and hope to find all of their wills. And we'd keep narrowing the search of each subsequent generation only to the people who were named as beneficiaries of the previous heirs. Have I got that right?"

"Clearly," deadpanned Andy, "you are not only graceful but clever."

"Okay, you're describing a search, then, that both widens and narrows with each generation. That's an interesting twist. You said the file you saw was from, when, around 1914?"

"Not quite. Actually, the hypothetical person in question hypothetically died in the Spanish flu pandemic in 1918."

"And did he or she leave a will?"

"Now, that's one of those fuzzy areas. I think he had one, but not from the state he was living in when he died. So that first bit of legal research will be a little complicated. But that's why I get the big bucks . . . or why I used to." Andy's turn to flash a small, self-deprecating smile. "But I do know the names of his wife and children when he passed. Hypothetically speaking, of course."

"Well, if we are only talking about a little over a hundred years, and we are looking for someone who is still alive today and possibly the oldest member of their particular generation within the family, that's probably . . . four, maybe even three generations. Piece of cake—if we can find the records."

"And how would you go about that?"

Scouting Report

It was not lost on Andy that he was treading a fine ethical line in pursuing the kind of research he had discussed with Keiley. In effect, he was trolling for a potential client, or more likely a group of clients, who might or might not be willing to pursue a claim that they might or might not have, based on records he had seen in a law firm archive while that firm employed him. To pursue such a thing was the legal equivalent of driving down a main road and running one red light after another, hoping against hope that the cops were elsewhere at the time. But if he had learned one thing during his brief sojourn at Stetson, Varney, it was that lawyers could often find some logic by which they might circumvent almost any constraint.

After turning the matter over in his head for several days and an equal number of sleepless nights, Andy decided that the ethical problem troubling him did not arise yet. There was, after all, no client, nor was there a case. So there could be no conflict of interest. There was, of course, the small matter of how Andy came to know of the Grissom file and its key document, which had been left in the stewardship of a firm that was now part of Stetson, Varney, but he thought he saw a way to deal with that one when the time came. Having been inside the firm for that one year, he thought he had an ace in the hole. Following this logic, Andy decided that he was just playing a hunch and doing a little historical research with the assistance of a genealogist of whom he knew he was growing quite fond.

Ah, he thought. *If we did this and things somehow went sideways, would Keiley have any legal liability?* Since she was not a lawyer, probably not.

But still, he ought to find a way to make sure she was protected. And he hit on the solution right away.

"Keiley," he said into the telephone, "I want to hire you as a legal assistant."

"What are you talking about? I already have a job. Did you forget?"

"No, I didn't forget. But I want to hire you part-time. I have decided to take a look at that hypothetical case we were talking about over dinner last week, and I could use your help. I think we'd be fine given that, at this point, it is more historical research than anything else. But there are some issues that could come up for me if we do determine that someone we can identify could have a claim to the . . . treasure map. It's a lawyer thing, and I think I can handle it. But I want to be sure you wouldn't have any legal liability if that happened. And I also want to be free to share the non-hypothetical details with you. I can only do all of that if you're an employee of D'Antonio & Dennum. Think you could work for a lawyer?"

"Depends. What kind of boss are you?"

"I have no idea. You'll have to ask Betty, who, by the way, I'm sure would be delighted to have your company around the office once in a while. In fact, since I'm going to be moving into Lou's old office in a few days, you could even have my old space if you want a place to land."

"Is this 'thing' you're talking about really worth all of this trouble?"

"I've been thinking about that. It could be a total blind alley. But there's also a scenario in which it could be worth literally millions of dollars."

"Are you serious? There *is* a treasure map? And you think there really might be a treasure?"

"Yes, sort of. It's not buried treasure or anything like that. But I could foresee some legal claims that would be a real gold mine for a potential client."

"And lawyers get . . . ?"

"Enough to buy their legal assistants a nice collection of genuine antique maps."

"It sounds intriguing, Andy, but I never make decisions like this on the spur of the moment. Give me a couple of days to decide, will you?"

"Of course. Oh, did I mention the free pizza every Friday?"

Betty was both curious and pleased when Andy told her the next week that Keiley would be moving into his old office—curious about what this young woman brought to the practice but pleased to have another female around the office, albeit part-time. Besides, she could sense this was a good thing for Andy as well, and after watching Lou become more and more insular as the years passed, if there was something personal in this for her new boss, she was all for that. She did her best to open up the small office once Andy had moved next door and to get Keiley set up with a clean desk, a decent chair, and a functioning computer. Theirs was a small operation—almost as small as they come—but she and Lou had always been careful to maintain two separate computer networks, one connected to the outside world through the internet for sending messages and doing research, and one restricted to the office proper for maintaining legal and other confidential records. Following Andy's instructions, she made sure Keiley's computer only had access to the outside network.

When Keiley showed up at the office a couple of days later, she could settle right in, and Betty went out of her way to make her feel at ease. An hour or so later, Andy called both women into his office to tell them about what he called his special project.

"A year or so ago," he began, "when I was working at Stetson, Varney, I came across a client file from more than a hundred years ago. It was a strange file, because there was almost nothing in it—just three pieces of paper. One was a cover memo from the lawyer handling the matter, one was an agreement the client had signed and wanted kept confidential, and one was a death notice from the local newspaper. The client, a fellow named Parker T. Grissom, who lived out in Kansas City, had died of the flu just days after he had visited the firm to open the file. And the lawyer he dealt with, a guy named Orren Davis, died shortly after that, also of the flu. That was at the beginning of the pandemic back then. Everyone calls it the Spanish flu, but these days, as I found out, a lot of experts think it, in fact, started in Kansas. Anyway, the result was that this became an orphan file. There was no living client, no living attorney. So it simply got buried in the firm's archives and, after a series of mergers, ended up in the archives of Stetson, Varney. That's how I happened to stumble across it."

"I was getting incredibly bored with my work at that point, just going through year after year of old documents. But that one file tweaked my interest, so I made a copy of the papers and took them home to do a little research. I probably wasn't supposed to do that, but I thought maybe there might be something of interest to the firm. I guess maybe I saw myself uncovering this buried treasure in an old file and rising to managing partner on the fortune the firm would reap from my great insight. Anyhow, I poked around the internet a bit, and I found out that Grissom was a minority owner of an old baseball team they used to have out in Kansas City called the Packers. And the Packers used to play in something called the Federal League. Back around 1914 or so, that league decided it wanted to become one of the major leagues, like the American and National Leagues we have today. But those establishment guys weren't real keen on the idea, and they fought the Federal League tooth and nail. And somehow Grissom must have got himself into the middle of that, because the three fellows who ran Major League Baseball back then wrote up an agreement, really a personal services contract, with him."

Andy reached back, grabbed a piece of paper from the credenza behind him, and placed it on the desk facing Keiley and Betty. "This," he said, "is the photocopy I made of the agreement. I'd forgotten all about it until I was over at Keiley's studio looking at her maps, and I wasn't sure I'd kept it. But it was in a box of papers I'd brought with me when I moved out here from the city.

"Basically, this paper says that, in exchange for whatever it was Grissom was to do for them, the National Commission, which was the governing body of baseball back then, and the two major leagues—same ones we have now—promised that if there ever was a major league baseball team in Kansas City, that Grissom, or presumably his heirs, would get a ten-percent share for nothing. Now, those old fellows were smart and tough as could be—especially, from what I've read, this Ban Johnson guy from the American League—and they must have figured they put one over on old Grissom. From what I've read, the Packers were already failing, and they went bankrupt within a year or so of when this was signed, and Kansas City was so far away from civilization in those days and so small compared to the major league cities, I'm sure they figured they were giving him absolutely nothing of value.

"We'll never know what they got in return, but not only did the Kansas City club go under financially, they even sued the league, claiming it was a forced bankruptcy. The Federal League eventually took the major leagues to court, but they ended up in the courtroom of a dyed-in-the-wool baseball fan, Judge Kenesaw Mountain Landis, and after a few days of hearings, he just let the case rot on his docket until the Federal League itself couldn't hold out any longer.

"Maybe it was just coincidental, maybe not, but a few years later, after a big gambling scandal involving the Chicago White Sox, Landis got himself named as the first Commissioner of Baseball. In any event, there was a big settlement of that case that helped out some of the Federal owners and helped out some teams in the majors who needed cash to keep going. And the whole thing just went away. Only two teams got left out. One was in Baltimore, and they were offered in on the deal but apparently didn't like the terms and said no. Later on, they sued the major leagues with the same kind of claim the Federal League had made for antitrust violations. But they lost when the courts decided baseball was entitled to be exempt from that law. That's a whole other story. The other big loser was the Kansas City club, because they got nothing at all.

"That's all ancient history, of course. But here's the deal. In 1955, one of the old American League teams that used to be in Philadelphia, the Athletics, moved to Kansas City, and they played there until 1967 when they moved on to Oakland, which is where they are today. The Oakland A's. They never amounted to much in Kansas City, but they had some really good years out in Oakland. And when they left for the coast in 1967, baseball came under pressure to put another team in Kansas City, which they did with an expansion franchise, either in that same year or in 1969, depending on how you interpret it. They called it the Royals. And that team—it's still there—has been pretty successful over the years, even been in three or four World Series.

"Now here's the thing. If we could validate this document somehow, and if we could find Parker Grissom's heirs, and if we could show a clear line of successorship for this claim, well, we might just find ourselves with some clients who could lay claim to ten-percent ownership of, not one, but two, major league baseball clubs, *and* ten percent of all the net revenues and distributed capital gains that both have earned over the years. And that, dear ladies, will add up to a tidy sum. We can also bring some justice for a family that the grand dons and self-appointed masters of baseball thought they were hornswoggling back in the day."

"Good gracious!" was all Betty could say when Andy appeared to have finished his narrative.

"Now I see why you were asking all those questions," said Keiley. "And I can see how we might be able to do this if you can find the way through those—what did you call them?—probate records. If nothing else, we could have some fun running all of this down. Count me in!"

"Now, I should mention that there is another wrinkle. It won't have any real bearing on figuring out the damages, if we ever get to that point. But we may need to take account of it in our legal filings. Technically, there was also a third major league team in Kansas City, not at the time they played, but now. There was a really good team in the old Negro Leagues called the Kansas City Monarchs. And just a few years ago, Major League Baseball declared that, for a certain period of years that ended, basically, when the majors themselves began to integrate, the Negro League teams were, in reality, Major League teams. So, technically, the Grissom family, or whoever they may be today, might have had a claim on that team as well. But legally, it was not a Major League franchise in its day, and there is no surviving entity against which to make a claim today, if we or they even wanted to. I just need to figure out how we have to deal with that legally, or I will if any of this goes anywhere."

"Heck," said Keiley. "What are we waiting for? Let's get to work!"

⊰⊱

Meeting one-on-one a few minutes later, Andy passed a second piece of paper to Keiley.

"This is a copy of the newspaper obituary for Parker Grissom. You'll see that he left a wife, a son, and a daughter. That should give you a starting point for your research."

"Any idea whether he just left everything to his wife or what was in the will? That might narrow it even more right from the start."

"Now, that's an added complication I didn't mention before. According to the third document, which is a note from the lawyer who started the file, Parker may have written a will years before, when he lived in Illinois. And it looks like the law firm was in the process of retrieving that when he died suddenly. Now, since his lawyer died almost immediately afterward, there was probably no one at the firm who knew to follow up, and the firm itself wouldn't have had any reason to do so once this file was archived, which happened right away as well. Grissom lived in a suburb on the Kansas side of the line that divides the city, and I need to do some research on Kansas law. It might be that he would have been treated as having died intestate without a will since he did not have one written in Kansas. Or, they might have accepted a will written in Illinois, if there even was one. While you are busy tracking down Annette, Arlene, and Raymond and any progeny who may have issued, I will be burying myself in some of the most arcane bits of state law you can imagine."

"I have to confess, I never did any probate work before I moved out here," Andy said to Keiley one morning the following week. "I mean, I understood the basics from my classes, but I am more or less learning on the fly, and it's a lot more complicated than I thought. Take Parker Grissom, for example. When he died, the Kansas City lawyer he was working with thought Grissom had written a will in Illinois, and there was a specific firm that supposedly had custody. Since I had his date of death, it was easy to go into the Illinois records, but I did not know exactly where he lived there, and after looking at the files for all of the counties where the lawyer might have filed it, I came up empty. But that turned out to be okay, because when I moved on to Kansas, it turned out that, back then, if you didn't have a Kansas will, you didn't have a will. You died what they called intestate. And that meant that the default distribution of assets specified in the state law of succession would apply. I've got it right here. By law, half of everything would have gone to his widow, Annette, and the other half would have been split between his two children. So that gives you three starting points for the first round of your research."

"Actually, I'm way ahead of you," Keiley replied. "You remember that Grissom's son, Raymond, was over in France in the Army. Well, unfortunately, he didn't make it back. He was killed in action about a month before the Armistice."

"That's too bad. But it does mean that his share of the original estate would have . . . that's a surprise. It would have reverted to his mother. So at that point, she had a seventy-five-percent share, and the daughter had the rest."

"Hold on. I'm not done. I played a hunch and focused on the local newspaper obituaries for a period of time after he was killed. You have to realize that, in less than a year, this poor woman, Annette, lost her husband and provider and her only son. She had to be under tremendous stress, and doctors weren't very good back then at treating stress. For that matter, they hardly bothered with diagnosing it in women. And sure enough, I found a small death notice for her in early 1920. It didn't say much, but it identified her lone survivor as her daughter, Arlene Colbert, who was still living in Kansas City at that time. So she obviously never moved or remarried and, for that matter, survived only a couple of years after her husband died."

"Interesting, and it probably keeps things simple. I'll check to make sure, but it seems unlikely that Annette made out a will, especially since she had only one prospective heir. So let's assume for now that she, too, died intestate. By the end of 1920, all of Parker's possessions, presumably including his contract with baseball, were the property of this daughter."

"Right. Now, she had a different last name, Colbert, so we can assume she was married when all this happened. That gives me a couple of places to start the next round of the search—marriage records and birth records. How old was Grissom when he died?"

"Let me look. . . . The newspaper said he was . . . fifty-seven."

"So, that would make Arlene no older than what, forty? And it's unlikely that she would have married before she was seventeen or eighteen, if even then. So to be safe, if I started searching records from about 1895 onward, I'd have a good chance of finding whatever is there. And as far as birth records, chances are she wasn't still pumping out babies when she hit fifty, but I'll go that far forward just to be sure."

"Those sound like the right parameters. But here's one more. We know Arlene lived in Kansas City, but remember that there are two of those, one in Kansas and one in Missouri. I'd almost bet on Missouri. Close to mama, but not too close. But you'll need to check in both states to be safe."

"See, back then," she said, "I'd go the other way—close to mama, period. But the implication for the search is the same. And you?"

"I'm going to start in both states and the nearby counties and move forward from 1920 looking for a probate file. If you find the marriage info, let me know, because we might want to see if the husband shows up in some other location later in life. If she was still alive then, we'd need to move the search."

⬥

"Close to mama," Keiley said, walking into Andy's office a couple of days later.

"Beg your pardon?" said Andy.

"I found Arlene. She stayed close to mama. And at the time, dad as well. She was twenty-four when she got married in June 1912 to Robert Charles Colbert, Jr. He was a clerk or bank teller or something like that. The happy couple settled in Kansas City, *Kansas*. They had a daughter in 1914, unnamed, who was stillborn. They actually put that in the death records. Then they had twin boys, Robert Charles, III, and Parker Thomas, born in 1917. Obviously named for the parents' respective fathers. RC III was listed first in the birth records and was born about two minutes before his brother, if that makes any difference. Then Arlene and Robert had a little girl, Francis Jean, in 1918. But she died of measles when she was three. I'm telling you, this family was star-crossed. But remember, this was all while Annette was still around and was no doubt helping with all of the birthing and child care. That's why women stayed close to mama back in the day. So, by the time her husband died of the flu, those two deaths would have weighed on her all those years, too, adding to the stress. My money is on depression. And if I had to guess,

I'd say Arlene was probably pretty devastated, too. I looked ahead for the next ten years, and if she and Robert still lived in the area through that time, there were no other children."

"Wow. You've been busy. I think you can jump ahead and look for any death notices. You'll need to search for both parents, even though we are mainly following Annette. I'll check, but I don't think Kansas was ever a community property state."

The search continued along both tracks, legal and genealogical, and, between small families and early deaths, it remained surprisingly narrow as it moved through the years. By 1985, the residuary estate of Parker T. Grissom, along with all of the elements added to it by his heirs and successors, passed into the hands of one young woman, Kathleen Proctor, the daughter of a mill worker and a librarian in Pittsburgh, Pennsylvania. She was just eighteen years old and finishing up her first year at Penn State when her parents were among those killed by a tornado, one in the most deadly cluster of such storms ever to hit Pennsylvania, which struck without warning and destroyed their home just outside the small town of Farrell in the western part of the state.

"So," Andy wondered aloud as Keiley settled in across the desk. "Is Kathleen Proctor the one? She would have been born in . . . 1967, so there's a good chance she's still alive and kicking and, arguably, the sole owner of parts of two Major League Baseball teams."

"Andy, that's what I wanted to talk with you about. And it's a serious conversation."

"Okay," he said, wondering at her tone of voice, one he had never heard before.

"Have you just been putting me on all this time? Did you invent this whole baseball inheritance thing because you were being cute, thinking it would bring the two of us close?"

"What are you talking about? I *love* that we are close. But invent a scheme to make that happen? What kind of person do you think I am?"

"That, Andy, is what I am beginning to wonder. I wonder if I'm just being used . . . and on so many levels!"

"Whoa! Slow down! What's going on here?"

She stared at him across the desk in a new way, a hard way. Judgmental. Disapproving.

"Tell me again," she said, an edge evident in her voice, "how you were never curious about your birth parents. How you never asked your adoptive parents about them, how you ended up working with Lou D'Antonio just by chance, and how just by chance he had done some of the legal work back when you were adopted, and how you never had the chance to ask him about that, and how, even after he died, and as recently as last week, you've never even looked back to see if the records of his work are somewhere in the files? Somewhere within maybe ten feet of where we are sitting? And you expect me to believe that?"

"Honest to God, Keiley, every bit of that is true. I never knew who they were, and I never cared. I had the great good fortune to grow up from my earliest memories in a loving household. I know there are a lot of grown-up adoptees these days who are fixated on finding their birth parents, but I'm not one of them. I never gave a damn about that, and I still don't. I almost don't want to know, and that's the reason I have never even glanced into those old files. What? You think I invented this whole thing so I could learn about how to do genealogical research? I could have read a damn book! You're right about one thing. I got interested in genealogy because you're interested in genealogy. But I got you involved in this case because, when I saw that chart in that old book you had and heard you talk about working backward, I flashed back to the file I'd seen at my old law firm, and I made the connection. Did it bother me that pursuing that idea would mean I'd have to work with you? Hell no! Have I enjoyed working on it with you? Hell yes! And that is all I have to say on the matter. Except this. Honestly, I don't have any idea what has upset you so much."

By this point, Keiley was in tears, and Andy felt them coming on as well. Their hands met over the box of tissues Andy kept on his desk for emotional clients. They stayed close momentarily, then each retrieved a tissue.

"Keiley, what the heck is going on?"

"Andy, if you're telling me the truth, then you're going to love this. I followed up on this Kathleen Proctor just the same as I have everybody else. Only child. She graduated from Penn State in eighty-nine—found her in the yearbook and on the alumni list. Pleasant-looking girl. She married a fellow named . . ." She paused to check her notes. "Donnelly, Tom Donnelly, in . . . 1995, and two years later they had a baby boy. So he'd be in his early thirties by now. They lived down around Carlisle. Anyway, about six months later, well, there was an auto wreck on the Pennsylvania Turnpike. Some truck jack-knifed, couple of cars rolled over. They shut the turnpike for something like six hours to get it all cleaned up. Six people killed, including both Kathleen and Tom. There was a big article in the papers when it happened, even ran on the AP wire. Ran in the Baltimore paper, the Jersey papers, and of course in Pittsburgh and Philly. Probably elsewhere. This family really *was* star-crossed! And I'm starting to find this whole search thing depressing."

"Ah," said Andy sympathetically. " *That's* what this was all about. Well, listen, I do get that. And now it looks like the whole thing was a total dead end. I'm sorry to have put you through a search that has ended up being such a complete downer. Can we just hug it out?" he asked, rising from his chair.

"Not yet," she replied, though more softly than before. "Because I'm not quite done. The only survivor was the baby. Somehow he got thrown clear of the wreck. Must have been when it was rolling over. Landed on a grassy median. According to the reports, they almost didn't see him in the long grass. And somehow, he wasn't even hurt, aside from a couple of bumps and bruises. So the bottom line is, here we are again with a sole heir."

"Well, goodness. Then there *is* a happy ending to this story, after all. Unless you're about to tell me that the kid died later, then we have an heir! Have you been able to track the kid? Well, I guess he's a grown man by now. Have you found him?"

"I think so. There's one last set of records I need to check."

"Well, don't keep me in suspense. What's his name?"

"Andrew . . ."

"What?" he asked cautiously, unaccustomed to hearing Keiley use his formal given name. "What's his name?"

"Andy, Andrew . . . *that's* his name. He would be about your age. He was orphaned when he was only six months old, so he never knew his parents. The Orphans Court records in the Pennsylvania county where they lived show that he was adopted, but beyond that, all the records are sealed. They always are. But the adoption notice itself was signed by two attorneys, one representing the county child welfare service that would have arranged for the adoption, and the other signed by the attorney representing the adoptive parents."

Andy sat quietly for a long moment, internalizing everything that Keiley was saying. It made no sense, and yet it made perfect sense. It explained nothing, and yet it explained everything.

"Tell me," was all he could think of to say.

"Louis Tomaso D'Antonio, Esquire," was all she replied.

Setting the Lineup

A man who is his own lawyer has a fool for a client. *It's an adage as old as the law itself*, thought Andy. But what of a man who *discovers* late in the game that he is his own lawyer? No conventional wisdom on that one.

As he thought further, Andy came to realize that, strange as his new situation was, it held at least one advantage. Lingering in the background throughout his search for the Grissom heir had been an awareness that, even if he located that person or persons, his ability to advise them of their good fortune might come with attendant ethical risks to himself and his career. After all, he only knew of the critical document because he had come across it while fulfilling his responsibilities to Stetson, Varney, in whose files he had found it. And clearly, Joey Coy was not inclined to pursue the matter, at least as far as Andy knew. To the contrary, his instruction had been clear. Bury it. Though he had not confronted this problem head-on, by some lights it was fairly black and white. Ethical lawyers didn't do what he was doing. Of course, ethical lawyers didn't do what Joey was doing, either.

But now, in this new world where he found himself, black and white had turned to shades of gray. For what he had discovered in the Stetson, Varney archives now turned out to be evidence of his own inheritance, evidence the firm, not realizing (as he did not at the time) who he was and how he was connected to the matter, essentially ordered him to destroy. At that point, or at the very least not later than his most recent conversation with Keiley, he had become the client. Well, *someone's* client, and arguably *Stetson, Varney's* client, at least in the eyes of the bar association, "arguably" being the operative term. If he was in the line of Grissom's heirs and successors, did the firm not have a fiduciary responsibility to protect *his* interests? To be sure, there was a lot of noodling to do over all these twists and turns. But at the very least, Andy thought there was surely enough ambiguity, and he had enough of a defense, that he was now insulated from any ethics violations. This left him free to focus on formulating a legal strategy. Who were his allies in the matter, who were his opponents, and how could he turn these two sets of parties, the facts, and the law to his advantage?

First things first.

"Keiley," he said, opening the meeting he had called on short notice. "I think you have done some terrific detective work in tracking down all of these . . . hell, all of my relatives from a life I never knew existed. And as we start to figure out where we can take all of this, I want you to find an effective way of mapping out what you found.

"But here's the thing. This case is inevitably going to involve some big-time adversaries with deep pockets and a lot at risk, and big-time adversaries with deep pockets facing a lot at risk tend to spend a lot of that money on high-priced legal talent. I've met some of those guys. Heck, I worked for some of those guys, at least briefly. They are tough as nails and scary good. And, they will hire highly credentialed consultants for every conceivable purpose, especially for giving depositions and, if we get to court, actual testimony. And judges really like credentials. They see them almost as substitutes for actual expert testimony, of which they have no real comprehension. And as good a genealogist as you are, you don't have a credential that says so. But you probably know who does—surely better than I do.

"So, I want you to find us one or two of those people—two is better—and I want you to sit down with them and show them what we have, including all of the news articles and obituaries, the vital statistics records, the probate documents, just everything. And then ask them to replicate the search and the data in ways that would allow them to give testimony independently of you and one another. Then, once they have that, put your graphic genius to work. I don't know . . . pictures of all these people in the line, artsy flourishes, whatever you think best illustrates the argument. Page through all those Tufte books and find us something outstanding. Can you do that?"

"Are you joking? I've already started, and I'm way ahead of you. I've got video conferences set up with three of the top people in the field—a couple of academics and the woman who founded one of the first commercial services. I should have it sorted out in the next day or two."

"Keiley Barefoot, I love you!"

"Isn't that sexual harassment?"

"Not yet."

"Hush. Betty will hear us."

"What? You don't think she knows?"

———

With that detail taken care of, Andy turned his attention to identifying the interested parties he would need to deal with one way or another.

At the top of his list was Stetson, Varney. Since Parker Grissom had been a client of one of the predecessor law firms, if only for the blink of an eye, he would have a basis to approach his old employer to represent him in any matters that flowed from the century-old personal services contract. But he knew, because Joey had already told him, that the firm would choose to opt out, citing potential conflicts with other clients. He knew that such a claim would only hold to the extent that his targets in any litigation, whoever they might be, were, in fact, clients of the firm. But he also knew that Stetson, Varney would extend that net as far as they could stretch it and that, given the circumstances, no judge would support him should he try to challenge the decision. Indeed, getting such a question before a judge at all was almost unheard of.

Andy also harbored a secret hope that Stetson, Varney would actually end up representing one or more of his targets. *Sure*, he thought, *I would like nothing more than to stuff a good loss down their throats*. But more to the point, of all the law firms he might face in a dispute, at least he understood the culture and capabilities of this one and personally knew some of the players. He wondered if Joey himself might be lead counsel.

Andy also suspected that, given its knowledge of the situation, Stetson, Varney might seek out such an opportunity, first because, having ordered it destroyed, they would be confident there was no evidence to support the claim he might make, and second, because they had made clear their assumption that they were all better lawyers than he was. True, Andy had in his possession a photocopy of the old contract, which was enough to legitimize the filing of a lawsuit in the expectation of finding better evidence through discovery. But in a case of the magnitude Andy thought this one might reach, any judge would be reluctant to accept such a copy as meeting the best-evidence standard required in court. That, he knew, would be the line taken by Stetson, Varney. Dennum, they would argue, is just a disgruntled former employee who has concocted this entire matter out of thin air. In fact, they would probably countersue for fraud just to throw him off balance.

Next on the list were the parties on the other side of the actual 1914 agreement—Major League Baseball and the two major leagues themselves. On the plus side, there was a pretty straight line of succession there. In fact, no succession whatsoever, since all three entities were still around and in the same line of business. The only wrinkle he could see was the transition at the top of Major League Baseball from the National Commission structure to being headed by a single, all-powerful commissioner. But that was simply a reorganization at the top of a business with organizational continuity—same component leagues, same teams before and after, and so forth. These were the parties to the agreement itself, and they had deep enough pockets to make the effort worthwhile and enough clout to impose any requisite financial obligations on their component teams. Moreover, and of particular legal significance, they had retained throughout the power to approve the creation, assignment, and relocation of franchises, a power they had exercised in every such occurrence. So not only were they parties to the 1914 contract, but they had exercised authority over each instance in which it was violated. Of course, the National League had never placed a franchise in Kansas City, and he would need to use discovery cleverly to determine that league's degree of culpability. *But clearly*, thought Andy, *at the very least, I will be making claims against the American League and the umbrella organization.*

At that point, though, some ambiguities began to emerge in his thinking. Andy knew that Kansas City had been awarded two separate franchises over the years. The A's had moved there from Philadelphia, an existing team awarded a new home by the league. And when they left for the West Coast, the league compensated Kansas City with an expansion franchise that became the Royals. His preliminary research had shown that the Athletics had been acquired by a Chicago real estate guy named Arnold Johnson in 1954 and that he had moved the A's to Kansas City from Philadelphia the next year. Charles O. Finley had tried to buy the team when they were still in Philadelphia, but Johnson had the inside track. Under baseball's territorial control system, because the Yankees owned the minor league team that was playing in Kansas City at the time, they held a right of refusal. That is, they had the right to prevent a Major League team from relocating to Kansas City. And clearly, the Yankees did not like Finley. But Johnson had strong connections with the Yankees—he owned Yankee Stadium and was friends with the club's top brass. So Johnson got the franchise. Finley was apparently not one to give up, though, and by 1960, he had managed to buy a controlling interest in the A's from Johnson.

Despite promises to the city and its fans that he was in Kansas City for the long haul, Finley began looking early on for a bigger market to which he could move the team. These efforts became increasingly public, which had the predictable effect of reducing attendance, until finally, in 1967, the league granted him permission to move the team to Oakland. In the meantime, in an effort to keep the team, Kansas City voters had approved a bond issue to build a new stadium. With all of this occurring on his home turf, Missouri's then-powerful Senator Stuart Symington threatened to revoke baseball's antitrust exemption—the same one established in the last bit of litigation arising from the demise of the Federal League—if Kansas City was left without a team. Major League Baseball capitulated, which opened the way for the Royals to begin play in 1969.

As Andy remembered it, the Grissom contract was pretty clear in its language, but he pulled it out once more to refresh his memory. Just as he recalled, it read, in part: ". . . Parker T. Grissom, his heirs and legal successors, will be entitled in perpetuity, or until disposed of, to ownership of ten percent of any affiliated Major League Baseball franchise that may, at some future and undetermined date, be awarded to the city of Kansas City, Missouri, or the surrounding metropolitan area to a radius of 25 miles from the city center, by this Commission, by the American or National Baseball Leagues, or by any of their successor organizations, and to any revenues and ancillary benefits that may attend to such ownership." That meant that Andy could reasonably claim that he owned ten percent, not just of the Royals, the team currently in Kansas City, but also of the Athletics, despite the fact they were now located in Oakland. The Oakland claim might be a little more tenuous for the years after 1967 when the team moved. But Andy could see an argument that the language granted ownership in the *franchise*, and the Oakland franchise was the very one that had once been in Kansas City. Moreover, his claim would not be limited to current ownership but to any benefits that might have accrued to ownership from 1954 to the present. Though he had no idea what the ultimate number would be, something he would have to determine through discovery, he was pretty sure it was a big one. Very big.

But then there was the question that had caused him some doubt already. None of this franchising activity took place until forty and more years after the Grissom agreement was signed. And while the agreement would surely (at least in his view) be binding throughout that time—that's what perpetuity meant, for goodness sake—he doubted that Johnson, or Finley, or anyone associated with the Royals would have had any idea it existed. It was possible, he knew, that Major League Baseball or the American League would have disclosed its existence to one or both during negotiations over granting the franchises—again, something to keep in mind during discovery—but he thought that was unlikely. In fact, he thought, the people who granted those franchises after so many years probably didn't know of the commitment their predecessors had made on a single, obscure piece of paper that they had regarded at the time as a valueless, meaningless dodge. For all he knew, the old baseball brain trust had never even bothered to file the document at all. (He made another note for discovery.)

Was it, then, fair of him to expect the two current ownership groups simply to hand over ten percent of their positions *and* compensatory payments for past profits when they had no knowledge of their respective obligations? He was sure he had the law on his side but not so sure of justice. Just then, an idea occurred to him. If he could convince the Oakland and Kansas City ownership groups of the validity of his claim, rather than suing them for damages, might he recruit them as co-claimants against the American League and Major League Baseball, which, together, would then doubtless move to share the pain of any damages across all of the remaining teams? That was a question worth pondering.

Lastly, there was the situation with the Kansas City Monarchs, which, as he learned, had two runs in the Negro Leagues, from 1920 to 1930 in the Negro National League, and then, after some years of barnstorming, from 1937 until 1955 in the Negro American League. The likes of Ernie Banks, Cool Papa Bell, Elston Howard, Buck O'Neil, and Satchell Page had played for the Monarchs, and it was from that team, in 1946, that Branch Rickey had brought Jackie Robinson to the Brooklyn Dodgers, breaking the color barrier in the major leagues. Of course, as Andy well knew, the Monarchs and the other Negro League teams were purposely *excluded* from the major leagues. But then, back in 2020, a complication arose when, long after the fact, Major League Baseball ruled that these leagues had, in fact, been major leagues and remained such until Robinson, and then other players, were called up in the mid-1940s. Did that constitute Major League Baseball establishing a post facto franchise in Kansas City? And if so, how should Andy treat that in the litigation he was considering? He knew it was not a claim he wanted to make. What he did not know, and would need to seek some advice on, was whether it was a claim he would *have* to make in order to retain the validity of his argument about the Grissom contract.

It was time to pay a visit to Mumbles and Sajak.

—◆—

When you studied law at The House of Torts, you didn't run into many constitutional scholars, let alone those who would opine nightly on Fox News or CNN. And you didn't end up with a network of classmates who clerked for the Supremes. But what you did get, along with your degree, was the chance to pick the brains of some gritty lawyers whose *practical* street-level knowledge of the law was pretty damn good. In fact, if you wanted to find them during the day, when they weren't moonlighting to pick up a few extra bucks through teaching, you didn't go back to campus. You went to a courthouse, or to their offices, both of which tended to be in neighborhoods known more for the clusters of pawn shops and bail bondsmen than for purveyors of sushi and lattes.

"Mumbles," as he was known by generations of students and the occasional juror, was Vincent Morgan Rose, Esquire, king of contracts at Madison-Jefferson but merely a prince of personal injuries in the real world he also inhabited. The true origins of his nickname, which one *never* used in his presence, were lost in the haze of rumors and student gossip that passed from one class to the next. But around them, a myth had grown in which a young Mumbles had suffered an accident that injured his tongue to the extent it required surgery. The surgery, according to the myth, was badly botched, leaving him with a scarred and discolored muscle that impeded his speech, a malady he attempted to mask by speaking through clenched lips. The effect of that, or of whatever had truly happened in his youth, in addition to fostering his passion for personal injury cases, was that his speech came out somewhat garbled and barely projected into the surrounding space. No wonder students who managed to claim seats in the first three rows of his classroom universally fared better than those consigned to seats further back. But when you could hear him and figure out what he was saying, you knew you were in the presence of a legal genius. The man could write a contract in spirals, concentric circles, or any other geometric use of language the human brain could conceive. It took another equally brilliant lawyer to interpret his constructions, which was precisely the point, and a twisted one at that.

Professor "Sajak" was attorney Gwynyth Dyfodwg, a delightful and knowledgeable woman of Welsh origin and a tenacious litigator. She was an exception to the rule at Mad-Jeff in that she taught night school because she enjoyed it. Of course, she'd only been there for a couple of years. Perhaps she'd learn. She was also an exception because her office was located in a modest professional building in the East Twenties, a good ten blocks or more from the nearest bail shop. She was known to have a good sense of humor about her name, and it was actually she herself who planted the seed of her campus nickname the first time a student tried in class to address her as Professor Dyfodwg. After three tries, the most elegant of which came out as "Professor Dufusdog," she simply blurted out, "Buy a vowel, for god's sake!" From that day forth, she was known both privately and in class as Professor Sajak, after the long-time host of the television quiz show *Wheel of Fortune*, where the phrase was, if not born, at least nurtured.

As expected, Andy found Mumbles in a hallway outside one of the smaller courtrooms in the Jersey City Municipal Courthouse on Summit Avenue. It was where he did some of his best work and, as some wags suggested, where his inability to communicate clearly was something of an advantage.

"Professor Rose, how are you?" Andy nearly shouted to attract his attention. The object of his greeting turned to stare. A moment passed, then came tentative recognition.

"Mr. Dennum?" Then further recollection. "Andrew? What's a nice kid like you doing in a place like this? You decide to be a real lawyer, after all?"

Andy knew he had this coming. Graduates of The Emergency Room just did not take jobs at white-shoe firms like Stetson, Varney. They would, of course. But the offers never came. So they ended up chasing ambulances just like Mumbles. He had broken the mold, he knew, and now here he was, back at street level.

"It's a long story, I'm afraid. Or maybe a short one. But in a way, it's why I'm here. I could use a little advice, and I'm willing to buy a cup of coffee to pay for it."

"Coffee, hell, Andrew. I'm done for the day. Let's find a bar and you can pay for the first round."

They ended up cabbing it to Fire & Oak, where Andy discovered that Mumbles had a taste for expensive single malts. But so be it. Andy was, after all, about to join the ranks of the nation's billionaires. Then the fantasy passed and he thought of the balance already owed on the single piece of plastic in his wallet. *To hell with it*, he said to himself as he raised his hand to call the waiter over for another round.

Over their drinks, Andy regaled Mumbles with stories of life in the fast lane. Then, midway through the second round, he came to the part about the detour. That, in turn, gave him a point of entry for the story of the Grissom contract. By the time he made it through the details of the genealogical record, the two had ordered and consumed a dinner of burgers and brews. Between the lateness of the hour and the effects of the alcohol, it was all Andy could do to keep his wits about him as he finally got to the point of asking Mumbles the question on which he had come to seek advice.

"So, Professor, from what I've told you, do you think this old contract is valid? And if it is, who is really on the other end of the deal? Is the National League part of it? I mean, they signed the thing. But then they never put a team in KC. And what about the teams? Are they legally responsible?"

Vincent Morgan Rose pondered the question for some time, long enough, in fact, to order and consume a modest after-dinner drink. He then rendered an opinion that gave Andy not only the legal advice he sought but some fresh ideas for ways to play the game out going forward. What Andy hadn't thought to ask him about but what occurred to Rose immediately was the question of evidence, of which the contract was but a small, albeit essential, part. Rose saw other possibilities, not only in what to bring in but in some possible ways to use it, and his suggestions set Andy's brain whirling. Or maybe that was just the booze. Still, Andy had the good sense to order coffee as his own after-dinner drink, and by the time the duo cabbed back to the courthouse and Andy retrieved his car, he was in full control of his faculties and ready for the drive back to Mendham.

⬬⬬⬬

Dealing with Sajak was different. To begin with, Andy needed to make an appointment to see her. And that appointment would be at her office. No booze, which was just as well. Rather than drive, Andy took the bus into the city, then the subway to reach her building. He presented his card to the receptionist, then took a seat and waited.

The office itself was nothing fancy. None of the wood paneling and giant, highly polished conference tables that characterized the offices of Stetson, Varney and its ilk. No vases of flowers, no elevator music, no glass-enclosed law library and reading room. No, this was a utilitarian space, pleasant and businesslike as befit the enterprise, but spare and functional in every way. Andy barely had time to register these observations when a door off to one side of the modest reception area opened, and out stepped Sajak herself. Andy wasn't sure whether that was simply her way of greeting clients and visitors or whether she did this because, like her students, her receptionist could not pronounce her name and she was unwilling to risk having a client greeted with the statement, "Ms. Dufusdog will see you now." But whatever the reason, the effect was both charming and reassuring.

Once again, Andy repeated his tale of woe from life in the big leagues of law, then used that as a segue to talk about those other big leagues and his prospective dealings with them. Sajak was a litigator. She was a skilled and experienced courtroom hand, not on slips and falls like Mumbles but on bigger and more serious matters that required actual strategy. In this conversation, it was that experience he was hoping to tap into.

"I could really use your advice, Professor, first, on whether I want to set my priority as litigating or negotiating, and then fall back on the other as need or opportunity presents itself. And second, I could use some advice on the strategy I should use in going in one direction or the other. I mean, this is David and Goliath stuff, and I know I have the stones, but I'm not sure I have the slingshot."

"Andy, have you ever read anything about military strategy?"

"Not really. I read Sun Tzu in college years ago, but that's about it."

"Well, a little more recently than 500 BC, and in truth, just over the last twenty years or so, there's been a lot of writing in those circles about what the military calls 'asymmetric warfare.' Not my usual reading material, but I had to get up to speed on it for a case a few years ago. Apparently, the impetus was when some higher-ups realized that armies needed to be capable of fighting terrorists and cyberattackers and all sorts of irregular and nonstate enemies. You can't nuke them, for god's sake, and really, you can't use a lot of large-scale conventional weapons against them. It would be like taking a sledgehammer to crush an ant, and the ant might be able to duck into a crack in the sidewalk to avoid the blow anyway. In effect, they realized that their big standing armies were musclebound and simply not agile enough to deal with the new threat. So they started coming up with ways of still controlling the battlefield—right out of Sun Tzu—but of countering these smaller and often more agile enemies by other means. Also out of Sun Tzu, by the way. It's taken them a long time to figure out, and I suspect they still have problems."

"Okay, I follow you. But I'm not the Army here. I'm the little guy."

"Exactly! And my point is, that can be your advantage. Big law firms like Stetson, Varney are set up to fight big wars. That's why they exist, and they are often pretty good at it. But what they are not set up to do and what they are not experienced at is fighting asymmetric wars. Of course, we're not talking military conflict here, but the same thing has been happening in civil society. Big institutions like corporations and powerful interest groups have been getting pecked to death, or at least forced to change their ways, by smaller and seemingly inconsequential antagonists who find ways to make them respond to pressure. I think you need to study the strategies and tactics of those small, smart, more agile antagonists so you can carry the fight to your baseball powers and their lawyers in ways they don't expect or have little experience with. It could be something as complicated as generating political pressure, or as simple as causing the other side embarrassment, or something else altogether. My take on that, from the few cases I've studied that got into the courts, is that the tactics have a lot to do with hiding behind third parties, parties that have no particular interest in the dispute itself, whatever it might be, but who have other interests of their own that could generate pressure on the big and powerful target if you can figure out how to mobilize them. They find ways to get these seemingly disinterested actors to do things for their own reasons that somehow advance the interests of the real agency behind the attack. Think of it like this. You're a kid playing with a friend. Your friend has built a castle out of blocks, but there are a bunch of leftover blocks strewn across the table between you. You decide to knock the castle over, but the table's pretty big and you can't reach it. So what do you do?"

Andy thought for a moment. "You push against the leftover blocks that you can reach, and they, in turn, push against the blocks a little further away, and eventually, in a kind of chain reaction, you are pushing against blocks that are close enough to push the castle itself over. . . . Then your friend gets up, comes around the table, and punches you in the face."

"Well, let's hope that last part doesn't happen, though you can bet they'll try, and you'll want to be ready for it. But yes, that's what you do. Now those blocks on the table weren't put there to be weapons. They were leftovers. And some, even most of them, will be so far off to the side that they never come into play. But you find a way to use the rest to push on one another until your reach is extended all the way to that castle. That's the essence of the strategy these smaller enemies tend to employ. And that, Mr. Dennum, in my view, is the approach you should take. Find your blocks in unexpected places, and push them across the table.

"And one last thing, Andrew. It's something every good litigator knows to guard against for himself and be ready for on the other side. Litigation generates pressures far beyond the courtroom. And the parties to litigation, especially their lawyers, can make mistakes. Some of those mistakes—a small number—can be the things on which a case turns. Sometimes it just takes one. You must tune your ear to hear everything, and your brain to process everything. And as you do it, keep your eye out for that one critical mistake that will affect the outcome."

Andy left the meeting with a whole new understanding of the anatomy of a lawsuit.

Fast Ball, High and Tight

"What the fuck is this?" The Commissioner's voice rang through the offices with unmistakable anger. The attorney seated across the large desk had expected such an outburst and, while waiting to gain admission to the inner sanctum, had steeled himself before presenting the sheaf of papers to his employer. Now, watching the man's face redden as he read, the attorney had known it was coming.

"It's a legal service, sir," the lawyer said, choosing a straightforward description over any effort at explanation. His luck at avoidance did not last long.

"I know it's a damn legal service, you twit. While you were sitting there adjusting your tie for the last ten minutes, I've been reading it. What I asked you was, 'What the fuck is this?' Am I to believe that some yokel out in Northern Jersey thinks he owns a share of . . . wait for it . . . not one but two Major League franchises? And if that's not enough, he thinks we are supposed to pay him some indeterminately large sum of money for having overlooked that fact for what . . . more than a hundred years?"

"Yes, sir. That's what it says."

"And what do you say? You are, after all, my general counsel. So, counsel me."

"On the surface, Commissioner, it looks to be an absurd claim. I could write this fellow Dennum a cease and desist letter or something like that, threatening him with all manner of legal harm if he continues to harass us with this bogus claim."

"All right, then. Do it."

"But," continued the general counsel, "I'm not sure yet that doing so is our best course of action. I did a little checking in our files before I brought this to you, and . . ."

"You mean he's right?" shouted the Commissioner. "He has a claim?"

"As I was saying, sir, I did some preliminary research. Our on-site files don't go back anywhere near the time period mentioned in the filing, but I did come across some references from many years ago—long before your term began—where apparently Johnson and some of the other powers of the day had entered into certain . . . ah . . . loose agreements on behalf of the leagues or the enterprise for which there was no direct documentation in the files, but when they were brought forward for implementation, counsel at the time found secondary documents in our files that were consistent with the various claims. It appears that during the period of the National Commission, either parts of the central files went missing sometime in the past or some documents were simply never filed."

"Jesus Christ in Heaven. So you're telling me this guy might actually have a valid claim?"

"What I'm telling you, sir, is that we cannot be sure, and we may never be sure. If he has an original document and the signatures on it are validated—and if he can prove he is the rightful successor to the fellow who signed it back in 1914—we might have a serious problem to deal with."

The Commissioner sat back in his chair and became lost in thought. It was at precisely times like this that he missed having CI around. Since his earliest House and Senate days, CI had been his closest and most trusted aide. As Chief Investigator for the Senator and his committees as he rose to the pinnacle of congressional power, CI had dug the dirt, papered over the problems, and performed just about any other metaphorical act that came to mind. Damn! They had always agreed that should one of their schemes go badly and there was a price to pay, that if two men were at risk and one had to fall, it would be the loyal CI who would step forward and take the hit. The Senator was to be protected at all costs. That loyalty had carried over when the Senator became the

Commissioner, a change of career that was itself helped along by CI himself. But then, they had gone too far. They had spun a dark tale of the origins of the game—of Albert Spalding and Abner Doubleday and an obscure pseudo-religious movement and a conspiracy for the ages. They'd even "documented" it! It was, the Commissioner thought, pure hubris. And for what? The so-called good of the game? Unfortunately, they'd been caught in the act involving a little forgery and a little fraud, or so claimed the Attorney General. True to form, CI had been the good soldier, taking the whole thing on himself and protecting his boss. And now he sat rotting through the second of his three years in federal prison. Just when the Commissioner thought, *I need his help. Shit.*

All of this passed through his mind in a flash. It was the need to frame a suitable action that took more thought. He looked up at the waiting lawyer.

"Here's what I want you to do. First, tell this guy Dennum he can go screw himself using any device or assistance he might choose. If he's serious about this, that won't stop him. Probably won't surprise him. But it might slow him down a little. That will tell us two things. First, how big his cojones are. And second, how smart he is and how confident he is in his claim. It will also buy us some time to get into the off-site records—I assume we have off-site records?—and see if we have any paper of any kind that speaks to this claim one way or another.

"Then, I want you to find out everything you can about this guy. Personal life, career, everything. I want to know if he wears boxers or briefs. I want to know who he's screwing when he takes them off. If I'm seeing this correctly, the guy is serving as his own lawyer. See if he's been disbarred somewhere or whatever explanation for that there is. Use the Philadelphia firm, not the one here. Those people are more ruthless when it comes to this sort of thing. Find us a handwriting expert, and have these signatures verified.

"And find out exactly what his claim is to having inherited this so-called contract. If Johnson and those idiots really did sign this and it was never rescinded, that's where we're going to have to fight this thing. I want to know everything there is to know about that. Got it?"

"Yes, sir, I do."

"Then why the hell are you still sitting there?"

———◆———

To help him think through his plan, Andy did the first logical thing that came to mind. He went to the Learning Express toy store over in Morristown, bought the biggest set of building blocks he could find, then returned to his office and turned the top of his desk into a faux construction zone. On the far side, he stacked a few rows of blocks to form a sort of castle. He scattered the rest of the blocks randomly across the remainder of the surface. Then he started pushing here and there, this way and that, to see if he could detect any one pattern of pressure that was more effective than the rest. The obvious path, he knew from the outset, was straight ahead toward the imaginary gate of the castle. But because the blocks never aligned in a perfect linear array, flat side to flat side, corners squared, even that approach had its inefficiencies. Yet as he pushed here and there, always resetting the game after a successful breach, he realized that it was not, in fact, either necessary or, in the circumstances, wise to bring the whole construction tumbling down. Ten percent of nothing, after all, is nothing. No, all he needed to do was to find some way, any way, to get inside that gate. Poke a small hole in a remote corner of the wall and crawl in. Tunnel under the wall, fly over it. A direct assault on the gate only magnified the power of the defenders and taxed the resources of the attacker. In other words, it amplified the weakness at the heart of the asymmetry. What he needed was something different, something unexpected, something almost . . . subversive. *Thank you, Sajak.*

Having achieved enlightenment, or what passed for it, Andy next set out to study the blueprints of the castle itself to find its strong and weak points. There was a king within this particular redoubt, of course, the Commissioner, and as Andy extended his research, he came to see that the power of the king was at once great and limited. Back in 1914, when Parker Grissom had done his deal, there were three power centers in the game—the American League, the National League, and the National Commission. Andy knew that the National Commission had evolved into a single, powerful Commissioner of Baseball when Judge Landis had taken that position with a promise to clean up the game after the Black

Sox scandal of 1919–1920. What he had not realized until now was that power had been further centralized in 1999 when the two leagues gave up their quasi-independence and merged their authorities into that of the Commissioner. An oligarchy had become a monarchy. That was a boon to Andy's effort because it meant that he needed to focus on only one primary target for his litigation.

He then turned to the question of just how centralized the power within this particular fiefdom actually was. He tried to determine, for example, just how the Commissioner had come to his position. Obviously, he was voted in by the ownership of the many teams in the two leagues, but beyond that, he could find only scattered rumblings in the baseball press about the dynamics of the search and selection process that somehow convinced a sitting and, by all accounts, a powerful United States senator to accept the job. Andy did learn one thing of which he had been totally unaware until then—that the Commissioner had suffered a major embarrassment not that long ago when he had made some claims about the origins of the game that turned out to be based on some sort of cultish conspiracy that was proven, or so he said, by what turned out to be a counterfeit document. One of his staff people had actually gone to prison over that. How that played within the game, he had no idea. But, he decided, there must be some level of support from some number of teams that the Commissioner had to retain in order to stay in power. Perhaps somewhere in some of that analysis, Andy might find a vulnerability he could exploit. On the other hand, the Commissioner was still the Commissioner, so whatever balance of factors might have been in play seemed still to be in his favor.

As he pondered all that, Andy decided he needed to consult with people who might know more about such matters than he did or might even have some personal interest in them. Based on his research and a few well-placed phone calls, he compiled a list, then set about traveling here and there to meet with those who were willing to speak with him and to try to figure out where they lay in the tabletop geography of his venture. As he went, he asked everyone to hold their conversations in confidence, but these were strangers with their own calculi of interests, and he could not be sure his requests would be honored.

Finally he was ready to commit the litigation to paper. But even that was slow as he thought of more and more prospective elements of the case, each of which had to be weighed and tested, retained or rejected. The drafts began to pile up one on the other, until finally Andy had something he couldn't tweak any further. This was it, and Andy thought it was some of his finest work, though, as he would be the first to admit, he was sampling from a very small population. It was the only lawsuit he had ever drafted. He once again read through the main element of the filing, the "Complaint."

Complaint

Whereas, upon information and belief, the following facts are true:

1. On 7 January 1914 a valid contract (Appendix A) was established between Parker T. Grissom, resident of Kansas City, Kansas, (hereafter Decedent) and the National Commission and the American and National Leagues of Professional Baseball Teams and their respective successors (hereafter Respondent);

2. Said Agreement granted to Decedent and his heirs and successors "in perpetuity" "ownership of ten percent of any affiliated Major League Baseball franchise that may, at some future and undetermined date, be awarded to the city of Kansas City, Missouri, or the surrounding metropolitan area to a radius of 25 miles from the city center";

3. The organization known today and since 1920 as Major League Baseball, including all of its current franchise holders, is the direct and immediate successor to the National Commission that was signatory to the said Agreement, and is therefore responsible for its continued execution;

4. In 1999, the American League and the National League ceased independent operations and were merged into Major League Baseball, leaving that organization as the sole and unified successor to all three signatories to the 1914 Agreement;

5. In 1955 Respondent did relocate, franchise, and establish in Kansas City, Missouri, a baseball team known as the Athletics, which operated until 1967, at which time it relocated to Oakland, California, but retained the franchised name "Athletics";

6. In 1967–1969 Respondent did franchise and establish in Kansas City, Missouri, a second baseball team known as the Royals, which continues in operation;

7. In the relocation and/or establishment of neither of the referenced franchises did Respondent inform either the franchise holder or grantee, or the heirs and successors of Decedent, of its obligations under said Agreement, thereby depriving each franchisee of the opportunity to consider the referenced obligation in its valuation of the franchise and depriving the heirs and successors of Decedent of their rightful inheritance;

8. Complainant is the true and sole surviving heir and successor to Decedent, and is therefore entitled to the full benefits of the said Agreement;

9. Said benefits, subject to verification through discovery, are estimated to be the sum of one-tenth of the apparent net value of the first Kansas City franchise, now located in Oakland, California, of $1,100,000,000 [$110,000,000]; one-tenth of the apparent net value of the second Kansas City franchise of $1,025,000,000 [$102,500,000]; one-tenth of the average annual net revenue of the first Kansas City franchise from 1955 to the present, or approximately $10,000,000, multiplied by the number of years of franchise operation, or seventy [$70,000,000]; and one-tenth of the average annual net revenue of the second Kansas City franchise from 1969 to the present, or approximately $27,000,000, multiplied by the number of years of franchise operation, or fifty-six [$151,200,000]; which total sum equals $433,700,000. All estimates herein are derived from the most recent annual listing of same by Forbes Magazine.

Therefore, doth Complainant hereby pray the Court for Judgment against Respondent in the amount of $433,700,000, plus interest and court costs.

Andy would have liked to file this action in Missouri, where he might hope for a judge or jury friendly to the local franchise, or even in Kansas, on the theory that his distant relative, Parker Grissom, was a resident of that state. He thought, too, of filing in New York, which was now home to the Baseball offices, and where the courts might be more accustomed to litigation with such a substantial financial claim. But in the end, he was persuaded by Mumbles' advice and filed in the Cook County Circuit Court in Illinois because the original contract of 1914 had been executed under the laws of that state, though he was not sure why that had been the case.

⚬⚬⚬

"Commissioner, we've hit a few dead ends. For starters, the lawyer was an orphan, and those kinds of records are sealed and almost impossible to break. So our people are working it from the other end. There was a fellow by this name in Kansas City back around this time. He died in the flu pandemic in 1918. We're just getting started trying to trace any survivors or other relatives he might have had.

"Also, we thoroughly surveyed the few old records we have from around 1914. It's all pure boilerplate—copies of player contracts, official score sheets. There's nothing in there that's out of the ordinary. If I had to guess, back in the day these fellows probably wrote off the chance they would ever put a team out in the middle of the prairie. They probably ripped up their copy of the agreement, if there was one, as soon as Grissom walked out the door. That's bad news in a sense, but we can argue that the absence of 'so important' a commitment in the 'official files'—if you take my meaning—is *prima facie* evidence that it never existed. That puts all the pressure on Dennum to prove otherwise. If he has an original of some sort, that'll be show and tell day.

"Now, I have to advise you, there is one little wrinkle that's come up in our research already. Since you came from outside the game, I'm not sure how much baseball history you know. But back around the time in question, there was a third league, called the Federal League, that claimed to be a 'major' league. They were stealing players and causing all sorts of problems for the American and National Leagues. It was what you might call a litigation-rich environment." The general counsel went on to describe the history of the Federal League litigation, the special circumstances of the Baltimore and Kansas City clubs, and the role played by Judge Landis and, later, the US Supreme Court, concluding by telling the Commissioner that, "it wasn't so much that baseball was exempt from the law as that, in the opinion of the Court, the law simply didn't apply."

"And you're telling me all this because?"

"Well, Commissioner, though we don't know a great deal about this Parker Grissom yet, one thing we did discover is that he was one of a number of minority owners in the Kansas City Federal League team. It was called the Packers. I'm not sure at this point what that means. He doesn't appear to have been a principal owner, and he's not named in any capacity in any of the litigation. But it does suggest that we may need to be careful of our ground as we proceed here."

"Shit," was all the Commissioner said. But once again, he found himself missing the steady hand and impure heart of good old CI.

Andy read the letter a second time, just to make sure he had not overlooked any nuance. Nuance, he concluded once again, was the one thing that was entirely missing from the text. It read:

Be advised that we are in receipt of service of your lawsuit and will be timely responding to the court. I must strongly caution you, however, that we take the filing of frivolous and self-evidently fallacious litigation against this enterprise with the utmost seriousness, and we generally issue only one warning before taking appropriate steps to punish the offending false filer or filers to the fullest extent afforded under the law. That includes but is not limited to: filing potential criminal complaints and claims for civil damages against any Complainant making a false claim under law, as well as potential sanctions, up to and including disbarment, for any attorney engaging in unethical behavior in connection with such actions. For Complainants filing *pro se*, which appears to be the case here, we are fully prepared to pursue both avenues of response. This letter places you on notice.

This response, or one like it, of course, was to be expected. That was why lawyers generally kept a supply of antacids on hand at home and in the office. Still, letters like this were never easy to read and harder to laugh off. That, of course, was the reason they were written, and this general counsel for Baseball was good at what he did. Still, Andy knew, as perhaps the general counsel as of yet did not, that this claim was far from frivolous. What the letter really said was that he had their attention.

He walked from his office to Keiley's and placed the letter on her desk.

"Check this out," he said.

As Keiley read the letter, the color drained from her face. "Oh, Andy! This is awful!"

"Actually, it's not. This is the kind of thing lawyers do among themselves for sport. And I confess this guy is pretty good. So now you know why I wanted to take you on as an employee of the law firm. No matter what happens, there's no threat here that can touch you. And what they will eventually find out is that there's no threat here that can touch me, either. We have a real case with real damages, and once they figure that out, they will change their tune. Just wait and you'll see."

⊷⊶

A week had passed, and the Commissioner, never a patient man in the best of times, was showing his increasing irritation daily.

"Where the hell are we on this thing?" he queried the general counsel. "How long can it take to get something we can work with?"

"Actually, sir, I just this morning got the preliminary report from the investigators, and I think it points us toward a strategy we can use to make this lawsuit disappear."

"I'm listening."

"It's this Dennum fellow. Leaving aside all the questions about whether he is a valid heir to that guy Grissom, whose name is on the so-called contract, he's apparently not much of a lawyer. He got his degree from Madison-Jefferson a couple of—"

"From where?" the Commissioner demanded.

"Madison-Jefferson School of Law, sir. It's a nights-only law school with a crappy reputation that's well deserved if you ask me. Faculty's a bunch of drunks and miscreants with law degrees, and the graduates almost all aspire to be ambulance chasers in the purest sense of the term.

"Now, this Dennum took a different path and somehow got himself hired at Stetson, Varney, and Handelmann down in the financial district. But he was obviously a bust. Got himself fired after his first year. Guess they figured out why nobody decent hires Mad-Jeff grads. That's when he went home—we found out he grew up in Mendham, New Jersey. That's where the adoptive parents lived. So he went home and ended up in a tiny local practice where the guy who hired him died not long afterward. So he is now the smallest of small-town lawyers and scrambling to make a living. That gives us a motive we can pin on him for engaging in what we can portray as an attempted shakedown of the enterprise here."

"Now *that*," said the Commissioner, seeing the first bright spot on this particular horizon, "is something I can work with."

"Indeed. And here's a thought on one way to do that. Back before you became Commissioner, whenever we had a problem that required outside counsel, we used to rely on one firm in particular: Stetson, Varney. Nothing like a good coincidence. They have come to understand our business, and they've always done well by us. Plus, in this case, they will know the opposing advocate better than anyone else, and I'd bet their presence will give that guy the night sweats. I think we should bring them in and let them handle the response to this suit for us."

"I like that," said the Commissioner. "First bright idea you've had about this thing. Anybody in particular you want to work with?"

"Yeah. There's a really sharp guy over there and he can be a real sonofabitch if you're on the other side. Name is Joey Coy."

"Give Mr. Coy a call and get him over here. I want to have a chat with him."

※ ※

Andy was pleased when Betty told him that the judge's office in Chicago had phoned to arrange a meeting of the parties to discuss the outlines of the case, clarify the issues, and begin the discovery process—the routine exchange of files and other information between the parties to a lawsuit. The call indicated that the matter was relatively high on the judge's docket. He instructed Betty to phone back and accept any of the three dates that had been suggested.

Ten days later, he found himself walking into an ornate courtroom in the Windy City, where he saw the advocates' tables at the front of the room had been pushed together and several chairs arranged around them. Three men, presumably the lawyers for Major League Baseball, had arrived earlier and were seated with their backs to him. He walked down the center aisle of the courtroom and through the old wooden gate. As he moved toward the table, the three men turned and faced him.

"Hello, Andy." Joey Coy stuck out his hand. "You remember James and Jake here, I trust?" James and Jake were two of Joey's star associates, just a step down from Andy's old coworker Janine.

113

Andy was taken aback momentarily at this unexpected but not entirely surprising, turn of events, and he did his best to cover it up, not sure how well he had succeeded.

"Joey. So nice to see you again. Jimmy, Jake." He shook the proffered hands all around.

Suddenly, everything was brought home to Andy in a flash. Andy knew that Joey knew that the central document in this case had once existed, and he knew that Joey surely realized he had ordered it destroyed. That could result in Joey's being sanctioned or disbarred. Joey knew that Andy knew that the document had only turned up in a search conducted while Andy was employed by and working on behalf of Stetson, Varney, and that any reference he might make to it outside the firm, let alone using a copy of the document to file a lawsuit, could easily result in Andy's being sanctioned or disbarred. Leaving aside the mind-blowing concatenation of ethical issues arising from all of this, there was also a complicated strategic dilemma for both sides. Andy needed the best evidence to prove his case, and the best evidence is almost always the original document. Joey was entirely confident that the original document didn't exist but could not acknowledge that Andy's photocopy was a true one. Andy faced an added complication because he was serving as both attorney and client. But Joey faced an added complication because he had to defend both his client and his and the firm's actions. They both knew much of this had to play out without the judge becoming any the wiser.

Let the games begin.

It was at this point in their respective silences that the attorneys were joined by a distinguished-looking man of perhaps forty or forty-five, who entered the courtroom from behind the bench, walked to the conference table, and seated himself at the end.

"Good morning, gentlemen," he said. "I don't think I've had the pleasure of meeting any of you before. I'm Judge Keyser, and I'm delighted to welcome you to Chicago on such a nice, sunny day to get this little matter underway." Hands were shaken and introductions were made around the table.

"As I'm sure my clerk will have told you, we have three items of business for today. To be clear, this meeting is not a formal hearing, and the discussion is off the record. I simply want to educate myself as to the nature and intent of the litigation and, of course, to have the opportunity to meet each of you.

"The first item on the table is the essence of the case itself. I have read both the complaint and the response, but I'd like to hear this directly from the parties, through counsel, of course. Mr. Dennum, since you filed this action, why don't you start us off by summarizing your case in chief."

"Thank you, Your Honor. I was orphaned and adopted at an early age. I recently learned that I am a direct descendant of a man named Parker T. Grissom, who died in Overland Park, Kansas, in 1918. That's a suburb of Kansas City. I also came into possession of a photocopy of a contract that Mr. Grissom had signed in 1914, granting him a perpetual interest in any Major League Baseball franchise that might in future be established in the Kansas City metropolitan area. In the intervening years, two such teams have been established there, both franchised by the American League as agent of the respondent. I believe the 1914 contract is still valid and that Major League Baseball has never acknowledged or fulfilled its obligations with respect to the two franchises in question. I am suing to demand enforcement and compensation."

"Thank you for that succinct summary. Let me ask you two questions. First, do you possess an original copy of the document at the heart of this case?"

"No, Your Honor, but I believe it to be a valid agreement, and I hope to recover through discovery an original copy bearing the signatures of all four parties to the agreement."

"I see. And also, I am curious. You are seeking relief in an amount exceeding $400 million. How did you arrive at that number?"

Andy explained his reliance on recently published estimates of the valuation of both the Oakland and the Kansas City baseball teams, adding, "I believe, Your Honor, that those valuations will adequately reflect the net current result of whatever changes in valuations have occurred in the two organizations. As for the revenue estimates, those are also based on the most recent published data. I did not have access to the true data for either club for the periods in question, and I anticipate that I will revise this portion of my claim once I obtain those records through discovery."

"Very well. And Mr. Coy, as lead counsel for the respondent in this case, please summarize your response."

"Certainly, Your Honor. It is our position that Mr. Dennum does not have standing to bring this lawsuit because he is not the direct or sole heir of the deceased Mr. Grissom. Further, it is our position that there exists no original copy of the contract Mr. Dennum has presented because no such contract exists or ever did. Mr. Dennum may, as he says, believe he has presented the court with an honest and true copy of the said document, Your Honor, but we do not. And finally, *arguendo*, if such a document ever did exist, its nonenforcement in the century and more that has passed since the purported date of the agreement renders it unenforceable at this time. The claim was never timely asserted. In sum, Your Honor, at the first formal hearing on the matter, should there be one, we will be filing a motion to dismiss."

Andy knew the term "arguendo" was lawyer talk for "just for laughs, let's say this claim was true." And as for the threatened motion to dismiss the case without proceedings, that came as no surprise. Any defense attorney worth his or her salt always filed such a motion. It was, he knew, the legal equivalent of spinning a gigantic wheel of fortune and hoping that one number in a thousand, maybe ten thousand, would come up. As for the rest, he was fully confident of his ground.

"Okay. Thank you. I will await your motion with bated breath, Mr. Coy. But in the meantime, let's see if we can't focus on the justiciable issues presented here. That should help us frame the discovery I am sure both of you will be seeking.

"As I see it, Mr. Dennum, it will be incumbent upon you to demonstrate to the satisfaction of the court that you are not only descended from Mr. Grissom but that you are the rightful and sole successor to the benefits promised in the contract. And you will need to come up with something more than this photocopy to document the contract itself. We'll need to get over those two hurdles before we get to the question of timeliness—and I will eventually want briefs on that, so you'd both best be thinking about it—and only then might we get to damages.

"Now, Mr. Coy, you may draft your motion to dismiss, of course, but I will tell you that, for the moment and subject to validation, the court sees enough substance here to doubt that Mr. Dennum's claim is *prima facie* frivolous. If I were your client, I would be tasking you with taking this matter seriously. For the moment, the onus has fallen largely on the complainant. But that moment could pass in an instant. Of course, you will have every opportunity to contest Mr. Dennum's documentation.

"Now, gentlemen, let's get to the real business of the day. I will be expecting briefs encompassing your discovery requests by, let's say, two weeks from today, and you can expect the court to rule on both sets of requests within five days thereafter. And be on notice that the court will set an early deadline and will expect your full compliance. Clear?"

Nods all around.

"All right. Now just between us, I would like to have a sense of where the discovery in this case is headed. I won't hold you to what you say informally today, and I know you will both be giving more detailed thought to the question over the next fortnight, but I do not especially like surprises. So kindly enlighten me to the extent that you are able. Let's begin with Mr. Coy this time."

"Your Honor . . . Our discovery requests will be fairly modest, simply because we don't believe there is anything real to discover from Mr. Dennum. We will be seeking documentation of his claim to be the lawful and sole successor to Mr. Grissom, and of course we will want to have a chance to conduct a forensic examination of the original copy of this so-called contract. We will also want to know, probably through a deposition, just how it was that Mr. Dennum learned that he was descended from Mr. Grissom as asserted, why he asserts that the relocation of the first Kansas City franchise did not terminate the interest he claims in that franchise, and, importantly, how and from whom he came into possession of this supposedly valid century-old contract."

Boom! Shot across Andy's bow. *How'd you get this piece of paper, sport?*

"Thank you. And Mr. Dennum?"

"Your Honor, we will be seeking the franchise agreements by which Major League Baseball established both the first and second clubs in Kansas City, where we expect to find an absence of notice to the franchisees dating to the 1950s or much closer to the date of the contract. We will also want to see the documents moving the first Kansas City franchise to Oakland to determine whether any agreement was included that sought to terminate in any way the perpetual rights promised to Mr. Grissom. In addition, we will be seeking the financial records of both baseball clubs for all the years since each was first franchised in Kansas City, so as to permit a corrected calculation of the portion of damages attributable to net revenues. We will want to see any and all documents pertaining to organizational successorship within Major League Baseball and its component leagues so as to demonstrate continuity of liability, as well as a complete listing by date of the establishment and relocation or termination of all its franchises. Finally, we will demand a search of the complete records of the respondent, its predecessor organizations, and the firms that have provided it with outside legal counsel on any franchising or other related contractual matters through the years, which, upon information and belief, includes current counsel, for the purpose of locating any documents or correspondence relating to the contract in question. We reserve the right to seek depositions as required, and, because the confidential records of law firms are involved, we will readily accede to the court's appointment of a special master to oversee those aspects of discovery should that be your decision."

Joey, secure in his confidence, did not realize it, but Andy had just returned fire. Still, as any lawyer would, he objected at once to having the files of Stetson, Varney pillaged.

"Your Honor!" Coy exclaimed. The judge held up his hand.

"I can anticipate your objection, Mr. Coy. Mr. Dennum, is that last not a rather sweeping expectation? Why should the court grant you license to search through the files of present and past counsel to the respondent? Surely you recognize that such a search could expose highly confidential information."

"Indeed, Your Honor. As to the first point, the complainant is concerned that variations in the respondent's relationship with its outside counsel over the years, which counsel we are not at present able to list, might have included some provision for the storage of legal records which, through the passage of so much time, dating fully back to 1914 and the signing of the contract, may have passed from the conscious awareness of the respondent and its employees. As to the second point, it is the complainant's belief that the interposition of a special master empowered to determine the relevance and admissibility of any documents or other records that may be encountered provides sufficient protections against any abuse of this process."

"All right. This sort of thing is precisely why I like to have these little informal chats at the outset. This will give me an opportunity to think through this issue of access and a special master even as I await your briefs.

In the meantime, since everyone's cats are out of the bag, I order both parties to preserve any and all records that have already been identified here, as well as any other records that existed at the time this litigation was filed with the court."

He looked sternly around the table. "Mr. Dennum, Mr. Coy, do I make myself clear?"

In unison, both replied in the affirmative.

"Very well, then. Again, thank you all for coming out to Chicago. This looks to be a most interesting case. Let's get started."

With that, he rose and returned to his chambers, leaving Andy and Joey to engage in only the briefest of stare-downs. It was Joey who broke the silence.

"See you in court, sport."

Runners on Base

"CI, get in here!" shouted the Commissioner. There was no response.

Shit, he thought to himself. Over so many years and facing so many challenges and opportunities, it was a habit he found hard to break. He couldn't even visit the man to seek his advice. He was in a place where the Commissioner of Baseball could not afford to be seen, especially in the circumstances. After all, he was the victim of CI's deceit, right? Wasn't that the whole point of the exercise, the sword on which his closest confidant had fallen? The story was that CI had betrayed his longtime friend and benefactor—had sold him on a bogus document that the Commissioner had made public, much to his personal embarrassment. What would it look like if the Commissioner were then to visit with the man in prison? Sin and redemption? Injury and forgiveness? He might be able to sell that, but it was still too soon. Better to steer the ship on his own for yet a while longer.

But this morning's surprise was almost too much to bear. Why hadn't the damn lawyers seen this coming, warned him? He could understand it from the general counsel, a fellow good at pushing routine paperwork around on his desk and not a great deal more. *But what about this so-called hotshot outside guy, Coy? Isn't he supposed to be the sharp end of the legal stick?*

What occasioned both the discomfort and the reflection were a couple of legal papers that his secretary had routinely left on the "IN" pile on his desk during the two days he'd been out of the office traveling. *Not even a phone call heads up*, he thought angrily until he realized that the entire matter was still being treated confidentially within the office, and it was unreasonable to expect she would understand the significance of the papers. The Commissioner liked to think he was a reasonable man.

The first paper was a fairly brief legal filing from the Kansas City team's attorney. The gist was pretty simple. The team had received the discovery request from Dennum seeking the profit and loss statements from each year of its existence dating back to the 1960s. That should not have come as a surprise since all of the teams had been informed of the litigation when it was first filed, and the general counsel had followed up with the Kansas City and Oakland franchises immediately after the discovery conference to give them a heads up on the request. And indeed, the filing advised the complainant, the respondent, and the court that the team would make its best effort to comply, though some of the earliest records might be difficult or even impossible to retrieve. It was unusual that such a formal notice of compliance would be filed, but not unheard of.

No, it was the second part of the filing that had caught him off guard, and it explained the reason for the first. Kansas City was asking the court to separate it from the enterprise and absolve it of any legal or financial responsibility for any adjudged violation of the 1914 contract that might result in damages. The team's stated grounds were that it had not been in existence on the contract date and had received no notification of the document's existence or terms in the 1960s when the team was awarded its franchise from Major League Baseball. In effect, the team was claiming that, rather than being responsible in whole or in part for fulfillment of the contract, it was itself a victim of misfeasance or malfeasance on the part of what was then the American League, and what is now, following the 1999 consolidation and reorganization, Major League Baseball. This amounted not only to a crack in the foundation of the enterprise but a direct challenge to the unity of the game and to his own personal authority. Damn them!

Slightly further down the stack of papers was the second filing, this one from the Oakland ball club. The language was similar. Remarkably. But Oakland's claim was more extensive. First, wrote their attorney, the team had not been informed of any obligation toward Mr. Grissom or his heirs when the franchise was moved from Philadelphia to Kansas City in the 1950s. Nor, said the filing, doubling down on the point, had the team been advised that this unknown obligation would carry over when its franchise was relocated a second time, to Oakland a decade later. This issue arose uniquely in this instance because the original contract, if judged valid, provided an ownership share, not in any team located in Kansas City but in any *franchise* that might be awarded to the city. Though the point could, and surely would, be litigated if necessary, the plain language of the contract could be interpreted to extend to the operations on the West Coast after Kansas City was abandoned. The team also promised the court that it would make a determined and bona fide effort to locate the records that were sought in discovery but pointed out the difficulty it faced in doing so across two geographically and operationally distinct management teams and accountants over the better part of a century.

Sonofabitch! They're in it together! Of course, thought the Commissioner, *I can't blame them for trying to wiggle out of this thing. They are, after all, the ones who'd feel the sting if things go the wrong way. But still! How fucking dare they break ranks!*

"Sharon," he said, picking up his phone. "Get me whoever you can find in the owners group out in Kansas City. I want somebody on the line right this instant."

⸺ ⸺

Once the formal discovery motions were filed with the court, it had taken the judge a few days to locate and appoint a special master. His choice was Professor Margaret Hanson, a retired litigator who now taught legal ethics at the state university's law school. The fact he had chosen to follow this path was a win for Andy since he was the one seeking access to the records of other law firms. In his motion, he had limited his request to three time periods: from 1914 through 1918, the years between the signing of the contract and Parker Grissom's death; the years surrounding the establishment of the first Kansas City franchise in the 1950s; and the years surrounding the relocation of that franchise and the establishment of the second Kansas City franchise in the 1960s. He had been careful in his choice of language—thank you, Mumbles—seeking not just the records of the leagues and the parent organization but any and all records from whatever source pertaining to the matters at hand. And he was careful to include Stetson, Varney in the records request on the grounds that the firm might have become the repository of related documents in connection with its current or past representation of Major League Baseball. Somehow, Professor Hanson, who knew nothing of the history of the case, approved all of these requests.

A clever Stetson, Varney lawyer receiving such a demand for documents would immediately challenge the demand on any number of grounds, beginning with client confidentiality and running a full gamut of rationales beyond that one. It might not be enough to halt the discovery, but even a small win could make a difference, and most special masters, when challenged, were inclined toward compromise. And Joey Coy was nothing if not a clever lawyer. But he read the request rather casually, concluding that the firm had nothing to hide—at least nothing that Andy would dare to challenge them on. The discovery request did not reference the original contract, which Joey took as a sign of weakness on Andy's part. So after a cursory look, he passed the request to a first-year associate with a simple instruction: "I don't think you'll find anything. But see what we have and send it over. Draft a cover letter and I'll sign it."

Joey, of course, had dispatched his own discovery request to Andy, asking for the original copy of the contract, the source who provided it to Andy, and the legal and genealogical records that led him to advance his claim to successorship in that agreement.

As to the claim of family lineage, Andy was locked and loaded. Keiley had spent several weeks producing a beautiful map of the Grissom family line from the death of Parker forward. This was supported by two highly detailed expert reports, both of which mimicked her earlier research. One report had identified a previously unrecognized branch of the family tree but not one that presented any issues once the second basket of evidence, the extensive collection of probate records that Andy had gathered, came into consideration. The icing on the cake was the file Lou had retained pertaining to Andy's adoption by the Dennums. There was, if one were honest, a potential area of ambiguity in that both Keiley and Andy had leaped to the conclusion that the timing of the automobile accident and the adoption was not coincidental. But in looking over the few pre-adoption family pictures Keiley had come across and saved during her research, Andy noticed a tiny detail—a small and rather unusual medallion that showed up across two generations. It was the same medallion his adoptive parents had given him when he was young, telling him it would surely bring him luck. He had kept it all these years and included the family photos and a photo of the medallion in his discovery production.

With respect to the contract, Andy stated, as he had before, that he was not in possession of an original signed copy. But it was the related request—for information on how he had obtained his photocopy of the agreement—that gave him pause. He knew how he wanted to handle this, but doing so would require more than a little finesse. First and foremost, he needed to be sure that Stetson, Varney's response to his discovery motion was submitted before his own production left the office.

⎯⎯⊂⊃⎯⎯

A few days after the Kansas City and Oakland filings hit his desk, the Commissioner received some more bad news, this time in the form of a filing by the Tampa Bay team claiming that it should be excluded from legal and financial responsibility for any share of any award of damages because the team had not been franchised until 1995 and had not begun play until 1998. For that reason, argued their attorney in the filing, the team could hardly be expected to honor an obligation that was made some eighty years before it existed. The brief also noted that the franchise had not been advised of any such obligation or commitment by the American League or by Major League Baseball at the time its franchise was granted.

He called in the general counsel and laid down the law. "Get your ass back to your office and get on the phone to the clubs. I don't want to see another filing like this, period. And get that asshole lawyer down in Tampa to retract this sucker. Do it!"

Too late.

Over the next three days, the Commissioner's office was deluged with similar demurrals—from both teams in Texas, from three on the West

Coast, from New York and Miami, from the mountains to the deserts, from sea to fucking sea. And they all said the same thing—that their team had not existed at the time of the 1914 contract, and if it was real and valid, they should not be held responsible for any obligations it might produce. The Canadians went one step further, claiming they could hardly be held to the terms of a contract made under American law, an odd argument since the franchise they held was itself created under American law. But that wasn't the point. The rats were on the run. This damn lawsuit was splitting baseball apart. It was nearly a disaster.

Then it became one. There were some teams—sixteen, to be precise—from whom the Commissioner and the court had not heard. No filings, no nothing. As the bad paper started piling up on his desk, he began to realize what these other teams—teams whose numbers might still give him a working majority within the enterprise—had in common. They were the franchises that had been around as far back as 1914, or in several cases, the successors to those teams. They were the core of Major League Baseball, and they were, he could see, standing by their commissioner.

Those teams, however, had an altogether different view of the situation. So it was that late that very afternoon, an unexpected visitor arrived at the office asking to see the Commissioner on urgent business. It was a member of the old guard, no longer an owner, but nonetheless well connected. He quickly made clear that he had been dispatched as an emissary and that he spoke for most, if not all, of the original sixteen franchises. He wasted no time coming to the point of his visit.

"Commissioner, I'm here representing to you informally the views of a good half of the teams in the game. I'm sure you know exactly whom I mean. They have sent me as a sort of outside insider, I suppose you could say, because they did not want to start adding to the blizzard of paper they have reason to believe you have been receiving. Owners do talk among themselves, you know. But, they wanted to convey to you in the strongest terms their common concern that if this Kansas City litigation, which you earlier told them was frivolous, turns out to be something real, they do not want to be left alone on the hook for what could be massive financial damages. They were in the leagues in 1914, and they were the franchises that put Ban Johnson and Garry Herrmann and John Tener in charge of the game, so they can't easily disclaim responsibility for any stupid thing those fellows might have done. But in their view, they cannot be left alone to bear the burden of any judgment or settlement. After all, these other teams, the Johnny-come-lately bunch of expansion teams, have benefitted immensely from their admission to the game, and they need to stand up and pay their share. And Commissioner, it's up to you to see that they do."

"Now, Bill," the Commissioner replied, using the man's first name as a way to communicate that he was spitting down and not sucking up, "you just tell those boys that we have this whole thing well in hand. All this not-me crap is just a bunch of lawyers curling up into the fetal position and sucking their thumbs. I can tell you with confidence that our own legal folks are on top of this, and they have assured me that it's not going anywhere. This Dennum fellow is some sort of huckster or faker, and by the time we get through with him, he'll be example number one that you don't fuck around with us. So you go back, and you tell those boys that they need to just straighten out their shorts and show a little patience."

"Commissioner, I'll tell them what you said. But I have to caution you that they are very concerned, and at some point they may feel as if they have to act on that concern."

"Bill, are you threatening me? Is that what they did? They sent you here to threaten me? Well, you remind those motherf—"

The visitor raised both hands, and the Commissioner stopped in mid-expletive. From there, the conversation wound down quickly, and the emissary from the old guard promptly departed.

Once he had left, the Commissioner picked up the phone and dialed the general counsel's direct line.

"I want Coy in my office first thing in the morning. Make it happen."

⚅ ⚅

Andy did not know, of course, of the emissary's visit to the Commissioner. But he did receive copies of all of the filings from the various teams—Kansas City first and Oakland second, then the blizzard of briefs from the post-1914 members of each league.

What was it Sajak had said? Something to the effect that you need to find players who may not be sympathetic to your cause but who have their own interests, relationships, and influence. Then you need to start moving them around the board, always working for themselves alone but in ways that advance your cause of action.

A couple of those trips he had made earlier looked like they might be paying off. The pieces were beginning to move. And he had Sajak to thank for that.

"Commissioner." It was the general counsel, standing in the office doorway and looking as if he were afraid to enter. "You'll probably want to see this before your meeting with Coy."

City, County May Sue MLB

Special To *The Star*

Informed sources within the offices of both the Jackson County Executive and Mayor have confirmed that staff attorneys are examining the potential for filing a joint, multimillion-dollar lawsuit against Major League Baseball. The sources have been granted anonymity because they are not authorized to speak on matters of pending litigation.

The potential suit arises from a separate lawsuit filed by a descendant of former Kansas City resident Parker T. Grissom, who died during the influenza pandemic of 1918. According to that lawsuit, a copy of which has been reviewed by *The Star*, Mr. Grissom entered into a personal services contract with the National Commission, which was at the time the governing body of Major League Baseball. In exchange for unspecified services, Baseball promised to provide a one-tenth ownership stake in any future baseball franchise that might be granted to the metro area. The suit contends that, even as two separate franchises were located in the city over the years following, this was never done, and seeks damages from Major League Baseball in the amount of $400 million.

Attorneys for the current Kansas City ownership group have indicated that the team was never notified of this obligation when the franchise was established and that they have asked the state court in Illinois, where the case is being heard, to exclude them from any award of damages. Efforts to contact the owners of the Oakland franchise, formerly located in Kansas City, have so far been unsuccessful.

Local authorities are considering legal action because both Municipal Stadium, in 1955, and the current stadium, in 1967, as well as the 2007 renovation of the latter, were built using bond proceeds and other public funds. Attorneys are working to determine whether the failure of Major League Baseball to disclose a material obligation to an unidentified additional owner of each franchise represented a *de jure* or *de facto* fraud upon the public, and if so, what level of damages might have been sustained. At the very least, our sources indicate, the local governments plan to file amicus curiae, or friend of the court, briefs, stating that they had no knowledge of any such additional ownership stake.

It is known that the State of Missouri is also considering entering the matter because any undisclosed owner may be liable for income or other taxes.

The Commissioner glanced over the article, then looked up from his desk.

"This is all we need. The media have the story. And since it's the KC paper, we probably have to assume that it wasn't Dennum who leaked it, although it is interesting that his name never appears here. But more likely, it was someone out there, and probably the ball club trying to cover its ass. Can this shit storm get any worse?"

As time passed, the anxiety rose among the Federal League owners as they watched their financial situation deteriorate. Week by week, the number of teams on the brink of bankruptcy increased, yet their lawyer, Edward Gates, urged caution.

"This judge is very temperamental," he told them repeatedly. "He's fair-minded, as far as I know. But he is a real stickler for procedure and decorum, and if you cross him or push him. . . . Well, let's just say that you don't want to do that."

The 1915 baseball season ended, and still nothing happened.

"Surely by year's end, we can expect a decision," wrote James Gilmore, the league president, in a Thanksgiving missive to his colleagues.

New Year's Day 1916 came and went, and still nothing happened.

Ban Johnson and his fellow members of the National Commission watched the pages of the calendar turn and eyed the beginning of spring workouts for the coming season. Gilmore and his Federal League owners watched the same pages turn with a growing sense of dread. They knew they had a winning argument, and they simply could not get their day in court.

Finally, the pressure reached a breaking point. Gilmore wrote to Herrmann, the correct official point of contact, essentially suing for peace. Was there, he wondered, some sort of middle ground we might achieve and end all of this conflict?

This was the moment Johnson had been waiting for. He knew that the major leagues—the real ones, as he thought of them—were not without their own challenges. There were owners among his own group who wanted out or who were, at the very least, in weak financial positions. And the Federals had two things of worth: some valuable franchises of their own and a small number of financial backers, like Weeghman and Sinclair, whose wealth was independent of their baseball operations and substantial enough to be of use. There were, then, things he wanted, gains he could achieve, even as he proceeded to destroy this upstart Federal League. It was time to deal.

The Federals went into the negotiations with eight established franchises, the Baltimore Terrapins, Brooklyn Tip-Tops, Buffalo Blues, Chicago Whales, Kansas City Packers, Newark Peppers, Pittsburgh Rebels, and St. Louis Terriers. Acting collectively, the American and National League owners bought out four of these groups, in Brooklyn, Buffalo, Newark, and Pittsburgh. That eliminated direct competition to the majors in two cities, Brooklyn and Pittsburgh, while demoting the other two cities to minor league status forevermore. Phil Ball, the presumed driving force behind the Federal League's ambitions, was allowed to purchase the St. Louis Browns of the American League, and

Charles Weeghman, owner of the Whales, was allowed to buy the Cubs, who moved to a new home in Weeghman Park, renamed years later for a new owner as Wrigley Field. Two more points of competition were eliminated. After a legal struggle, the financially bankrupt Kansas City team had been taken over by the league office and ceased altogether to be a factor. That left only the Terrapins, whose ownership declined to participate in the settlement. The Baltimore team would sue the major leagues a few years later, reasserting the antitrust claim that underlay the Federal League lawsuit, something Johnson should have anticipated given the intense personal acrimony between himself and the Baltimore ownership. But for the moment, he was greatly pleased. He had, in one turn, eliminated the competition and strengthened both the baseball establishment and his own hand. All in all, a good day's work.

Equally pleased was Judge Landis. By letting the matter gestate for a year, he had birthed a satisfactory outcome that preserved the game he loved. More than that, it particularly benefitted his favorite team, the Cubs, who got a new, special stadium and stronger financial backing in the deal. Before long, in 1919, his good friend, William Veeck, Sr., would be named president of the club, and the two would share many happy days together at the stadium. And the next year, Landis himself, on Veeck's recommendation among others, would be named the first Commissioner of Baseball.

***

Judge Keyser was not one to sit on his hands, especially not when he smelled a rat. Days after the first round of discovery production had been concluded, Joey Coy had filed a motion seeking a hearing on one item Andy had delivered at the last moment: an affidavit claiming to have obtained his copy of the Grissom contract while he was employed by Stetson, Varney. Coy's sputtering anger almost visibly dripped from every word of the short and pointed brief, but Keyser didn't need that to set him on edge. In the guise of a claim of authenticity, Dennum was, at the very least, acknowledging he had breached professional standards of ethics. At worst, he could be determined to have fabricated his most essential piece of evidence. *There is a reason*, thought the judge, *that lawyers are not supposed to represent themselves.* It keeps them out of logical pretzel knots like the one revealed in Dennum's affidavit.

Once both parties were settled in their respective places in his courtroom, Judge Keyser opened the hearing.

"Mr. Coy. We are here today pursuant to your three-part motion to exclude from evidence the affidavit filed by the claimant and the claimant's counsel, whom, we shall note once again for the record, are one and the same person, to dismiss this case with prejudice and to refer Mr. Dennum to the bar associations of Illinois, New Jersey, and New York for disciplinary action. The court is unsure of its authority to make such referrals to out-of-state entities and would gladly receive briefs from the parties as to that. As for the rest, let us proceed. Please state the basis for your motion."

It was early yet, but they had arrived at the nub of the case. Joey and Andy had been eager to reach this point, each in his own way and each with his own expectations. For his part, the judge had been far less eager to confront an inconsistency he had referenced from the outset in the hope that it would resolve itself, but now that it was before him, he, too, understood that this could well be the point on which the case would turn.

"Thank you, Your Honor. As counsel for the respondent, I feel the obligation—and as opposing counsel is a former colleague of mine and, I thought, a friend—it pains me to make this argument. However, I have a clear duty to my client to do so.

"The complainant's affidavit raises two crucial questions. First and foremost, it suggests that Mr. Grissom was at one time a client of a firm that was later merged into Stetson, Varney and that a signed original of the so-called Grissom contract exists or existed in the files of my law firm, a fact that the complainant claims is known to me personally, and that I ordered him to destroy that document and others that accompanied it. All of this search and destroy activity allegedly occurred last year, during the time when our firm employed the complainant. He is correct in stating that his responsibility during the year of his employment was to comb through archived files from many years ago to determine what they contained. This, of course, is customary practice in our profession.

He is incorrect, however, in stating that Mr. Grissom was a client of the firm or that there is any file in that archive pertaining to Mr. Grissom or his contract. I assure the court that I am unaware of any such file that we possess. If we had it, we would have produced it in our own discovery.

"Of primary import here, since the alleged signed original of the contract upon which he bases his entire case does not exist, by entering his claim in the form of his affidavit, the complainant, or should I say, the complainant's counsel," Joey continued with a sneer, "has in effect knowingly introduced false evidence before this court and, in the same act, has committed perjury. That is *prima facie* grounds for dismissal with prejudice, followed by whatever subsequent legal sanctions the court might regard as appropriate.

"But let us say, arguendo, that the document did exist, that the complainant made a photocopy for his own benefit, and that he then made a public show of this photocopy by using it as the basis for this litigation. In bringing his assertion before the court by means of this affidavit, the complainant, an attorney who was extended a courtesy affiliation with the Illinois State Bar Association so that he might participate in these very proceedings, has committed a serious breach of professional ethics. He has used information he acknowledges having purloined from a confidential file of a firm that was, at the time, his employer and used that file for unauthorized purposes. And to be clear, I make this argument only to make the point and not to suggest in any way that such a document exists.

"My distinguished opponent and former colleague has used his previous association with my firm to add credibility to a claim that he has based on a document that is pure fabrication. One can speculate on his reasons for doing so—revenge against a firm that separated him from its employ, financial greed, an effort to connect with imagined birth parents he never knew, or some other deep psychological need that I, for one, do not understand. Whatever it was, this litigation is misguided, and the respondent prays the court to bring it to a halt here today. Thank you, Your Honor."

"All right, Mr. Dennum," the judge said, turning his gaze toward Andy. "What have you got to say for yourself?"

"Your Honor," Andy began.

Andy had been more than a little nervous as he prepared for the motions hearing. He knew that everything—*everything*—would be on the line . . . knew because he had been the one squarely to place it there. At some point, it would be necessary to confess his sins to the judge, to acknowledge that he had stretched the boundaries of legal ethics, though that had never been his intent. So far as he knew, though Joey had indicated that if pressed, they would do so to preserve other client interests, neither Coy nor the firm had taken any concrete steps to disassociate itself from Parker Grissom and his heirs. And Andy was still employed by Stetson, Varney at the time he had done his basic research on Grissom and his contract. Moreover, the photocopy he now possessed had been made in connection with a firm matter and had been duly logged to the appropriate accounting code. And Joey had been so anxious to toss him out on his ear when his first year expired that he had neglected to ask that any firm-related materials Andy had outside the office be returned. Hell, Joey had effectively banned him from the building. He could feel that line brushing against his skin.

The problem arose from that point forward. Because Andy had retained that contract—all three documents, actually—when he knew better, and he had probably broken through that razor-thin line itself when he became interested in tracking down the heirs of Parker T. Grissom. Truth be told, of course—and it was a truth that he simply could not relate in court—he had decided to do that on the fly as the quickest and best excuse he could think of to spend some time with Keiley. One thing had led to another, not only with her but with the quest for an heir, and then, all of a sudden, everything had come together in a most unexpected way, one he would never have guessed. Not only were he and Keiley becoming quite close indeed, but because of her efforts, he had solved not one but two mysteries. He had learned who his birth parents were, and he had become the sole heir to the Grissom legacy. Stuff like that only happened in novels.

In the circumstances, the best he could hope to do in court was to convince the judge of his honorable motives, plead coincidence, document his claims, and prove beyond any doubt that Joey Coy and Stetson, Varney were hiding the critical evidence supporting his case and undermining that of their own client. The key to that was proving the link between Grissom in 1918 and the Stetson firm today.

It was Keiley who came up with an idea for that, and Keiley who executed it to perfection. She mapped the history of the firm as a genealogist would a family tree, borrowing from her old friend Edward Tufte the idea of illustrating it in the form of a subway map showing all of the various mergers and acquisitions in the firm's history and the areas of practice associated with each. In itself, the map did not prove that Grissom had been a client of a predecessor firm; that would have to wait until a bit of drama played itself out. But it did make clear that, once that fact was established, Joey would have some serious explaining to do. And that, hoped Andy, was only the beginning of his troubles.

———

"Your Honor, as I stated in my affidavit—"

"Let me stop you right there," said the judge. "Obviously, the court has read your affidavit. What I am trying to do here is figure out why you think you have the right to bring this matter before this or any other court."

The judge's tone, as well as his words, set Andy back on his heels. Perhaps it had been a mere fantasy, but he had assumed all along that, at the very least, he would have a chance to establish his case. But Judge Keyser was showing more than a little attitude, and that did not bode well. Then it got worse.

"Mr. Coy, if you don't mind," the judge continued, turning to Joey, "I have a few questions of my own I'd like to pose to Mr. Dennum here."

"Not at all, Your Honor," Joey replied, attempting not to sound smug but not entirely succeeding.

"Mr. Dennum, let us begin with this matter of professional ethics. Were you employed by Mr. Coy's firm at the time you claim to have discovered this document, or rather, this set of three documents, one of which is the Grissom contract?"

"Yes, Your Honor. I—"

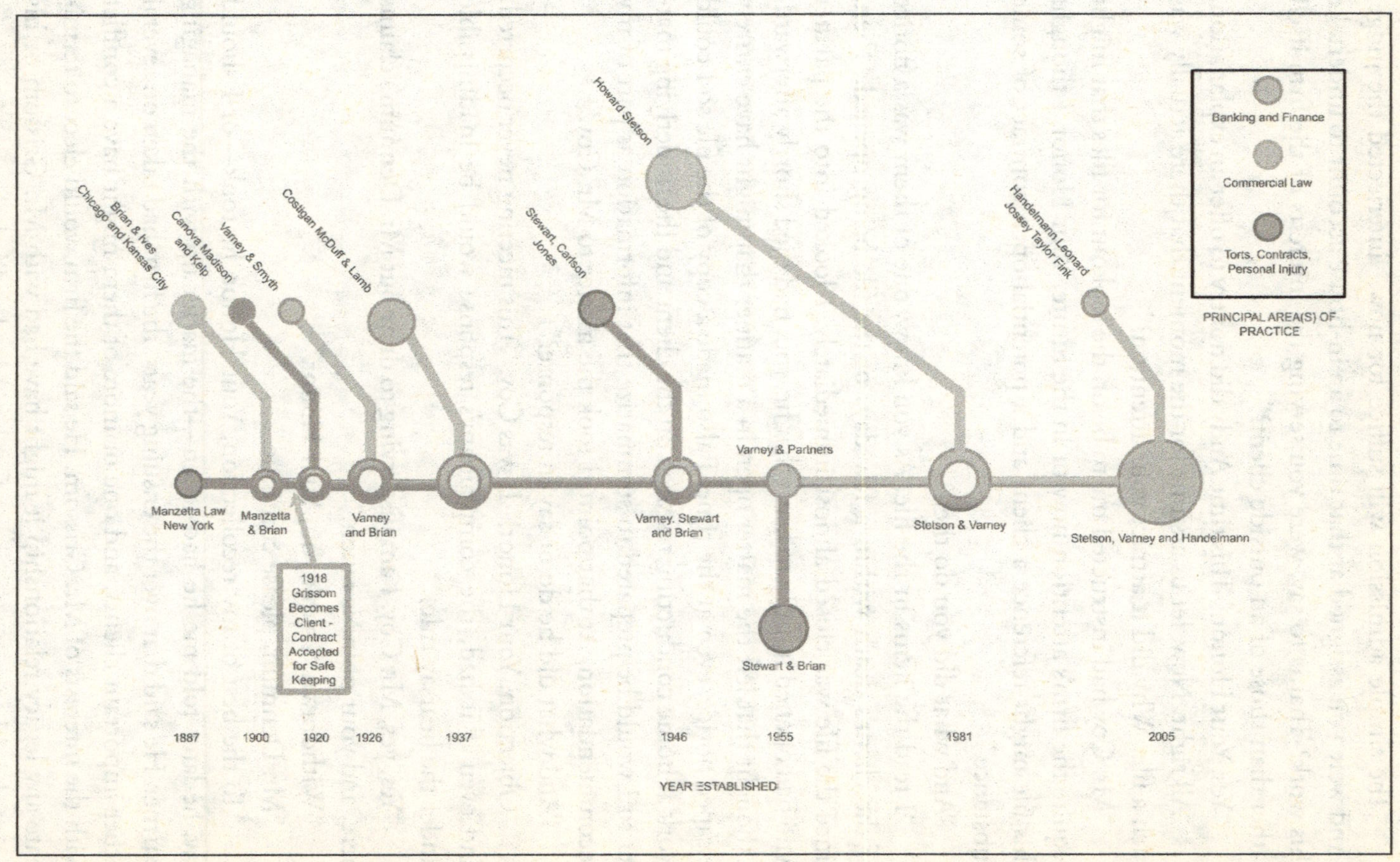
Banking and Finance
Commercial Law
Torts, Contracts, Personal Injury
PRINCIPAL AREA(S) OF PRACTICE
Howard Stetson
Handelmann Leonard Jossey Taylor Fink
Brian & Ives Chicago and Kansas City
Canova Madison and Kelp
Varney & Smyth
Costigan McDuff & Lamb
Stewart, Carlson Jones
Varney & Partners
Manzetta Law New York
Manzetta & Brian
Varney and Brian
Varney, Stewart and Brian
Stetson & Varney
Stetson, Varney and Handelmann
1918 Grissom Becomes Client - Contract Accepted for Safe Keeping
Stewart & Brian
1887
1900
1920
1926
1937
1946
1955
1981
2005
YEAR ESTABLISHED

"The simple admission will suffice for now," interjected the judge. "And were you assigned at that time to an in-house account to undertake this work? That is to say, were you serving the interests of the firm itself rather than those of an outside client?"

"Yes, Your Honor." This time Andy did not try to offer an explanation.

"All right. Now, let us assume for the moment that there actually was such a file. Why did it attract your attention?"

"Mr. Coy had instructed me to be on the lookout for files that might require the firm's attention now or in the future, Your Honor. I thought this file might reference a client and a potential open contract of some substance."

"And what did you do then?"

"I read the items in the file. As you know, one of them was a notice of the client's death within a few days of the file being opened. Then, since the file was closed almost immediately, I looked into the partner who had opened it, only to learn that he, too, had died shortly afterward. I thought that left the matter open in a manner that might have entirely escaped notice, even at the time. I also made a copy of the file so I could work at home conducting research on the client and the underlying matter so I would be prepared to summarize that information as part of my recommendation. At that point, I took the matter to Mr. Coy."

"And what did he do or say in response?"

"Objection, Your Honor!" It was Coy. "This meeting never occurred, and even if it had, the complainant's response would be inadmissible under the hearsay rule."

"Yes, yes, Mr. Coy. I am just trying to draw out Mr. Dennum's claims here, and your point is taken."

"Withdrawn. Thank you, Your Honor."

"Mr. Dennum, please continue."

"To the best of my recollection, Your Honor, he took—or I should say, he later told me he had taken—the matter up with the managing partner. He said that over the ensuing years, the firm had taken on several other important clients, and one or more of them might have a conflict with the interests of Mr. Grissom. He said the firm would elect to terminate any legacy relationship it might have had with Mr. Grissom or his heirs, should any ever appear, a fact he judged unlikely."

"And that was the end of it?" pressed the judge.

"No, Your Honor. At the end of that conversation, Mr. Coy instructed me to do four things: to return the Grissom file to its place in the archive, take the entire box in which I had found it and place it in the burn pile. Next, I was to return to the stacks in the archive and move the other nearby boxes around to mask the resulting gap. Finally, he instructed me to get back to work."

"Objection!"

"As I said, Mr. Coy, I've got this."

"Yes, Your Honor. Withdrawn."

"And did you follow those instructions, Mr. Dennum?"

"To the letter, Your Honor."

"And that was the end of the matter?"

"As far as I was concerned, it was, Your Honor. I just moved ahead—there were a great many files in the archive—and I forgot about the whole thing."

"Then, Mr. Dennum, how is it that we come to be here today?"

"Well, Your Honor, a few months after all of this happened, I was called up to Mr. Coy's office and told my services were no longer required. I was offered two weeks of severance and then given a few minutes to collect my things and leave the premises. I was accompanied by a security officer from that moment until I was out the main door."

"And is that when you managed to collect the copy of the Grissom file that you had made some months earlier?"

"No, Your Honor. I didn't realize I had neglected to return that copy to the firm when I first came across it and did that initial research. It had ended up in an unrelated stack of papers, and it wasn't until I found myself with time on my hands after being let go that I had occasion to take a look at that stack. I was actually trying to locate an old electric bill when I came across the file."

"And were you not obligated to return that file to the law firm?"

"On reflection today, Your Honor, I can see where that might have been the case. But my termination from Stetson, Varney had been so unexpected and so abrupt that I was not thinking that way. Mr. Coy had basically given me no notice and no time to think or respond. He practically had me thrown out of the building and for no reason other than . . .

well . . . I don't want to speculate on what his reasons might have been. I only know that I had performed the task that I was assigned."

"Okay, so you were going through papers looking for a utility bill and you came across this file."

"Yes, Your Honor. And I guess I just started thinking about it—about whether Grissom had any living heirs today and whether they might have some continuing property rights that had fallen between the cracks simply because the contract establishing those rights had been locked away for safekeeping by a lawyer who died one week later. It was at that point that I happened to meet a woman who was a genealogist. We were part of the same program at a community center. We got to talking, and I asked her if she could track Mr. Grissom's family forward from the little that I knew—more as a hypothetical than anything else. Well, one thing led to another, and between her tracing his family tree and my research in the probate records of each succeeding generation, we were able to plot out the line of inheritance until about thirty or forty years ago."

"And that, Mr. Dennum, is when you suddenly discovered that you yourself were the missing heir?" The judge's voice as he asked this particular question dripped with incredulity. And by now, Joey Coy was just sitting back and enjoying the show.

"No, Your Honor. Not exactly. You see, after I was fired from Stetson, Varney, I went home to New Jersey to look for a job. And I ended up in the office of an older local solo practitioner, Lou D'Antonio, who, it turned out, had health problems and was looking for a partner. We reached an agreement and I started work there. When we were first talking, Lou . . . er, Mr. D'Antonio, had mentioned to me that he knew my adoptive parents and that he had actually done a little of the paperwork when I was adopted. Now, I know that a lot of orphans can't wait to find out who their birth parents were, Your Honor, but for me, well, the Dennums were the only parents I had ever known, and I never had that kind of interest in tracking down some strangers. So I never even followed up with Lou about that. And then, just after I started work, he had a stroke and passed away. So I never could.

"Now, genealogists would hear me talk like that, about not having any interest in my birth parents, and think I'm nuts. And somewhere in that time frame, Ms. Barefoot, the genealogist I had consulted, asked if we might consult Lou's old files, because she had learned that a baby boy had survived an accident in which the last surviving Grissom heirs had been killed, that the accident had happened at roughly the same time as my adoption, and that Mr. D'Antonio's name was on some of the related legal papers. It turned out that D'Antonio's file was actually more complete than he had let on, which made the link look highly likely."

"Mr. Dennum," the judge interrupted. "This is quite a long chain of coincidences that you are asking the court to accept, don't you think?"

"Yes, Your Honor. I know it is. But let me just tell the court one more thing. When we were finished examining Mr. D'Antonio's file on the adoption, Ms. Barefoot produced a couple of old family photographs from newspapers that showed a particular medallion being held or worn in two separate generations of the Grissom family tree. I have appended them to my affidavit. Those photos reminded me of a good luck medallion the Dennums had given me as a young boy, one that I still have. It was this medallion, Your Honor."

And with that, Andy took the object out of his jacket pocket and handed it to the judge.

⬤◀▬▶⬤

"Your Honor!" It was Joey again, this time trying to break any momentum that Andy might have established for his tale.

"Okay, Mr. Coy. Okay. Now it's your turn. Let's keep it simple. Did Mr. Dennum ever bring you a file containing these three Grissom documents?"

"No, Your Honor, he never did that."

"All right, so then it would follow that it is your testimony that you never discussed such a file with your managing partner and never made any determination regarding Mr. Grissom's status as a legacy client of your firm?"

"Correct, Your Honor."

"And it is your testimony that you never instructed Mr. Dennum here to return the file to the archive and then destroy its file box?"

"Correct, Your Honor."

"So it would follow that the only way Mr. Dennum could have obtained these documents would have been by creating them himself?"

"As far as I know, Your Honor. I cannot say that he did not obtain them elsewhere or did not commission someone else to create them."

"Hmmm. So if the court were to instruct a third party, such as the special master, to enter your firm's archive and examine the files from this period, she would not find any evidence supporting Mr. Dennum's claim, correct?"

"Yes, Your Honor."

"And tell me, does your firm maintain any sort of record of the files and the like that it discards and burns? Is there a log listing the items?"

"No, Your Honor. That would seem to defeat the purpose."

"And would there be any way to determine whether, at any time during the course of his employment with your firm, Mr. Dennum made photocopies of these three documents?"

"Well . . . let me think about that. It would be possible, I suppose, to use the combination of Mr. Dennum's identification code and the account number assigned to internal archival work to create a listing of how many copies of documents he charged to that account and of the dates when he did so. But I know of no way to determine what specific documents were copied."

"Might I follow that up for just a moment, Your Honor?" asked Andy.

"Very well."

"Mr. Coy, do you know whether the firm integrates its copiers through an electronic network and whether that network does, in fact, capture and record every document that is copied?"

There was a pause as the significance of the question settled onto Joey's shoulders. This was something he had not anticipated. Hell, he'd never heard of such a thing. *Could there be a record of those documents? Andy is probably bluffing.*

"To my knowledge, we do not. I have never heard of such a system," he responded, hoping that would slide past the judge. Not quite.

"All right," Judge Keyser said. "I think I would like to adjourn these proceedings for a couple of days. In the meantime, everybody has homework. Mr. Dennum, I want you to put together any evidence you might have to support your claim that Mr. Coy knew of the file and ordered its destruction."

"Yes, Your Honor."

"And Mr. Coy, I want two things from you. First, I want you to investigate the possibility that electronic records of photocopied documents are maintained by your firm in the manner Mr. Dennum suggested. I want a written report on that signed by your managing partner and by you. And, in the event that such a system is operating, I want you to produce a complete file of every document Mr. Dennum photocopied and charged to the accounting code in question for the duration of his employment."

"Yes, Your Honor."

"How long will all of that take, do you think?"

"If there is no system of that kind, a day after I get back to New York. If there is a system, I would be guessing, but perhaps a week?"

"Very well. I'll instruct my clerk to schedule a continuation of this hearing one week from today. But there is a second thing I need from you, Mr. Coy. I will instruct Professor Hanson to conduct a personal search of the relevant areas of the Stetson, Varney archive. I want you to facilitate that. And I am issuing an order at the conclusion of our session today, which is to say, momentarily, that neither you nor any member of your firm, including staff, is to enter the firm's archive for any reason until that search has been completed."

"Yes, Your Honor."

"Now, Mr. Dennum, I understand that your task in the archives was to review all the case files from a particular period of time. Is that correct?

"Yes, Your Honor. I was to start with files dated 1914 and keep going."

"And how far did you get by the time you were, ah, separated from the firm?"

"I was into records from 1920, Your Honor. But—"

"No buts, Mr. Dennum. The court has the information it needs. I will pass those dates along to the special master as the parameters of her search. Since the contract itself dates from 1914—perhaps another of those nasty coincidences, Mr. Dennum?—that range should allow her to determine whether there are any files at Stetson, Varney that are germane to this case. I will look to her to advise the court as to her findings."

"Yes, Your Honor."

<hr>

By the time Andy landed back in Newark, it was all he could do to walk unassisted from the plane. He was physically exhausted as well as emotionally spent. He thought he could see a path forward, but with so many potential twists and turns, he wasn't sure he could follow it to the end. His spirits picked up when he saw Keiley waiting for him in the main area of the terminal, but by the time she had driven them back to Mendham, he was sound asleep in the passenger seat.

He woke up as Keiley was parking the car.

"Good thing you're awake," she deadpanned. "I was wondering how on earth I was going to carry you into the house."

"Sorry. I guess I was just really tired."

"So. . . . How was your day?"

"Long. It was just Joey and me with the judge in this big old court-room. More than a little intimidating, I have to confess. The whole thing didn't last more than a half hour or so, and the judge ended up doing pretty much all of the questioning. Mostly of me, as it turned out. He wanted me to go through every step of how I found the document, how I ended up with a copy of it after I left Stetson, Varney, why and how I tracked down the Grissom descendants, how I happened to end up working for Lou D'Antonio, who just happened to have the file from my adoption, and how I just happened to end up as the last living heir of Parker Grissom. It was all in my affidavit, of course, right down to the medallion, but he kept talking about all of these amazing coincidences—which they were—and I got the distinct impression he had his doubts about the claims. Joey just sat there smugly and smiled through the whole thing. Then it was his turn, and the judge laid out some things he had to do. But that part was all pretty short and sweet.

"I did have one interesting idea while I was testifying. I heard some-where that some law firms are now using a photocopying system that stores electronic images of whatever gets copied. I have no idea whether

Stetson uses something like that, or if they do, whether they had that last year. But I tossed it out there and the judge picked up on it. Joey has to check that out and report back when the hearing resumes next week."

"So you have to go back out there again next week?" she asked.

"Afraid so," Andy replied.

"Well," Keiley said, "I don't want to add to your burden, Andy, but I got this earlier today."

With that, she handed Andy the copy of a notice ordering her to appear at the offices of Stetson, Varney the day after next to be deposed.

"Shit," he said. "I was hoping you'd be spared all this aggravation. But I suppose this was inevitable. Just go in there and tell them the truth."

***

"Take a seat, Mr. Coy," said the Commissioner, indicating the empty chair beside the general counsel. He did not rise to shake his visitor's hand.

The three men were seated at the Commissioner's large desk, the Commissioner on one side in his elegant high-backed desk chair and the other two across from him in decidedly less posh seats. He had learned early in his political career that a conference table is a great equalizer, but a desk is a power plant for the one seated behind it. He was sending a message and wanted it to be clearly understood.

"Mr. Coy, I am not happy with the way this case seems to be proceeding, and the purpose of today's meeting is to determine whether I am about to fire your friend here, my general counsel, for having recommended you and your firm. He assured me that Stetson, Varney has—that *you* have—provided able assistance to us as outside counsel over many years and in the face of several critical challenges. But I am sitting here with a rebellion of sorts on my hands. I have filings, which I'm sure you have seen, from the clubs in Kansas City and Oakland claiming that, if the contract ends up being valid and enforceable, they are as much victims as Mr. Dennum. They want out of any responsibility for damages. Then I have a whole stack of filings from the other clubs in both leagues that were granted franchises after 1914 on essentially similar grounds. And I read in the papers recently that even the city and county governments out there are thinking of suing us because their facilities were built with public money. You have about ten minutes to convince me that whatever you are doing here is going to put an end to this whole thing, and quickly. Tick tock."

"Commissioner, I understand your concern. I do. But you have to know that these things take time, and they almost always follow a crooked path. I've looked at all of this paper you're talking about—the legal filings anyway—and I can tell you that all of that is just ass-covering by the lawyers for these teams. Over the years, I have had the opportunity to review a number of your franchise agreements, and in my view this is all bluster. But more importantly, it's all irrelevant. Because we are winning this case.

"I was out in Chicago yesterday for an evidentiary hearing, and it couldn't have gone better. Mr. Dennum has submitted an affidavit summarizing his case, and the whole damn thing is based on a bunch of suppositions and coincidences. A person would have a better chance of winning the lottery than all of these events would have of lining up the way he claims. And the judge saw right through it.

"I had asked for the hearing, and I went out to Chicago prepared to walk Dennum through all of these remarkable events, but I never got the chance. The judge himself stepped in, and I have to say, he did a better job poking holes at the story than I could have. I made a note. His exact words were, 'This is quite a long chain of coincidences that you are asking the court to accept, don't you think?' He also seemed reluctant to admit the so-called contract into evidence since there is no signed original. That would be required to meet the best evidence standard in a case this big. We are going back out there next week to wrap up the hearing, and it wouldn't surprise me if we walked out with a dismissal."

There was, of course, more to the hearing than Joey had relayed. But that was all outside baseball, all related to internal matters at Stetson, Varney itself, and he saw no reason to trouble his client with the details. Besides, he knew just how that would turn out, and it would not be a problem.

"One more thing, Commissioner. You know we had an investigator looking at this Dennum guy. Well, on a hunch, we added a second one to check out this genealogist who seems to have played some kind of role. Her name is Keiley Barefoot. On and off, we have had tails on both of them, and you know what? Those tails have spent a few nights sharing coffee in their cars because they both somehow ended up in the same place. We gave notice to Ms. Barefoot yesterday, and we have scheduled her deposition for tomorrow. I think the judge will be interested in that deposition, which I expect to take with me out to Chicago when the evidentiary hearing resumes next week."

Now, this was something the Commissioner could appreciate, and he seemed to relax a bit, almost smile.

"*That*," he said, "is just the sort of thing I wanted to hear. Perhaps you're right, and I'm being too hasty. Perhaps. So I'm going to give this a little more time. But, Mr. Coy, you are on the clock in more ways than one. And so is your friend here. Good day to you, gentlemen."

The Commissioner swept his hand outward in a clear gesture of dismissal and quickly found himself alone at the desk. *Shit*, he thought, not for the first time. *CI would know how to handle this.*

———— ————

"Ms. Barefoot, please come into the conference room," Joey Coy said in an ingratiatingly pleasant voice. "I apologize for keeping you waiting in the lobby for so long. It took us a while to get ourselves organized this morning."

Keiley took a seat at the center of the conference table, directly across from Joey. There was a video camera directly over his shoulder, pointed right at her. The red light was on. At the end of the table was a stenographer, and seated beside Joey was a young woman.

"For the record, I am Joseph Coy of the law firm Stetson, Varney, and Handelmann, and we are convened in the offices of that firm. I am accompanied by a colleague, Jill Parsons, who is assisting in this deposition. The session is being memorialized by James Hargus, a certified court recorder. The session is also being recorded on video. A transcript and a copy of the video will be provided to the deponent—that's you, Ms. Barefoot—as well as to the complainant's counsel and, of course, to the court.

"Ms. Barefoot, would you please state your name and also please acknowledge aloud that you are aware of the video recording of this deposition."

"My name is Keiley Barefoot. I live in Morristown, New Jersey. And yes, I know there is a video camera." Keiley hoped the nerves she felt did not come through in her voice, but she feared that she sounded more than a little shaky.

"Thank you. And would you identify for the record these two gentlemen who have accompanied you."

"Okay. On my left is Robert Timmons. He's my lawyer. And I think you know the gentleman on my right."

"Please identify him anyway."

Andy spoke for himself. "Andrew Dennum, and I'm here in my capacity as attorney for the complainant."

"Very well. Shall we begin? Ms. Barefoot, you hold a degree in genealogy, am I correct?"

"No," she responded. "I have an associate's degree in graphic arts and a bachelor's in geography."

"Wait, I'm confused," said Joey, though he clearly was nothing of the sort. "I thought that you were a professional genealogist. Are you saying that's not the case?"

"I'm a professional cartographer, Mr. Coy. I make maps for a living."

"Well then, have you had some other training in genealogy? Done some sort of apprenticeship with a professional genealogist, for example, or perhaps an internship? Even some kind of online genealogy course?"

"No, sir. None of those."

"Well, just what is your professional background, Ms. Barefoot? Where have you worked, for example?"

"I worked for several years for Morrison Gray Cartographers here in the city—sorry, in New York City—and about two years ago, I decided to go out on my own, so I established my own company, Barefoot Maps."

"I see. And where are your offices? How many people do you employ?"

"I work from home, and I have no other employees. Just me."

"Any other employment? I mean, it must be hard to earn a living by yourself just drawing maps."

"My mapping business is actually rather successful. But yes, I do also have another part-time job."

"And where is that?"

"I work for the D'Antonio Law Firm."

"That would be more properly known as D'Antonio and Dennum, LLC, would it not?"

"Yes, that's correct."

"So, just to be clear for the record, Ms. Barefoot, in addition to owning your own small mapping company, you work for the complainant in this case, Mr. Andrew Dennum. Is that correct?"

"Yes."

"So how did you become a genealogist?"

"I did some reading, and I simply became interested in it. So I did some more reading, and I started to see connections between what I was learning about family trees and my work in mapping. So I developed ways of using mapping and illustrating to represent family relationships through time."

"So is it fair to say that you are a professional mapmaker but an amateur genealogist?"

"Yes," she replied. "That's probably an accurate description."

"Okay, now let's take a walk, shall we, through the genealogical research you did that, as we know, led to Mr. Dennum, your employer, being identified as the sole and legitimate heir to this extraordinary claim that he has valued at the astronomical sum of more than $400 million."

"Objection," said Andy.

"Let me restate the question," said Joey. "Tell us about the research you did that found its way into this case."

The deposition continued along that line for another forty-five minutes or so, with Joey asking questions that were framed to minimize the apparent credibility of Keiley's work and asking them in a manner designed to intimidate her, and with Keiley trying hard to maintain her composure and to answer carefully but honestly. All of this was entirely routine for Coy, who had conducted dozens of depositions, perhaps hundreds, and had deposed hard-bitten corporate types and others, all but the toughest of whom eventually reached the point of mental exhaustion he sought. That, he knew, when they were most likely to be caught off guard, was the time for the unexpected question. He had figured that Keiley, inexperienced in these matters, would last not more than an hour or so before she reached this point of maximum vulnerability. And now, here they were, right on schedule.

"Ms. Barefoot, I want to say for the record that I have found you a most cooperative witness. And I thank you for that. I have just one more question, and we'll be finished. Ms. Barefoot, are you sleeping with Mr. Dennum, here? Are you involved in a sexual relationship with the complainant?"

Andy and Joey were eyeing one another angrily as they sat on opposite sides of the table, awaiting the arrival of the judge. Neither said a word.

"Gentlemen," said Judge Keyser as he closed the door to his chambers behind him and strode across the room. "Good morning. I have another matter pending today, so let's see if we can keep this brief.

"I have received a report from Professor Hanson, the special master. In her filing, she notes that she had full access to the archive, which, as expected, was organized by the dates on which the various matters were closed out. She examined all the file boxes dated from January 1914 through December 1920. She was unable to locate any box marked as relating to Mr. Parker T. Grissom. Of course, that absence was predicted in the complainant's various filings, including his affidavit, so it comes as no surprise. But Professor Hanson continues. With the assistance of the firm's archivist, she was able to decode the numbering system for the files, and applying that knowledge, she determined that there were seventeen missing boxes for the period 1914–1920, including five from the year 1918. She was also able to identify two boxes that had been filed or replaced in the archive outside of their proper locations, though apparently, none was more than three boxes or one shelf out of place.

"Professor Hanson then queried the archivist regarding the missing boxes. He reported that the firm routinely reviewed these files from time to time once they had been in the archive for at least seventy-five years, and when a matter was found that involved no living persons, no living counsel, no corporate or other entities that were still in operation, and no continuing legal issues, the files were routinely destroyed. The only two exceptions, he noted, were a group of approximately forty boxes from the mid-1950s that had been damaged years later when a fire sprinkler malfunctioned, and a smaller set from the 1960s, which were simply unaccounted for. By the time the first problem was recognized, those files had become so water-logged that they were unrecoverable, and they were viewed as a potential source of mold or mildew. So they were discarded. In the second instance, there was some sort of internal investigation, but the best guess was that the files had been accidentally placed in the burn pile and were destroyed.

"From this report, the court concludes that there were gaps in the record, including gaps in 1918 which might be pertinent. But the court also notes that, after spending a year in the archives, the complainant would have known that such gaps were not unusual. Sorry, Mr. Dennum, but I do not see anything in this report that directly supports your claim."

"But, Your Honor—"

The judge held up his hand. "Not now, Mr. Dennum. Not now."

He turned to Joey Coy. "Mr. Coy, what did you discover regarding the practice at your firm with respect to the electronic recording of photocopied documents?"

"As you'll see from this signed affidavit, Your Honor," Joey began, passing over a document to the judge and a copy to Andy, "Mr. Chester Kinnalley, our managing partner, and I affirm that Stetson, Varney does not employ any system of the type alleged by Mr. Dennum."

"I never *alleged* anything," Andy interjected, falling into the minor trap Joey had set. "I only—"

Again the judge held up his hand. "Please continue, Mr. Coy."

"Thank you, Your Honor. As I said, the firm does not use any system of this type and never has. So we have no related records to produce.

"What we do have, however, are two additional items. The first is an investigative report from the Burnside and Grove Detective Agency. We hired them on behalf of our client to undertake a basic investigation into the complainant—his personal affairs, business affairs, and the like—which, as the court will recognize, is fairly routine in high-leverage cases of this type. In the course of that investigation, the detectives took it upon themselves to conduct surveillance on the complainant and, after observing his behavior, added surveillance of another person at the center of this case, the cartographer cum genealogist, Ms. Barefoot. This produced information that we were able to corroborate in the course of deposing Ms. Barefoot during the past week.

"Let me put this delicately, Your Honor. Ah, Mr. Dennum here and Ms. Barefoot are, ah, boyfriend and girlfriend."

The judge sat back and paused for a beat. Then he leaned on the table and looked directly at Andy.

"Is that true, Mr. Dennum? Are you and Ms. Barefoot what one might call 'an item?'"

"Yes, Your Honor, but—"

"And did you ever consider that that fact might be of interest to the court, especially given the role . . . the central role that this woman has played, not only in giving evidence in your lawsuit but in your own *discovery* that you were yourself the long lost Grissom heir?"

Andy could almost see the sarcasm dripping from the judge's voice. He glanced at Joey, who was showing his best poker face. Andy knew that Joey often lost at poker, and in that instant, he understood why.

"Your Honor, I—" Again the hand.

"Mr. Dennum. Although the court finds your lawsuit highly imaginative, particularly given the almost total paucity of direct evidence that the contract at the heart of the matter ever existed. And although the court finds remarkable your ability to weave a chain of coincidences, ambiguities, and gaps in the record of which you would have had special knowledge into this tale of ancient and enduring malfeasance by a deeppocketed and, in some corners, perhaps even disliked respondent. For all of that, what we are left with is little more than innuendo, supposition, and in the worst case, pure invention. But for an occasional sustainable fact—each one subject to multiple interpretations—your case is more air than substance.

"Now, I think you are a serious young man but also an inexperienced advocate. You may emerge from this as a textbook example of the old fool-for-a-client adage. But I am close to concluding that you have wasted this court's time, not to mention that of Mr. Coy, and you have demeaned—I will not use a legal word here—*demeaned* the reputation of the respondent. That in itself may give rise to a later legal vulnerability.

"Only because I believe you have developed a sincere belief in this cause of action—perhaps one that has been influenced by your relationship with Ms. Barefoot, whose motives the court is not in a position to judge—I will defer the dismissal of this case with prejudice for a period of one week. If you have something, son, now is the time to bring it forward.

"This hearing is concluded. Court will convene one week from today, at which time I will either receive significant additional evidence from the complainant or I will issue my ruling. That's it, gentlemen." He stood and left the room.

"Welcome to the major leagues, sport," Joey sneered, not even recognizing his own play on words as he packed up his briefcase, grabbed his coat, and left the courtroom.

Andy sat there in stunned silence until the courtroom doors opened a few minutes later and people began to stream in for the next case on the judge's docket.

<hr>

"It was awful," Andy said, describing the legal colonoscopy he had undergone in Chicago. "It was just awful. And to make it worse, that asshole Joey dragged your name into it. He made it sound like because we are together, you might have made up the whole thing and then made me believe it so . . . I don't know . . . so you could get rich off me? I mean, he didn't say that, but he made it sound that way. And the judge, I think maybe he bought it."

"Andy," said Keiley, "I'm so sorry!"

"Don't be silly," he replied. "You didn't do anything wrong. Neither of us did. But by the end, the judge was so pissed at me he wouldn't let me get a word in. And then he told me if I couldn't prove my case by next week, he was going to toss it. I need to get some sleep and hopefully clear my head. I have to be in depositions tomorrow over at Morrow and

Long in the Pearson divorce case. Okay if I just head home? I'll see you in the afternoon."

Andy returned to his house, where he did eventually drop off to a troubled sleep. As for clearing his head, though, he thought that might require a plumber. Total clog.

Fortunately, the Pearson divorce was a relatively straightforward one. The husband had slept with his secretary, and his wife had found out. At about the same time, she had slept with her therapist, and her husband had found out. There were no children nor any real property. *A marriage made in heaven*, he thought as his client's lurid testimony continued for the appointed two hours. Mercifully, the deposition was concluded before noon, and he headed back to his office, intent on taking a nice nap on the sofa beside Betty's desk.

"Surprise!" Betty and Keiley had decorated the office with balloons and streamers, and on the reception area coffee table was an elaborately decorated cake topped by flaming candles. Betty had completed the preparations while Keiley kept watch for Andy's car. As he drove into view, Betty lit the candles.

"Happy birthday, Andy!" the pair said in unison.

"You look like you could use one," Betty continued.

"Jeez," Andy stammered. "I forgot all about that." It was, Andy realized, a made-up date, one his mother and father had guessed at way, way back, and one they all had treated as true and accurate ever since. Then, after a pause, he added, "Thank you, guys. Thank you. This is just what I needed today."

"Great," said Keiley. "Thanks for the philosophy. Now blow out the damn candles before they melt the frosting."

Andy followed orders, though it took two tries. *Getting too old for this*, he thought to himself. Betty did the honors while Keiley went into her office and returned with a container of Cold Stone Sweet Cream ice cream, the perfect complement, she had determined, for devil's food cake. The trio sat down to a relaxing treat. *Just what the doctor ordered,* he thought.

"I almost forgot," said Keiley, standing up and moving toward her office. "I got you something."

She was back in an instant bearing an oblong box wrapped in foil and topped by a big red bow. "Here. I hope you like it."

Andy tore away the wrapping and opened the thin box it had covered.

"A picture frame!" he said, smiling.

"Not just any old picture frame," Keiley replied. "It's one of those electronic frames. You know, you load a bunch of picture files into the thing, and it stores them, and when you turn it on, it displays them, kind of rotates through them. I thought it would be nice to keep on your desk. You know. Just in case you had some pictures you wanted to look at."

"I love it. But I'll need to take some pictures to put in it. I wonder who I should photograph. . . ."

"You bastard!" she laughed. "It better be me. You already have some shots on your phone you could use. And you can take one of this cake to get started."

Betty and Keiley posed themselves holding up the half-eaten cake. Andy took the picture and only afterward told Keiley that she had a big dab of ice cream on her nose. Everybody had a good laugh, and after the half hour or so of celebration, the mood in the office was lightened considerably. Andy retreated to his office to read the instructions that accompanied his new picture frame and see if he could get some of his photos to load for display.

Just as he sat down, his cell rang. Looking at the caller ID on the screen, he smiled.

"Dad, how are you?"

"I always freak out when you do that," came the reply. "But to answer your question, your mother and I are doing fine. We just called to wish you a happy birthday."

"Thanks. Love you guys."

"I also wanted to let you know that your mother's shopping gene has activated, and we're actually on the road on our way up there right now. Somewhere in Georgia, I think. Or maybe it's still Florida. She's driving, and you know how she gets. Won't even let me look at a map when she's got the wheel. Doesn't care about faster or better ways to get there, I suppose. Ouch!"

"Happy birthday, Andy," he heard her shout in the background.

"Anyway, we haven't heard from you in what, a couple of months? We knew you lost your job, and we were starting to worry about you."

"I'm really sorry about that. Things have been incredibly hectic here, but everything is fine. I have a lot to tell you and a couple of things to ask about."

"Well, once we get out of the Southeast Conference states, the traffic slows down, but we expect to get there day after tomorrow. Probably late afternoon. We'll stay a week or two, depending on how long it takes you-know-who to spend us into the poor house. Ow! Hope that's okay."

"It's perfect," said Andy, laughing, but also wondering privately how he could entertain his parents and figure out how to survive in court all at the same time. "I'll try to clean up a bit, and I'll see you then. Drive safe."

"Commissioner," Joey said, using the speakerphone in his office. "I wanted to bring you up to date on some developments in the case."

"I'm listening," came the reply.

"We completed the evidentiary hearing earlier today. I wish you could have been there. Basically, the judge tore Dennum a new one—told him that his case looked like a house of cards, a pure fantasy. The kicker was when I presented the evidence about Dennum and his girlfriend. There's one thing you don't want to do if you're a lawyer, and that's to give the impression you've been holding out on the judge, and basically, Dennum came away looking like that's just what he had done. The judge actually went a step further and suggested that the girlfriend might even have conned the guy into believing his own story so she could share the wealth if he won. I could almost hear the air coming out of the poor sap."

"Mr. Coy, that is excellent news. I'm sorry I doubted you before."

"Wait, Commissioner. You haven't heard the best part yet. At the end of the hearing, the judge told Dennum that he had one week to come up with something convincing enough to keep the case going or he was likely to dismiss with prejudice. Just throw the whole thing out. And not only that. He told Dennum that, if that happened, he would be lucky if you didn't come around behind and sue him for libel for having brought such a frivolous action."

"No kidding? Maybe we should think about that, eh? Does he have any assets that are worth the trouble?"

"No sir, not as far as we can tell. But sometimes it's just good to make an example of someone, don't you think?"

"I do indeed, sir. I do indeed. All right, now you keep me in the loop. I want to hear from you directly from now on. Do you understand?"

"Yes, Commissioner, I do."

"Good. Then I will expect to hear from you around this time next week. And after that, we can give some thought to how we'd like to deal with our young antagonist here. Good day, Mr. Coy." And the line went dead.

It was a spur-of-the-moment decision.

"Wake up, sleepy head," Andy said, gently pushing on Keiley's arm.

A groggy voice responded, "What time is it?"

"Six o'clock. Time to wake up."

"Are you crazy? Leave me alone."

"No, really. Wake up. Let's have some coffee and pack a lunch. We're taking a little road trip."

"Huh?"

"Listen. I've told you that I never thought anything about my birth parents—that phrase even sounds strange. But with everything that's happening, I have to admit I have been a little curious about some things. And now, with Mom and Dad coming tomorrow and everything else, I want to go out and see where it happened."

"Where what happened?"

"The accident."

"You want to drive to Pennsylvania? Just like that?"

"Yep. Assuming the Escape can make it there and back in one piece. You coming? It's a long drive each way, and we need to get started."

Andy was right. It was a long drive. Fortunately, it was all on interstates—287 to 78 to 81 to the Turnpike. The only real problem spot was Harrisburg. There was just no easy way to get into, around, or through Harrisburg. But after about three hours of driving, they found themselves on the Pennsylvania Turnpike headed west. One of the newspaper articles Keiley had located had actually identified a particular mile marker near where the accident that set his life on a new course had occurred so many years ago. They passed the marker, then used the next exit to turn around and head east. As they approached the spot from the other direction, Andy slowed the car and pulled to the shoulder.

"Look at that," he said, pointing to the side of the road. There in the scrub, about ten feet off the roadway, were two small crosses, and it appeared that someone, perhaps from one of the local churches, had been maintaining them over the years. The white paint looked fresh.

"This has to be it," he said quietly. Then he looked across the road to the median, freshly mowed now but apparently not so carefully manicured back then. "That has to be where they found me."

Keiley reached over and took his hand but said nothing.

Andy took out his phone and snapped a picture looking across the busy roadway to the median, then another of the two crosses. Then he turned to Keiley.

"Go stand over by the crosses, would you? I want to take your picture there."

She'd never seen Andy so sentimental before, and she did as he asked. Then she came back toward the car, and they stood there in silence for a minute or two.

"Okay," he said at last. "Let's go home."

⸺◆⸺

Andy and Keiley were sitting on the sofa watching some forgettable old movie on TV when they heard a key turn in the lock. It opened slowly, and two familiar faces appeared—familiar to Andy, at least.

"Mom! Dad! How was the trip?"

"It was long, like always," said his father.

"You have no idea how long," said his mother with a sideways glance at his father. This, remembered Andy, was how they were. "We kept running into—" His mother stopped in mid-sentence, noticing Keiley hanging back a bit. "And who is this beautiful young lady, Andrew?"

"Mom, Dad, this is Keiley. Keiley, this is my dad, Newt, and my mom, Nora." Hands were shaken all around, and a small glance passed between the new arrivals.

"Andy, you've been holding out on us," said his father.

"Dad, you have no idea. Why don't you two get settled in, and then I have a lot to tell you and a couple of questions to ask too."

It was two hours or so before Andy had finished catching his parents up on everything that had happened—getting fired from Stetson, Varney; finding a place with Lou D'Antonio, who seemed to know them; Lou's death; meeting Keiley; all the things she had uncovered in her research on an old case; and how that case ended up pointing to him. By the time he got to the lawsuit, they had finished the dinner that Keiley had excused herself some time into the narrative to prepare and were sitting down with the last of the wine.

"You know," Andy said a little nervously as his tale was winding down, "there is something we never ever talked about. I never thought or cared about it. But with everything that's happened, I guess it's something I'd like to know. It's about my adoption."

"Thank goodness," said his mother, which immediately lifted any concern he might have harbored that he would offend these people who had given him everything and whom he loved so much. "We've been sitting on that for all these years. We didn't want to burden you with it, and like you say, you never asked."

"What is it you'd like to know, son?" said his father.

"I guess I want to know if we've put the pieces together correctly. Am I really that baby that survived that car accident? And if I am, how did I end up here? I mean, in New Jersey? With you?"

"Well, to answer the first," said his father, "yes. The rest of it is a little more complicated."

"Your father," interrupted his mother, "and Lou D'Antonio were good friends back in the day. They and a couple of other men used to get together every weekend and play pinochle."

"Pinochle?" asked Andy.

"Pinochle," she continued. "What can I tell you? It was a thing. Anyway, Lou was a good friend, and he knew that we couldn't have a family. I had a miscarriage a couple of years before that, and, well, it just wasn't in the cards for us. So we were starting to think about adopting, and, of course, we talked to Lou about it. To get his advice on how things worked, get started on the paperwork. There was a lot of paperwork.

"Now, that accident with your parents, that was in all the papers. I guess it was a pretty dramatic accident they had, but that wasn't the story. The story was about what they called the 'miracle baby.' It was about this baby that had been thrown clear and was later found in the grass. That was you.

"Well, we saw the story, of course, but never really thought much about it. I mean, it was all so far away. But Lou, he had some old law school buddy or something out there in Pennsylvania, and I guess he got on the phone or did some other lawyer thing, because a week or so later, he came by the house unexpectedly, told us he knew of a baby boy who'd recently lost his parents in an accident, and asked if we would like to think about adopting him. A private adoption, he called it.

"Now, your dad and I, we thought about that for about twelve seconds before we said yes. Then Lou went off and did whatever magic he did, and a few days later, we drove out to Pennsylvania and met our new son for the first time. He must have really pulled some strings, because from what I've read, it just doesn't happen that way except in the movies. And the papers were right. You were our little miracle baby."

Then it was his father's turn. "Of course, look how that turned out," he joked. Then he turned to Keiley. "My dear, Nora and I sincerely apologize." Everyone had a good laugh. But then the others noted that Andy seemed to be tearing up a bit.

"What's the matter, son?" asked his father.

"Nothing. Really, nothing. It's just, the four of us here, this is the first time I ever felt truly surrounded by family."

At that point, it was Keiley's turn to show a little glisten in her eyes.

But the moment was fleeting, and Andy, aware of what the coming week held for him, which he had not fully shared with his parents, took a lawyerly turn.

"We found some old adoption papers in Lou's files after he passed away. Nothing that gave us any idea about everything you've told us, but enough to hint that he was a great deal more involved in all of that than he had let on in the one conversation he and I had. But there might be some questions about the adoption in this hearing I have to attend out in Chicago this week. Are there any other papers that you have? Any documentation of who my birth parents were?"

"Well," said his mother, "of course, they would never tell us that straight out back then. I think it was part of the arrangement. We have the adoption papers, but they're probably in our safety-deposit box down in Florida. We could look for them when we get home if that will help."

"Anything else? Any other kind of records that might be in the house here?"

"Well," said his father, "there was the trust fund."

"Trust fund?" asked Andy.

"Yeah, you know. That little trust fund we had for you—well, it wasn't really a trust fund, but that savings account we had for you. The one we signed over when you turned twenty-one."

"The one I used to help pay some of the law school tuition. That was, what, an inheritance?"

"We think so. But we were never sure. When you were, I don't know, one or two, Lou told us he had some money for you. Made us set up one of those, what do you call them . . . custodial accounts. Your money, our signatures sort of thing, until you were an adult. It wasn't a lot. Maybe a couple thousand dollars or so. And we just let it sit there until you were old enough, and then we gave it to you like we were supposed to."

"Was the check from somebody in Pennsylvania?"

"Whoa, Andy. This was a long time ago. But as I recall it," his father continued, "it was from Lou. Something about running the money through his client account at the law firm as some sort of legal thing. And again, we weren't supposed to know anything about who your parents had been, so that seemed to fit. Of course, Lou couldn't keep a secret on a bet—you probably didn't know him long enough to figure that out—so we knew more than we were supposed to. Just a little bit. Lou must have been surprised as hell when you walked into his office looking for a job."

"What goes around comes around, I guess," said Andy. "We didn't see any paperwork about an inheritance. But then, we weren't looking for it. Mom, Dad, I hate to do this since you just got here and all, but I need to ask you for a favor."

On the night before Andy was to fly back to Chicago for what he feared might be the final hearing in his lawsuit, the four of them sat around the dinner table, this time enjoying one of his mother's specialties. Keiley, who enjoyed cooking, had made a point of watching as Nora pinched this seasoning and seemingly randomly sprinkled that one—all very old school—and then found herself awestruck at the taste of the rib roast that resulted. She then found herself the subject of the dinnertime conversation.

Newt and Nora pronounced themselves fascinated by her interest in cartography, and Andy pulled out his phone to show them a couple of photos he had taken of the work in her studio.

"Wait!" she said. "That tiny screen won't do them justice. Go load them onto that picture frame I gave you and then we can see them a lot bigger."

"Here, here!" said Newt. "And you must have some pictures of this young lady on that phone as well. Load them all up and let's have a look."

Andy disappeared upstairs and was gone long enough that he was missed.

"Andy," Nora called out. "Everything all right up there?"

"Coming in a sec, Ma," came the reply, though to Nora's ear, her son's voice sounded a bit odd.

A moment later, Andy appeared at the top of the stairs. He made his way down, carrying both his cell phone and the new electronic picture frame.

"You're not going to believe this. I know I don't."

He sat back down at the dining table and turned on the display. The first photo to appear was a picture of Keiley, the one from the previous week, with the ice cream on her nose.

"You put *that* picture on there? I'm gonna get you!" said Keiley, laughing.

"You're right," said Newt. "I don't believe that. What I mean is, I don't believe you had the sheer audacity to put that in the frame and show it as the first picture. Good for you!"

"I warned you, Keiley," pitched in Nora. "He takes after his father." They all had another good laugh.

"Very funny. Very funny. But that's not the picture I'm talking about. Give me a second to page through here. . . . It's this one."

Bottom of the Ninth, Two Outs, Bases Empty

Andy knew this was it. The last chance to keep his case going. The last chance to keep his career going. He was surprised by how steady he felt as he walked into the courtroom, surprised that his nerves were under control. He hadn't known this kind of calm since . . . since high school. In high school, everybody was always nervous about taking tests, getting grades. But not Andy. He just took it all in stride, the good, the bad, the indifferent. Girls? They made him nervous. School? Not so much. Maybe he was finally learning to feel at home in a courtroom. Or maybe, just maybe, what he was feeling was a kind of confidence that surprised him and, had he known of it, would surely have surprised Joey Coy even more.

Speaking of Joey, he made his entrance just a moment before the appointed hour. And they both knew that it was a sign of confidence bordering on hubris. This courtroom was like all the others he had been in over the years. It was Joeyland.

This time, the judge kept them waiting. Five minutes. Ten minutes. And when he appeared, he had a court reporter in tow.

"Gentlemen," he said as he settled in, "today we are on the record. Mr. Dennum. I believe you have the floor. What do you have to say for yourself?"

"Thank you, Your Honor. Let me begin by saying that I appreciate the court's indulgence. I know that the case I have presented has required a few . . . leaps of faith, that there were so many coincidences as to require a suspension of disbelief on the part of a neutral observer such as Your Honor. For that, I apologize. What I hope to do today is present evidence to convince the court that, strange as my claim may be, it is true and valid.

"At the core of this matter are two critical claims. One is that I am, in fact, the successor to any and all claims that might accrue from the contract signed between professional baseball and Mr. Grissom back in 1914. The other pertains to the validity of that contract itself. With the court's permission, I would like to address each of those in turn.

"With respect to the matter of successorship, I would like to introduce four new pieces of evidence. The first, which I acknowledge was an oversight on my part, comprises documents from the files of my deceased partner, Mr. D'Antonio, that finalized my own adoption. I call the court's attention to the date and the signatures of Mr. D'Antonio and a second attorney, the latter identified as representing the social services office of Cumberland County, Pennsylvania. As indicated in newspaper accounts submitted previously, the automobile accident that seemingly ended the Grissom line occurred in that county mere weeks before these papers were executed. I had referenced these papers earlier, Your Honor, but had failed to provide them for the court."

"Your Honor!" objected Joey. "Surely, this is just another fabrication. Given enough time, who knows what evidence the complainant—or his lawyer—could manufacture."

"It does appear to be just one more timely coincidence, Mr. Dennum," said the judge.

"Well, Your Honor, if I may continue?" The judge nodded his affirmation.

"The second and third pieces of evidence I would like to introduce are two affidavits, one from my mother, Nora Benedict Dennum, and one from my father, Newton Breeze Dennum. Both were sworn before a notary, and I can make either or both of my parents available for depositions if necessary.

"As I told the court some time ago, I had never had any curiosity about my birth parents and had never asked about them or the circumstances of my adoption. Over the past week, Your Honor, as I prepared for this hearing, I had occasion to do that. And when I heard what they had to say, I asked them each to memorialize what they had told me in these statements. As Your Honor will see, they detail here, each in their own words, the circumstances of my adoption. Both state clearly that Mr. D'Antonio had arranged this privately in coordination with a colleague in Pennsylvania and that he had told them that I was, in fact, the child referred to in the news accounts from the then-recent fatal auto accident outside Carlisle. This was a critical missing link in the complainant's argument, as presented earlier, and has now been bridged.

"The statements also reference the payment of what was represented to be the proceeds of a small estate belonging to my birth parents, a sum of a few thousand dollars, which was presented to them by Mr. D'Antonio a year or two after the adoption. Upon his instruction, they deposited those funds in a custodial account, ownership of which was transferred to me upon my attaining the requisite legal age. Your Honor, we have searched Mr. D'Antonio's surviving records and found no reference to this transfer. However, I was able to locate a small number of statements from the custodial account itself. These I present to the court. I could not trace the origin of these funds or search the probate records of Cumberland County for the period in question during the limited time available this week. However, I would hope the court will agree that the evidence already provided on the issue of successorship is of sufficient import to justify continuation of these proceedings, at least long enough to permit such a search, and thereupon, if successful, to proceed to trial."

"Your Honor," Joey began, "I don't see how—" This time it was Joey who was halted mid-sentence by the judge's open palm.

"Patience, Mr. Coy. Patience. I'd like to see where this is going." Then, to Andy, "Please continue, Mr. Dennum."

"Thank you. Now as to the second issue, that of the contract. If the court will indulge me for a moment, last week was my birthday, or really just a date my family and I had settled on more or less at random when I was young since we did not know the real date, and as a gift, I received one of those electronic picture frames. This one, in fact." And with that, Andy pulled the frame from his briefcase. "In addition, my parents were in town for a visit, which was when I was able to have them sit for those sworn affidavits."

"Your Honor, please!"

"Point taken, Mr. Coy. Get to it, Mr. Dennum."

"Yes, Your Honor. Well, my . . . my visitors were interested in seeing some pictures I had taken on my phone of some examples of Ms. Barefoot's cartographic art. But the images were too small to appreciate fully, so I decided to transfer them to this frame where they would be much larger and easier to see. And in the course of doing that, I happened to browse back into some older photos I had taken with the phone, including one I had taken a year or so earlier and then forgotten altogether. It was one of the kind that people refer to as selfies. This one was of me, standing in front of a bunch of boxes in the Stetson, Varney archive."

Joey Coy sat up in his chair, then tried to mask the move by stretching a bit and resuming his earlier position. Andy could not tell if Judge Keyser had noticed the movement.

"It was intended as a kind of humorous photo, you know, showing off the work of a so-called big-time lawyer. And I might have glanced at it once or twice since I took it, but it was so small that any detail would have been lost on the phone. So I never gave it another thought.

"Now, Your Honor, I have to caution you that this is another one of those coincidences that have been such a big part of my . . . of the complainant's case. But if you look closely at this photograph, you will see, just over my right shoulder, a box clearly labeled February 1918. The client name associated with the file is identified as 'Grissom, Parker T.' Your Honor, this is a photograph of the actual file box which I reviewed—I have no idea whether that was just before or just after I took this photo— and which, I have claimed, Mr. Coy instructed me to destroy."

"Mr. Coy?" queried the judge. "Anything to say to that?"

"Let me see that," said Joey, reaching for the frame. He studied it for a moment.

"Your Honor, this is just another of Mr. Dennum's little games he is playing with the court. I mean, what do we have here? We have a set of steel shelves and a couple of rows of file boxes. And the whole thing just magically appears today, at the complainant's last gasp. I could stage this photo myself and set the time stamp to anything I wanted without much trouble. And as for the purported labels—and I acknowledge they do resemble those employed by my firm—as for those, we must remember that Mr. Dennum worked daily in that archive for a full year. He probably had visions of those labels in his eyes as he fell asleep at night. It would be no trouble at all for him to purloin a few or even counterfeit them. I mean, who knows at what point he became little more than a disaffected employee? He might even have staged the whole thing way back then and hatched this plan of his. What would he have needed to do, after all, but pick up one of our labels from the archivist's desk when he wasn't looking, slap it on an empty box, stick the box in a random spot on a shelf, and snap his little photo. I don't know which was the case, Your Honor, and it really doesn't matter. This box never existed, or if it did, Mr. Dennum never brought it to my attention. And I never ordered that he destroy it."

"Mr. Dennum, the respondent's counsel has a point. I'd like to believe you, son, I really would. But here we are again. You started out offering your girlfriend as a witness, and now you are offering your own parents. And your own bank account that could have come from anywhere, their testimony notwithstanding. We always look out for the ones we love. And now this rather generic photo. The court acknowledges that the details are potentially intriguing, but between the report of the special master as to what boxes she found in the file and the rather credible assertions of Mr. Coy here, in the context of all the many coincidences that underlie the complainant's case, I simply do not see how we have enough to keep going. Accordingly . . ."

That is when Joey Coy knew for certain that he had the case won.

"Accordingly . . ."

"Your Honor, please. Just one more minute. If you look closely at the photo here once again, you will see the box immediately to the left of the Grissom box on the shelf. The label reads *Madigan v. O'Hare*.' Chronologically, that would have been the last matter filed in the archive before the Grissom matter was put into deep storage.

"When exploring my claim earlier, the court asked me for clarification. Specifically, Your Honor, you asked me whether I had followed Mr. Coy's instructions regarding the disposition of the file, which I have said he reviewed at my suggestion and he has said he did not. My response was that I had followed his instructions to the letter. I stand by that. But, Your Honor, just what were those instructions?"

Joey was back on his guard.

"Mr. Coy instructed me to do two things. The first was to replace the Grissom *file* in the proper place in the archive. The second was to take the Grissom *box* and burn it, or rather, place it in the area where files are collected for burning. And that, as I stated, is precisely what I did.

"But when I placed the Grissom file in its proper chronological order, Your Honor, I confess, I did not place it back into its own box. I don't know why. I mean, I had no reason to do anything different at the time. But I guess I just thought that someday, years from now, the next grunt lawyer who got to spend a year in that part of the archives might come across it and agree with me that it was not entirely a dead issue, that there might still be someone with an interest that was captured in that file.

"So what I did, Your Honor, was I opened the box just to the left of the Grissom box's place on the shelf. I don't recall today what the label on that box was, but I'd stake my career—I *am* staking my career—on that being this box in the photo, the Madigan box. And I placed the Grissom file, comprising the originals of the three documents of which I have presented photocopies to the court, I placed that file at the very back of the Madigan box, which, one could argue, was, in fact, its proper chronological place in the archive. And only then did I remove the Grissom box for burning and, as instructed, move things around on the shelf so that its absence would not be noticed.

"Your Honor, it is my understanding that the special master, in her review of the archived files, examined only the placement of the boxes, not their content. And believe me, Your Honor, as the one person who read every page in those very boxes she examined, I understand why she would have proceeded in that manner. If the court would ask the special master to return to the archive and locate that Madigan box and then look at the actual files in that box, especially the file at the rear, I believe the court will be able to locate the original signed contract of which my submission was a copy."

By this point, Joey had been having increasing difficulty maintaining his composure and was nearly apoplectic. "Your Honor! This is ridiculous. If he claims that that file was there all along, in that specific location, why didn't Mr. Dennum tell us that and save the court and the special master a lot of time?"

"It's a fair point, Mr. Dennum," said the judge. "Why didn't you tell us this sooner?"

"With respect, Your Honor, when the court was outlining the instructions for the special master, I did try to offer a modification. However, at that particular time, the court had . . . ah . . . lost patience with the recurrence of coincidences in the case, and I was not permitted to address the issue."

"Fair enough," said the judge, remembering that particular portion of the previous discussion. "And I think this is an easy problem to resolve. But I warn you, Mr. Dennum. If the documents are not precisely where you have said they are, this case is over, and I *will* be referring you to the bar.

"Gentlemen, please excuse me for a moment while I see if I can reach Professor Hanson. As it happens, I believe she is actually in New York today on other business. Oh, and Mr. Coy, please hand me your cell phone, and please do not leave the courtroom for any reason until I return."

Ten minutes passed, during which Andy and Joey said nothing to one another. For the first time in weeks, Andy was starting to feel some hope. For the third or fourth time in, oh, ten or twenty minutes, Joey was starting to feel something far different. He tried mightily not to show it, but what he was feeling was panic, pure and simple panic. If that file was where Andy said it was, then he, Joey, was the one in real trouble, not Andy. Joey's client, of course, would be in trouble, too, but that was the furthest thing from his mind. *Shit*, he thought. *Shit, shit, shit!*

⋯⋯

The word both had awaited came a few days later in one of three attachments to an email from the Cook County Circuit of the Illinois State Court System. It was short and sweet. In the matter of *Dennum v. Major League Baseball*, the motion for dismissal was denied, and the complainant's case was certified to proceed to trial. Andy would get his day in court. *Obviously*, he thought with relief, *those documents were exactly where I said they would be*.

A second attachment gave notice that the court had found Joseph Coy, attorney for the respondent, to be in contempt of court, had imposed a fine on Mr. Coy in the amount of $25,000, and had referred him to the Illinois State Bar Association, recommending that it consider imposing sanctions and that it consider communicating its determination, if any, to New York State Bar Association, where Mr. Coy's practice was primarily centered. The court gave Mr. Coy seven days to appeal its ruling before the judgment became final.

Ultimately, it was the third attachment that mattered most. This was a brief report from the special master indicating that three documents comprising a file on Parker T. Grissom had been located in the archive of Stetson, Varney, and Handelmann appended to which were copies of the documents that had been recovered as well as a certification from the court that they were being held for safekeeping. The court indicated that it was awaiting the complainant's instructions for their transmission for forensic paper dating or handwriting analysis to one of the several authenticators that the court had approved for such work in prior cases. There was even a list of these experts, which Andy took to be a subtle gift from the judge who, he thought, might feel a little badly about having cast so much doubt on his word. It was thus clear just what his next step would be.

The options for Joey's next step were rather more constrained. He could choose between paying the fine and accepting sanction by the bar with whatever degree of grace or disgrace he might choose. Or he could appeal the judgment and fight like hell against the sanctions. By nature, by his very being, Joey Coy was a fighter. But before making the decision, he had the good sense, for once, to consult with his boss, Managing Partner Chet Kinnalley, on whose sage advice more than a year ago, after all, he had set himself up to be in this position. "Dump the client, burn the box," Chet had said. It was where Joey's head had been at the time as well, and he did it. Or rather, he instructed that twit Dennum to do it. In the end, dumping the client would have been easy to defend. Law firms made those decisions every day. Burning the box, though . . . they did that as well, but it was much harder to defend. Then there was the other thing, the thing he could not pin on Chet.

"You idiot. You don't lie to the court! You weasel. You have a memory failure or a brain cramp. You lose things. But you don't flat-out lie to the court." Chet's feelings on this were, Coy could see, quite clear. And, of course, Chet was right. And there was another thing, one Chet would not know, though he might guess at it. Joey Coy, master judge of people, had badly underestimated Andy Dennum, and in disposing of him as he had—as he was accustomed to doing with the night school types he brought in to do the work that was one step up from the paralegals—he had set the coals for the fire that was now about to burn him.

But Chet had one more question, one Joey had barely considered to that point. "How," he wanted to know, "are you going to tell the client what happened? More specifically, how will you explain this to the client without giving him a cause of action against the firm? That commissioner has a reputation as a real SOB when he thinks somebody has crossed him. So you'd better think it through real good before you talk to him. And he'd better hear it from you before some reporter out there in Chicago stumbles across this mess. Or Dennum decides to use it for leverage. Clear?"

"Crystal," said Joey, and he left Chet's office for his own.

⸺⸺

Two days later, while Andy was still formulating his next move in between meetings with clients seeking to do some estate planning—that talk at the community center had actually brought in several new clients—and dealing with the continuing fallout of the Pearson divorce petitions, Betty buzzed Andy to let him know he had a phone call.

"Who is it?" he asked. "Can it wait? Can I call them back?"

"I don't think that would be a good idea," Betty replied. "It's the Commissioner of Baseball on the line. I think it's the man himself."

Andy reached for the phone on his desk.

"Commissioner. This is an unexpected pleasure. Should we be talking without Mr. Coy on the line?"

"That is why I am calling. For reasons that I believe you know and I have only just discovered, Mr. Coy will not be on the line. He and his firm no longer represent us in this or any other matter."

"Honestly, sir, I can't say I am surprised."

"I thought not. It is now my understanding that the document you presented to us some months ago is likely genuine. I know there has been some controversy over that, but I want you to know that the obstinacy that has been displayed was not on our part. In effect, Mr. Coy was self-dealing. He was protecting his law firm at the expense of his client's interests, of our interests. That is now ended. I think you'll find that we are prepared to accept the document at face value."

"Well, I must say, that does come as a surprise. I mean, I knew that Joey, ah, Mr. Coy, was protecting the interests of his law firm, but I had been under the distinct impression that you knew of and had approved his strategy. It's nice to hear that was not the case."

"Indeed. And as a show of good faith in the matter, I was wondering if you might be willing to come over to our offices in New York—I believe you are not too far away, out in New Jersey. Is that correct?"

"Yes, I'm in Mendham. It's North Jersey just past Morristown," said Andy.

"Yes, good. As I was saying, I thought you might come to our offices and you and I could sit down together and see if we can arrive at a satisfactory solution to this nasty bit of business. I was hoping perhaps next Tuesday around eleven. Would that work for you?"

"Let me check my calendar for a moment. I have to be in court on a brief civil matter at nine. Shouldn't take more than an hour. With the traffic, I probably couldn't make eleven, but I could do, say, one in the afternoon, if that works for you."

"Even better. I'll arrange to have some lunch brought in. I've lost my Hale and Hearty. Their Tuscan white bean soup used to remind me of my Senate days. They seem to have closed. But there is a Cull & Pistol nearby. Clam chowder and lobster rolls work for you?"

"Yes, sir. That would be just fine."

"Excellent. See you then."

As he hung up the phone, the Commissioner tried to reconstruct the brief conversation as CI might have done. What was there that he could work with? Dennum had called him "sir." More than once. Good. That meant he respected the office. And he was clearly young and gave the impression he was easy to please. Also good. This would be easy pickings.

———❦———

Andy was on pins and needles waiting for Tuesday afternoon to roll around. He hardly slept the night before and floated through the court proceeding scheduled for that morning. Then he made an early start for the city, the better to be sure he arrived on time . . . and found parking within a mile or so of his objective, Chelsea Market, where the baseball offices were located. Finding himself with an hour to spare, he simply wandered the market shops. He found one he would hit on the way back out to pick up a small gift for Keiley and a smaller one for Betty. But who knew? If this meeting went well, there might be much bigger gifts in store.

For his part, the Commissioner was no fool. To the contrary, his decades in politics had given him a finely tuned sense of the trappings of power and how to use them to his best advantage. And this was a time for just that.

One of his innovations had been the creation of what he called the Alumni Association—a group of twenty or so former Major League players, none of them Hall of Famers or the like, but all of them recognizable, either by their faces or by their names when introduced. These men all now lived somewhere in the greater New York area, which is to say, within a couple of hours by train, and all were placed on retainer to the office for $25,000 a year. Their only responsibility was to serve as eye candy for times like this when it was necessary for the Commissioner to impress some outsider from whom he or the game wanted something important. They would meet for an hour or so before some appointed time—"meet" being a euphemism for having a big social hour and gab fest—then break up just in time to make an appearance so that, on their way out, they could "happen" to run into the designated guest. It made for an impressive display of elbow rubbing for those outside the game. When Andy's arrival was announced, the Commissioner rapped on the glass wall of the conference room as he walked toward reception—their signal that their meeting had concluded.

"Mr. Dennum?" he said, picking Andy out easily since he was the only one in the reception area. He didn't bother to introduce himself. "It's nice to meet you at last. Please come with me."

As they walked down the hall toward the Commissioner's corner office, they had to pass through a group of men whose meeting had evidently just ended. "Guys," said the Commissioner, "I'd like you to meet Andrew Dennum. Andrew is helping us out with a little problem that's come up. Andrew, allow me to introduce these fellows." Even Andy, not the biggest baseball fan in the world, knew these names, had seen these men perform on television or even one or two in person. What lucky timing. Perhaps it was an omen? This would be a great story when he got back home to tell it. Or at a bar with friends for the next, what, fifty years?

The hook was set. They moved on to the Commissioner's office. There, Andy was surprised to see another man at the wooden conference table.

"Andrew," said the Commissioner. "This is Mark Stephenson of Stephenson, Horner, and Hardart." Andy knew of the firm. It was a rival, perhaps the primary rival, to Stetson, Varney. The Commissioner was obviously trying to make a point with Joey.

"Mark is taking over the case from Mr. Coy. And since, in this rather unusual circumstance, you are here wearing two hats, as the complainant and as the complainant's attorney, I thought it best not to come unarmed to a gunfight."

Stephenson stood and offered his hand. "I'm sure you understand," he said. "We wouldn't want any *ex parte* communication. Not after everything else that has happened in this case."

Andy sat down and realized, suddenly, that this was not quite the friendly little tête-à-tête he had naively expected. Best be on his guard.

It was, in fact, Mark Stephenson, and not the Commissioner, who began to carry the meeting.

"Andrew, I believe the Commissioner here has told you, against my advice, I will say, that we are prepared to accept the validity of the Grissom contract, and we are prepared to accept, subject to your delivery of certain documents, that you are the sole legal heir and successor to Mr. Grissom. We could drag this out for a long time, of course, and cost everybody involved a lot of money—except me, I guess," he inserted with a lawyer's smile. The Commissioner did not smile. His only thought was that lawyers were even slimier than members of Congress, something he would have found counterintuitive not that long ago.

"As I was saying, we are prepared to accept both of those assertions, which are central to your claim. Given what's happened, the court is likely to accept them in any event. But what we are not prepared to do is to pay you $400 million and give you large ownership chunks of two Major League Baseball teams. Andrew, that is simply not going to happen. Even if we could do that, which we cannot because all of our franchisees are legally independent entities, and we cannot bind them in the way you demand, but even if we could, frankly, we would not. Surely you see this."

After a beat, he paused, and Andy filled the void as Stephenson knew he would.

"Of course I see that. And of course I don't expect to walk out of this room with half a billion dollars and passes to two owners' boxes. I got into this litigation just by trying to solve a century-old puzzle I had come across in a musty old box of legal papers. And the deeper I got into it, the more intriguing it became. And then, by sheer serendipity, it turned out that I had a more personal interest in the case than I ever would have guessed, even in my greatest flights of fancy.

"So, no. I don't expect to obtain all the damages to which I believe I am legally entitled. And, by the way, I do believe that. And if we did go to trial, I think I have a pretty good hand. No, for me, there is a whole other set of stakes. There was this poor man, Grissom, way back in 1914. And I still don't know the details and probably never will. But he performed some service for the predecessors of the Commissioner here, no idea what. And I have come to believe that Ban Johnson and the other men who signed that contract were out to flimflam old Mr. Grissom. I think they promised him something that they never, in their wildest imaginations, thought they or anyone else would ever have to deliver. In the world they inhabited, Kansas City was so small and so hard to reach that they thought it would never have major league baseball. But they sold Grissom the dream that it might . . . someday, and in return, they extracted something of value. I became interested in Mr. Grissom and his dream as a kind of . . . what did Albert Einstein call it . . . a kind of thought experiment. A what-would-happen-if sort of thing. And then, all of a sudden, it became much more real and much more personal.

"The short answer to the question I think you are asking, then, is yes. I am a reasonable person and I am open to a negotiation. What number did you have in mind?"

"Zero," said Stephenson.

"I beg your pardon? I thought you were opening a negotiation here. If it's not that, then why am I here?"

"Two reasons, Mr. Dennum." This time it was the Commissioner who spoke. "First, although Mr. Coy knew, or rather he claimed to know, you well, neither of us had ever had the pleasure. We wanted an opportunity to size you up, see what you're made of. And now we've had that chance. Second, we wanted to give you this." With that, he nodded to Stephenson, and the lawyer pushed a sheaf of legal papers across the table toward Andy.

"As you'll see," said Stephenson, "and as we said, we are stipulating to the fact of the contract, and we will, with proper support as is spelled out here, stipulate to your personal status as heir and successor. But we will not be making any concessions with respect to the underlying litigation. We have simply chosen to contest it on different grounds."

⟢ ⟣

Andy was more than a little dazed as he made his way back to his car and wove through the mid-afternoon traffic, which remained fairly heavy as far as Morristown. Rather than head straight home, he turned off and drove to Keiley's house. He figured he'd find her there, at work in the upstairs studio.

One look at him, and she knew something had not gone to plan. "What is it," she asked. "What's wrong? You look awful."

"I'm not sure yet." He took out the papers he'd been handed earlier in the afternoon. "I need to read this. But I'm pretty sure it's not good."

Andy proceeded to tell her about his visit downtown, how he'd met all of those famous baseball players and . . . As he relayed the story, he realized what the Commissioner had done. By his manner on the phone, by his friendly greeting, by running the gauntlet of famous players, he'd thrown Andy completely off balance. Andy was the one being played. When he thought about it, he realized that the Commissioner had manipulated him in exactly the way Joey Coy had when he'd hired him a year and a half ago and then summarily fired him after a year of good solid work. Stroke the ego, extract the price, lower the hammer. That he'd fallen for it yet again simply pissed him off. When would he learn?

Andy realized that he had stopped talking, and he looked up to see Keiley sitting there quietly and staring at him.

"You back with us?" she said gently.

"Yeah," Andy replied. "Yeah, I am. I have to go back home and read this brief. I'm not sure what'll come after that, but I think I know where to start. I'll give you a call later."

With that, Andy got into his car and headed back to his house. Then he poured himself a long glass of seltzer—nothing to further fog his mind—and settled down to read.

The first part of Stephenson's brief was pretty much what he'd been told. The new legal regime would no longer contest the authenticity of the original contract. While there did not appear to be a copy of the document in any organizational archive that had been searched, the signed copy that turned up in the Stetson, Varney files, paired with the note from the partner at Brian and Ives, which Keiley's map showed to be one of the two firms whose merger eventually led to the current configuration, would no longer be contested. So, too, would the respondent accept Andy's claim of successorship once he had delivered the requisite probate records from Pennsylvania as well as a complete copy of Lou's adoption file. So far, so good. But then he came to the real point of the brief.

While the baseball powers that be were no longer challenging the contract's authenticity, they were now challenging its enforceability. According to the brief, the contract clearly said it would hold in perpetuity. But according to Stephenson, the law said that could not be. He had cited what he said was a common law principle called the rule against perpetuities, the idea that "a contract cannot outlive the parties who agreed to it, or even in the most expansive interpretation, cannot exceed the lives of the signees by more than twenty-one years."

"Whereas," the brief continued, "Mr. Grissom died in February 1918, under this most permissive interpretation, the contract in question would have been valid and enforceable until, but not after, February 1939. And whereas no Major League Baseball team was franchised to or located in the Kansas City metropolitan area until 1954, long after the de facto termination of the contract, no obligation was incurred by Major League Baseball."

Andy had a sinking feeling that he had heard of this limitation on perpetuities before. And then it came to him. It had to have been something Mumbles had said in class. Andy pulled out a box and dug through to find his old law school notebooks, and sure enough, there it was. First year in law school, third class in contracts. He'd forgotten all about it—if he had ever internalized it in the first place. With Mumbles, you could be so focused on trying to figure out what he was saying that it was all you could do to get something in your notebook before he moved on. Damn! But there was more to the brief, and Andy forced himself to return to it.

Stephenson then noted that the original contract had been agreed upon and made justiciable under the laws of the State of Illinois, and Illinois, he said, had an explicit limitation on perpetuities. He cited a 1998 case that Andy, who'd never practiced in the Illinois courts before, was sure he had never heard of, *Jesperson v. Minnesota Mining and Manufacturing Company*, in which, Stephenson said, the Illinois Supreme Court had determined that an agreement with no termination date could be terminated at will by either of the parties and that such termination did not amount to a breach of contract. It was more complicated than that, but that was the gist of it. And if that weren't enough, the case had originated in the same Cook County Circuit Court where his challenge was being heard. Andy found the case online and read the decision. It was all rather confusing at first read, but he found it hard to argue with Stephenson's interpretation. Still, Andy did not trust himself. He needed help, and he knew where to find it.

His first call was to Mumbles, who was, at best, only mildly encouraging. "I would have to look again at the specific language in the contract," he said once Andy had filled him in on the developments to date and had sent him a copy of Stephenson's argument. "But it seems to me that you do have some counterarguments available. For one, the contract is not necessarily open-ended within the intent of the Illinois statute or the rule against perpetuities. It actually uses the phrase 'entitled in perpetuity.' So you could argue that the drafters of the contract explicitly intended to impose a transgenerational burden or property right on their respective successors, that they recognized that the anticipated event of the establishment of a franchise would not occur in the near term.

"Your second argument might be that while the individuals who signed the contract are no longer alive, the organization that was represented by three of them still is, and thus the twenty-one-year limit in Illinois law is not relevant. And on the other side, you can argue that the contract encompasses by direct reference the heirs and successors to Grissom, which at this time means you. And you are still alive, unless I am talking with a ghost. Andrew, I have to warn you, these may not be winning arguments. But they are reasonable, and they may be enough to keep you in the game, at least long enough to reach some settlement.

"One last thought. It's a longshot, because 1918 was a long time ago. But you might want to take a look at when those three baseball guys who signed the thing died. Anyway, Andrew, I wish you well. If nothing else, maybe you will, at last, have received a real education in contracts."

"Oh, Professor," said Andy. "I'm pretty sure I already had one. I appreciate your help. Thank you." And with that, the call ended.

Next up, Sajak.

⸺◆⸺

"Andrew. Nice to hear from you. How's that unusual case of yours going?"

"Actually," Andy said, "that's why I'm calling. That advice you gave me before was really, really useful. But the situation has evolved since then, and I'm hoping you might have another suggestion or two."

Once again, Andy laid out the chain of events that had transpired since their last conversation. He made a point of mentioning the briefs filed by several of the Major League teams and the hint in the local newspaper, as yet unfulfilled, that the governments out there that had funded the two stadiums might yet seek to place their interests before the court.

"Ah," she said. "The blocks on the table. I trust you had something to do with that. Very good, Andrew. Very good." Hearing those words from her, he felt a moment of warmth, of pride. Maybe he actually was learning to do this.

"I had a good teacher, Professor. And I appreciate it. But now I think I'm back in a legal cul-de-sac of sorts. The other side has accepted both of the key facts behind my case, but this new lawyer—Stephenson is his name—is arguing that—"

"Mark Stephenson?" she queried.

"Yes, that's him."

"How interesting. . . . Mark's an old friend of mine, and he is an extremely capable lawyer. He's argued before the US Supreme Court three or four times. And if you look him up, you'll see he is all over the top law journals, either publishing himself or having his cases cited. He is a worthy adversary, Andrew, a worthy adversary.

"But you know what? Like every lawyer, every adversary, he has his strengths and he has his weaknesses. On paper, or in an intellectual debate like at the Supreme Court, the man is brilliant—a fine legal mind. He can tie you in legal knots just trying to parse his arguments. But he's not a street fighter, Andrew. If you can get him outside his comfort zone, he can become flustered and risk-averse. Of course, getting him there is not easy."

She paused for a moment, then continued.

"Andrew, I'm sure you remember the old aphorism about the law. 'If the facts are against you, argue the law. If the law is against you, argue the facts. If the law and the facts are against you, pound the table and yell like hell.' Well, it sounds to me like the facts are on your side, and the other side knows it. And maybe the law is on their side, though it sounds as if my colleague, Professor Rose, might have at least created some room for hope on that score. Let's assume not, if only for the sake of argument. In effect, that's a standoff. You know what that leaves. I know someone you might want to talk with, but don't do that until you clearly understand how you want to proceed. There is a risk that once you make that call, you will lose control of your own narrative, and that can prove fatal to your case."

Sajak passed along a name and some contact information. Shortly after that, Andy thanked her profusely, and the call ended.

Walk-Off

From Miracle Baby to Millionaire
Orphaned boy, now grown, claims his legacy: not one, but two
Major League clubs

Rick Shaw, *Major Sport Weekly*

Three decades ago, he was nearly lost. His parents were killed in a terrible auto wreck, but Andrew Dennum, Andy to his friends, somehow survived. Thrown from the car as it rolled over and over, he landed in the tall grass of a highway median. All but overlooked, he was eventually rescued by a sharp-eyed fireman. Newspapers at the time called him the "Miracle Baby."

Young Andy was adopted by a working-class New Jersey couple he describes as the only parents he's ever known. In fact, he never knew his real identity until a strange series of coincidences led him on a path of discovery. And what he discovered is that he is the heir to partial ownership of not one but two Major League franchises.

The story begins in 1914, when a distant relative, Parker Grissom, signed a contract with Major League Baseball, which was run back then by something called the National Commission. Grissom apparently provided some services for the baseball establishment—Andy does not know what those were—and in exchange, the solons of the game guaranteed him or his heirs a ten-percent share of any Major League franchise that might ever be located in Kansas City, where Grissom lived. And Andy's got the contract to prove it, complete with the signatures of Ban Johnson and the other members of the commission.

Chances are that, way back then, baseball never expected it would put a team in Kansas City, so in their view, the promise of ownership provided in the contract was meaningless. But forty years later, there was a team out there on the banks of the Missouri, and when that team moved to the West Coast in the sixties, well, there was another. And from the way the contract reads, young Mr. Dennum owns parts of both of them. Given the valuations of Major League clubs these days, that makes him a millionaire many times over.

Of course, Baseball is fighting back. Dennum, a young lawyer just starting out, sued the sport for his rightful inheritance. The case has been in court in Chicago for a few months, and recently, Baseball acknowledged that the contract Mr. Dennum has is authentic and that Dennum is the sole surviving heir of old Mr. Grissom. But that's apparently not good enough. So the commissioner's office is now claiming that the central commitment in the contract, which was a grant of ownership to Grissom and his heirs in perpetuity—forever—is somehow invalid under Illinois law. Not since the days of Richard J. Daley has there been such a power play in Cook County.

The case is back in court next week, and Judge Warren Keyser will decide whether justice will prevail or whether powerful men like the commissioner and his high-priced legal talent can win on technicalities. It's a real tale of David and Goliath, and one you can bet the folks out in Kansas City and Oakland are watching with special interest.

Andy wasn't sure how many people actually read *Major Sport Weekly*, but as it turned out, that didn't seem to matter. For whatever reason— and he figured it was probably the words "Miracle Baby" in the head- line—the story went viral. To his utter amazement, he saw it on the news out of New York and Philly, and the reporters said there had been a social media storm—hundreds of thousands of postings and repostings. And then the phone began to ring. Old law school buddies offering their con- gratulations. Old high school chums trying to get a piece of the action. A couple of so-called investment advisors offering to help him manage his newfound fortune. *My god*, he thought, *you'd think I just won the lottery.*

Next came the media calls. Would he sit for an interview for the Kansas City paper? Absolutely. Oakland? Cleveland? Los Angeles? Houston? Denver? You bet. Anywhere there was a Major League team. But the one call he was waiting for was slow to come. And then it did. Ed Archer from *Beat on Sports* had his producer call to ask for an interview. This was the big one, the reason for the whole effort. Fifteen minutes of fame on the flagship program of the National Cable Sports Network, with its twenty-three million subscribers. The story was going national on the premier television sports network. The Commissioner was sure to see it or hear about it. And so was his lawyer.

"Folks," Archer began, "with me in our New York studio now is Andy Dennum. You might know him from the news as the Miracle Baby, but as you can see, he's all grown up. Welcome to *Beat on Sports*."

"Thank you, Ed. I'm happy to be here. I've never been on TV before."

"Well, don't be nervous. There are only about four or five million of your closest friends watching. So what's the real story here? You have a contract that gives you ten-percent ownership of two Major League ball clubs, the Royals and the A's?"

"I guess I do. In plain language, that's pretty much what it says."

"And this contract is how old?"

"It was signed more than a hundred years ago, Ed."

"And you think it's the real thing?"

"Well, the court seems to think so. But I have a copy of it right here, so judge for yourself."

Andy handed Ed the one-page document he had brought along, and Ed took just a moment to read it.

"Folks, what I'm reading here looks to be an agreement from 1914 that gives a fellow named Parker Grissom and his heirs forevermore an ownership share in any Major League Baseball franchise ever established in KC at any time in the future. And it's signed by Ban Johnson, August Herrmann, and John Tener on behalf of Major League Baseball and its two leagues. I bet the commissioner would like to see this."

"Actually, Ed, he has. As you probably know, this lawsuit was filed several months ago, and we briefly discussed the matter in the commissioner's office a while back. Since that meeting, baseball has filed a new brief that recognizes the authenticity of the contract."

"So what's the problem? Why aren't you moving back and forth between your two owners' boxes?"

"Well, the law's never simple, I guess. They said that the contract is legit, and they even agreed that I am the sole legal heir to Mr. Grissom. But they now say the contract is unenforceable under the law because of a technicality. I disagree, of course, so we fight on."

"If you're willing to say, just what are you asking for in your lawsuit, actual ownership of those teams?"

"No. I would be the first to admit that I don't know enough about baseball to make a very good owner. I told the commissioner as much when we met. But the suit does ask for monetary damages."

"And what's that number?"

"Well, for now, it's $433 million."

"Wow! I bet that got their attention."

"I know it's a big number, but really it's just a placeholder. It's sure to get smaller. But if you think about it, that contract gives me ten percent of the current values of both ball clubs plus ten percent of all their earnings over about three-quarters of a century."

"That would break the bank, wouldn't it?"

"Probably. And to be clear, that is not my intention. The real reason I'm pursuing this is to defend the rights of my family, a family I never knew I had until this thing came along. As you know, I was orphaned as a baby, so I never knew anything about those family roots. But Parker Grissom was, I think, my great-great-great grandfather or something like that. And he created this legacy for his family. And I am just trying to preserve that."

"Just so you folks know, Andy was thrown from the car in a wreck that killed both of his parents. He was found unhurt, lying in some tall grass near the highway, and he was later adopted by the Dennums. Now Andy, back to the money. If you're not trying to break the bank, what are you after?"

"Ed, as I told the commissioner, I expected to come down quite a bit once I had a look at the financials of the two teams. I'm still waiting for those documents."

"So let me get this straight. The commissioner has already agreed that you have a valid contract and also that you are the legal heir to the proceeds of the contract. And he knows you are willing to ask for a lot less than you say in the lawsuit. Wasn't there a negotiation based on all that?"

"Well, I thought that was why he had invited me to his office—to start those talks."

"And it wasn't?"

"Hardly. He had my number, and I asked him for his. It was zero. He said baseball wasn't going to pay a thin dime, and then he handed me a legal brief that set out this argument about technicalities in Illinois law. You'll see here in the contract that all this was done subject to Illinois law. Well, I feel an obligation here, and I'm not about to give up so easily."

"Okay, so let's look ahead a bit, and let's say that all of this is just posturing—like contracts between teams and players and their agents—and at the end, some deal gets done. What are you going to do with all that money?"

"You know, Ed, I've thought about that, though I don't want to get the cart out front of the horse. And I do want to make a point. Money seems to be the way we do that in our society. But I don't think I deserve all that money, however much it might end up being. And I do feel as if the two ball clubs have been put in the middle of something that, from their own legal filings in the case, I don't think they ever knew anything about. And I want to support baseball in both cities. So after I cover my legal expenses and the court costs, I plan to give a million dollars to each city to support youth baseball. They can use that money to build fields or train student athletes or whatever they think is needed. And then, because Kansas City is really the heart of all this, and the city itself might have been a victim of the greed of those guys who signed the contract, I've been looking for a way to do something useful out there. And I think I've found it. So, I plan to give half of whatever is left of any settlement to the Negro Leagues Baseball Museum to preserve the history of that dimension of the game, which was important in and to Kansas City. And, of course, the museum is out there as well."

"Am I hearing this right? You're going to give, what would you call them, Miracle Baby Grants, to Oakland and KC for youth baseball, and then split what's left with the Negro Leagues Museum? That's incredibly generous."

"Well, I just think of it as the right thing to do. And by the way, I'll have to remember that Miracle Baby Grants thing."

"Andy Dennum, thanks for joining us today on *Beat on Sports*. And good luck to you, my friend."

"Thanks, Ed."

The call came in about an hour after Andy returned to his office. It wasn't the call he had been expecting, hoping for, but it was an intriguing one nonetheless. "Please," the caller had said, "come out and see me." Andy decided he would comply with the request. He supposed that lawyers got these phone calls all the time, and he remembered some of Mumbles' stories from such meetings. Besides, it was only a short drive to the north.

Andy arrived at the Federal Correctional Institute at Otisville, New York, promptly at eleven the next morning. Though hardly open like a college campus, the place had a certain campus-like character, with a large lawn crisscrossed by walkways leading to clusters of remote cell blocks that served in lieu of dormitories, all fronted by a low-slung, contemporary-looking administration building. He passed through the sensors and searches of the visitors' entrance to the minimum security facility and was ushered into a large open room furnished with scattered small picnic-style tables, each with attached bench seating. He found his assigned table number and waited. A couple of minutes later, a guard directed an olive-green-clad inmate in his direction.

"You know who I am?" asked the man once he had settled onto the bench opposite Andy.

"I didn't at first. But I looked you up. So, yes, I do."

"Well, don't think you're here to be my lawyer. That's not happening. But I saw you on TV yesterday. You seemed like a square guy. Thank you for coming up here."

"Okay. So I'm here. What is it you wanted to talk about?"

"Nah, I don't want to talk. I want to give you something."

With that, he raised high one hand in which he held an envelope and waved it around to attract the guard's attention. This exchange had obviously been pre-arranged. *Perhaps*, thought Andy, *this is the way it is here*. The guard nodded his assent, and the man gave the sealed envelope to Andy.

"Now, look carefully at the back of that envelope, and you'll see it's been hand-stamped, kind of like a postmark but not really."

Andy turned the envelope over and noted the stamp, a sort of shield surrounded by the words "Approved—FCI Otisville" and the day's date.

"Listen closely. Don't you mess with that seal, and don't you look inside this envelope. Now, sooner or later, you're going to have another sit-down with my old boss. And when you do, I want you to give him this envelope. No need to tell him where you got it. He'll know. And he'll know if it's been tampered with.

"Now get the hell out of here before somebody thinks I'm talking to a lawyer about making some kind of deal." And with that, he got up and returned through the door he had entered not five minutes before.

Perplexed, but with no other option and, in truth, with no interest in staying in that place any longer than necessary, Andy exited the facility and headed home. The whole thing took maybe three, three and a half hours. And all the way home, his mind kept churning. *What the heck is in that envelope, and why should I do this guy's bidding?*

The other call—the one he *had* been waiting and hoping for—came a couple of days later. Mark Stephenson had read Andy's response to the new set of legal arguments, and he and the Commissioner wondered if Andy would be willing to have a second meeting in the city. Andy said he would be willing but suggested the discussion should take place at Stephenson's law firm. That was apparently agreeable and had probably been anticipated, and the session was scheduled two days hence.

Those two days, like the two before them—like the week before them—had been among the least pleasant in the Commissioner's tenure. Once Dennum went public with his claims, it seemed like every newspaper in the country ran the story. And every time that story appeared in the morning paper in one of his cities, the Commissioner got at least one phone call, often more, from the local ownership group demanding that he make this thing disappear. To a one, they were concerned that the publicity would hurt ticket sales, not to mention the image of the game. He expected that from Kansas City, maybe even Oakland. And he understood it. The enterprise did not look very good right now in those two cities. But when he heard from most of his owners, his concern began to grow. So far, he had turned down every request for an interview. *Pending legal matter, can't comment.* And so far that had worked. Almost too well. Because, as should not have surprised him given his long political experience, when only one side is speaking to the media, only one story is being told. Still, if he talked to those jackals, what could he say that would make things any better? *Maybe*, he thought, *Stephenson has an idea of how we can fight this out.*

On the appointed day, Andy drove into the city, parked, and headed to the Stephenson, Horner, and Hardart offices on the top floors of a midtown building. He started at reception, on the fifty-first floor, and was accompanied on an internal elevator that took him to the fifty-seventh floor and the office of the senior named partner and founder of the firm, whose office occupied half of the floor with a broad panoramic view, mainly to the north and west. Andy wondered idly if he could see his house from there.

"Andy," said his host. "Thanks for coming over. Let's go sit in the corner conference area over here." He led Andy to an area of well-padded leather chairs, and as they approached, the Commissioner, who had been hidden by the back of his chosen seat, rose to shake his hand. The limited pleasantries thus accomplished and the customary bottled water and snacks pointed out, Stephenson opened the meeting.

"Andy, we have read your latest brief. And I must say, it's very clever. You may be right that the direct references to perpetuities and inheritability in the contract might overcome the limitations established in the Illinois statute, but I don't think so. And noting that the Illinois Supreme Court did not set the precedent until 1998, well, that's just disingenuous. As we have argued, the underlying principle goes back long before this contract was signed in 1914, and, of course, a precedent is a precedent. Doesn't really matter when it's established.

"I can't speak for the Commissioner, but I particularly enjoyed your arguments about the twenty-one-year limitation. Yes, it's true, one of the executives who signed your agreement, John Tener, lived a long and fruitful life and died only in 1946. So I suppose one could employ sophistry and argue that because both the A's franchise in 1954 and the initial moves toward the Royals franchise in 1967 occurred within twenty-one years of his death, both would fall under even the strictest common law limitation. Oh, wait. That is, in fact, what you did. Employ sophistry, that is. As you know well, Mr. Tener was long retired from his baseball responsibilities when he passed. Another non-starter.

"Now, that leaves only the claim that the actual counterparty to your contract was Major League Baseball, which, of course, is still in existence. Again, nice try. But it is, and will remain, our position that it was actually the death of your apparent ancestor, Parker Grissom, in 1918 that started the twenty-one-year clock. So the clock ran out all the way back in 1939. And in 1939, Kansas City was every bit the minor league town that the National Commission had anticipated it would be. I can tell you that our Chicago office has been all over this case since we came on board. That includes a couple of retired state judges who are of counsel to us. And they think you haven't got a leg to stand on. Sorry, Andy, but you don't."

"Then why am I here?" Andy asked, his frustration and anger growing by the minute. "I didn't need to come all this way for another sham negotiation, let alone to be lectured on the law."

"Oh," said the Commissioner, entering the conversation for the first time. "This is no sham negotiation. It's not a negotiation at all. Stephenson here, he wants me to settle this thing to make it go away. He's lucky he's still on the case. But me? I don't settle.

"What I *do* do, though, is express myself clearly. I'm an old hand at this sort of thing, Andrew, and I know how to fight dirty if I have to. Now, you must think you're pretty smart starting this big media campaign like you have, getting in all the papers and on television. It's actually a pretty sophisticated tactic for a young fellow like you. But it's not going to work. I am hearing from my ball clubs every day, and the message is clear. Commissioner, they say, hold your ground. We're with you. And son, that's just what I intend to do."

"Well," Andy responded, "I might as well leave then. Because I don't see this meeting going anywhere." And he started to rise.

"That would be a mistake, Andy." Stephenson was back in the conversation. "There is something we want to tell you, and you'll want to listen closely and think about it. Because you took this dispute to the media and because you have been speaking about the Commissioner and the baseball enterprise in disparaging terms, you have laid yourself open for a defamation action. We do not want to go to court over that. Yet. But if this media campaign continues, we will. And we will bring the full force of the resources of both baseball and this firm down on you like a sack of rocks. Believe me, Andy, you do not want to be standing under that sack of rocks if it falls."

Andy found his courage, which had lain only slightly hidden beneath his rising anger. "Gee, Mark," he said. "Can you see me trembling? You want to bring a defamation action? Bring it."

"Okay, Andy. Perhaps I put it too strongly. But I want to be sure you understand that this litigation thing, it's a two-way street, and the Commissioner here, well he's been standing out in the field until now taking ground balls, but he's about ready to come into the dugout and grab a bat. That's all I want you to understand."

Andy just stared at Mark, then at the Commissioner. Then once again he made as if to leave.

"Andy." Mark again. "As long as you're here, what is your real number? It won't change anything, but we—well, *I*—would just like to know what this is really about."

Now Andy understood what was really happening here. *We're just playing a game of good cop, bad cop.*

"What this is really about, Mark, as I have been telling the reporters who ask, is the honor of my family, even if I didn't even know they were my family until a couple of months ago. And as for my number . . . my bottom line no-negotiations number . . . it's thirty-one million, plus expenses and court costs. That's my number."

"Well, that's certainly a lot better than $433 million," said Stephenson. "But it's an odd sort of number. If you don't mind my asking, how did you arrive at that?"

"Simple, really. I don't have any interest in owning part of one ball club, let alone two. But I do have an interest, as I have said, in standing up for the principle that your client owes case debt to my family. There are thirty franchised clubs on your side of the table, and I think each one ought to be responsible for a million dollars. It's not a number they can't all meet, yet it's a big enough number to remind them that they need to pay attention to whatever actions are being taken in their name."

At that last, he turned to face the Commissioner. "And the last million, well, I figure the—what was your term? The enterprise, yes, that was it. The enterprise should have some skin of its own in the game as well. Now, do I really care whether the financial burden on your side falls out just that way? Not really. That's not my business. But I would imagine it would end up with a similar kind of split. So that's my number. Thirty-one million to make this go away.

"So, Commissioner, here we are once again. Dare I ask, sir," Andy spoke the last word with just a touch of derision in his voice, "what your bottom line is now?"

"I can tell you straight out," said the Commissioner. "It was zero a few weeks ago, and it's zero now. I don't care how you decide to frame it, and I don't care who you promise to share it with. We are not going to give you a dime." And with that, the Commissioner stood and prepared to leave the room, depriving Andy of the pleasure of being the first to leave.

Andy was nonplussed at first but recovered his senses enough to remember one final task.

"Commissioner," he said. "I almost forgot. I was asked to give you this envelope."

The Commissioner gave Andy a quizzical look, but he took the proffered envelope, then he turned and stalked out of the room.

"Well," said Stephenson with distinct irony, "I thought that went well. What the hell was that envelope? I don't want any *ex parte* communication with my client."

"Mark," Andy retorted, "I honestly have no idea what is in that envelope, and I can assure you that it's not from me, either as the complainant or as the complainant's counsel. It's something I was asked to pass along, and I don't even know if it has anything to do with this case. Now, don't bother calling me again until you have something to put on the table. And failing that, I'll see you in court."

Andy grabbed his briefcase and followed the Commissioner's path to the internal elevator and thence through reception and out of the building.

"Fuck," Mark muttered to himself. The bravado he had laid on in front of his client notwithstanding, he was not at all sure that one or more of Dennum's latest arguments would not carry the day. And if it came to that, he knew that this informal number Andy had stated was not binding in any way. Legally, it did not exist. Best get ready.

The Commissioner had never forgotten the lessons he'd learned during his years in the Senate. One of the most useful of those was knowing when to take out the trash, the politicians' term for releasing bad news, which they invariably did around six o'clock on Friday evenings in the hope it would escape notice in the more limited weekend news coverage. So it was that, just before dark on this particular Friday evening, the Baseball office issued a press release. It was brief and to the point.

The Commissioner of Baseball is pleased to announce an agreement in principle with Andrew Dennum under which Mr. Dennum will terminate his pending legal action against the game arising from a 1914 contract which he has sought, at this late date, to enforce, and will surrender his claims against the sport. In exchange, Major League Baseball agrees to compensate Mr. Dennum in the amount of fourteen and one half million dollars, plus expenses and court costs. At its own initiative, Baseball is also committing to issue local development grants totaling one million dollars each to the cities of Kansas City and Oakland to support youth baseball activities. We'll be working with our teams and the local governments in both areas to iron out the details. Finally, and consistent with its belated recognition of the Major League status of the Negro Leagues, Baseball will be providing a gift in the amount of fourteen and one half million dollars to the Negro Leagues Baseball Museum in Kansas City. Our feeling was that if Mr. Dennum was entitled to compensation for his long-ago contract, then we ought to provide a like amount to support an appreciation of baseball in Kansas City, the one place most directly affected by the terms of that century-old agreement, and we thought this was the best way to do that.

"Andy, congratulations! You did it!" It was his father on the phone. "Did what, Dad? What are you talking about?"

"The settlement, son. Of *course* I'm talking about the settlement. What did you think I was calling about?"

"I'm sorry, Dad. What settlement? I have no idea what you're talking about."

"I just saw it on the news. You settled your case. Were you not supposed to tell anyone until they announced it? You could have told us!"

"Dad, I can honestly say, if I settled that case, I'm the last one to know about it. No one has told me."

"Well, how can that be? Turn on the news, look it up online, do something! They said they're giving you a lot of money. And they didn't tell you?"

"Okay, okay. Calm down. If it will make you happy, I'll see if I can find anything online. You're probably just misreading a story, or some idiot reporter is making one up. I was just there talking with the Commissioner, and believe me when I tell you, there is no settlement happening. If anything, we are probably further away from that than ever."

"Andy, they quoted the Commissioner in the story. Something about a press release. Do me a favor. Just get on your computer or something and take a look."

"Okay. I will. I'll call you back later."

Andy turned on his computer and went to one of the sports news websites, and sure enough, there was the text of the Commissioner's release. And his father was right. It said Andy had struck a deal. Reading the release, he was struck by two things in particular. First, the number was right. It was the same number he had mentioned in the discussion in Stephenson's office. And second, the Commissioner must have been watching his interview on *Beat on Sports*, because this so-called settlement included all of the charitable initiatives he had indicated that he planned to undertake with the money and in the precise detail he had spelled out. The only difference was that the Commissioner claimed credit for all of those charitable acts. Son of a bitch.

Before he could digest the news and consider its implications, the phone rang again. *Dad probably can't wait any longer*, he thought. But when he looked at his caller ID, it showed a New York number he couldn't quite place.

"This is Andrew Dennum. Who's calling?"

"Andy, it's Mark Stephenson. I just saw the news—I assume you've seen it—and I wanted to let you know that I didn't know anything about this. And that's the truth. My client has gone rogue, and I'm at a loss. I am so sorry about this. Obviously, I plan to resign from the case. But I wanted to talk to you first to assure you that I am as shocked as you are."

Andy considered that for a moment. "Well, Mark," he said at last, "I have to say it has come as a pretty big surprise. I literally just saw the news, and I haven't had even a minute to think about it. At one level, of course, it's pretty satisfying, and it does accord with what we discussed— and the Commissioner pretty clearly rejected. On the other hand, it's not really an agreement. And the way your client has gone about it, well, he's put me in a corner. All of a sudden, he's trying to do all these charitable things, and if I don't go along, I look like the villain. That sucks."

"Yes, yes, I can see that it does. But you do have to hand it to the old goat. He's no amateur. You can see why he was such a power in the Senate before he moved over to baseball."

"Listen, Mark. I understand why you want to get out of this thing. I'd do the same thing if I were in your situation. But could you hold off for a day or two? Let me have a chance to think about this. If I do decide to let this little fait accompli stand, I'd much rather work through the details with you than with the next lawyer in line, if you know what I mean."

"Okay, Andy. I can do that. And listen. If I don't get a chance to tell you this later, I want to say that I have been very impressed by the way you've advanced this case, both the legal filings and the . . . ah . . . extracurriculars. You have a great future ahead in law. When this is over, I'd like to get together for lunch or something and talk about that."

"That's really flattering, Mark, especially coming from you. Let's get through this cleanup on aisle thirteen and see where we are. As you know, I've spent some time in one of the big firms, and I can't say that ended well."

"Times and circumstances change, Andy. Times and circumstances change. Let's get this thing worked out."

And on that note, one that Andy later realized was likely a double entendre, they ended the conversation.

The Commissioner took the envelope out of his pocket, looked again at the FCI stamp over the seal, opened it again, and read the note one last time. It was classic CI—no wasted words, just their long-standing personal code for communicating that it was time to walk away from some challenge. The note was unsigned, the message a simple one:

He put a match to it and tossed it into the can beside his desk.

The Box Score

Acknowledgments

That Andy Dennum has chosen to return to the Borough of Mendham in northern New Jersey is no accident. Andy may be a fictional character, but there is nothing fictional about the welcoming nature of Mendham and its residents. Particular thanks go once again to Pat Serrano, without whose friendship I might never have discovered this special place. And thanks as well to Mayor Christine Glassner; to Bob Diffin, Greg Bock, Heather Holzwarth, and Tony Sarno of the Mendham Business Association; and to Bill Westhoven, Pat Robinson, John Rollins, and everyone else who made my wife, Amy, and me feel at home when we visited. Last, a call out to Tony Sarno and Lisa Durso of Dante's Restaurant. Oh, what those people can do with fresh tomatoes and an old family recipe.

I particularly want to thank singer-songwriter John Gorka for permission to quote from his tongue-in-cheek anthem to his home state, "I'm From New Jersey." I am not from New Jersey, but I am a big Gorka fan. Thanks, too, to John's representative, David Tamulevich, for facilitating use of the quotation.

I also want to express my appreciation to publisher Lawrence Knorr, who saw the potential in the book, to my editor, Sarah Peachey, who made it better, to Crystal Devine, who made it look like a book, and to Taylor Berger-Knorr and the rest of the staff at Sunbury Press. It is always a pleasure to work with people who know what they are doing.

Finally, and as always, thanks to my patient wife (and valued editor), Amy, who was undoubtedly saddened to see yet another writing project reach its end, thus leaving me free to pester her.

Notes

<table>
<tr><td>**Pg.**</td><td>Note</td></tr>
</table>

xi   "Professionalism—pay for play"—For a thorough discussion of this transition from amateurism to professionalism with a particular emphasis on baseball as a club sport, see Gilbert, passim.

xi   "The National League of Professional Baseball Clubs"—For brief but more extensive histories of the National, American, and Federal Leagues, see https://en.wikipedia.org/wiki/National_League; https://en.wikipedia.org/wiki/American_League; and https://en.wikipedia.org/wiki/Federal_League, respectively, all found online, December 30, 2020.

2   "Both sides must understand"—These words were actually spoken in court during the January 23, 1915, hearing. See, for example, Pietrusza, p. 156.

6   "Old Mr. Spalding"—See Ross, p. 38.

9   "the Brooklyn Tip-Tops"—Owners and managing partners of the several teams in the Federal League as of 1914 were found in Wiggins, passim.

10   "The president of the club"—The leadership and representation of the Kansas City Packers are found in Grow, pp. 359–371, passim.

14   "Teach you to get hooked up"—To appreciate Ward's role in this rebel league, see Wiggins, passim, but especially pages 51–134.

16   "Haskell County, Kansas"—While several hypotheses have been offered regarding the geographic origin of the 1918 influenza pandemic, ranging from areas of China to a British military post in France, recent analysis suggests that the virus actually first appeared in Haskell County, an isolated livestock-raising area in the southwest corner of Kansas, in January 1918. As chronicled by a local physician, numerous patients developed debilitating symptoms during January and February, then began to die. At the same time, local enlistees and draftees were being funneled through a training center at Camp Funston, near Junction City, Kansas, which emerged as a key vector for transmission of the disease to other troops as the trainees went on to their wartime assignments. See Barry, passim. See also, Adler, passim; and Berry, passim.

17   "The Federals are trying to buy"—This list is compiled from several sources, principal among them Wiggins, pp. 173, passim.

19   "Speaking from bitter experience"—For a treatment of the National League's legal counterattack against the Players League rebellion in 1890, see Ross, pp. 124–125.

20   "One is George Johnson"—Wiggins, pp. 74–78.

20   "Hal Chase is another"—Wiggins, pp. 128–134.

20   "I like Armando Marsans"—Wiggins, pp. 125–127.

21   "the last one on my list, is Lee Magee"—Details of the divorce allegation were found online, January 11, 2021, at https://en.wikipedia.org/wiki/Lee_Magee.

22   "It was the biggest and grandest"—See the description of the hotel during that period at https://www.arlingtonhotel.com/history/, found online, January 15, 2021.

26   "longer and richer profile"—This profile, accompanied by the text of the book itself, is available through the Online Library of Liberty, found online January 15, 2021, at http://files.libertyfund.org/files/680/Zane_0027.pdf.

29   "But there's this other guy"—For a thumbnail sketch of Mr. Shannon and his rivalry with the Pendergast machine, see https://pendergastkc.org/article/biography/joseph-b-shannon, found online January 15, 2021.

30   "Zane was apparently mentioned"—See Grow, p. 363 et passim.

31   The "legal" documents reproduced here and on page 44 are purely fictional. No such agreements are known to have existed.

52   "I'm from New Jersey"—This partial lyric from the song "I'm From New Jersey," reprinted with permission of the artist and composer, John Gorka.

62   "His presentation touched on"—A description of the Senior Resource Center and its programs as of January 2021 was found online at http://www.srcnj.org.

72   "a family history of the Cartiers"—The books cited here are those by Brickell; Lind; Akerman and Karrow; Harris; and the four titles by Edward R. Tufte, all of which included in the bibliography.

72   "She opened the book"—To pages 90–91, where this graphic is found.

83   "I am more or less learning on the fly"—The probate rules, processes, and records vary from one state to another, and have evolved over time—certainly over the last century or more. A general overview of the process and associated terms was found on February 1, 2021, at https://www.familysearch.org/wiki/en/U.S._Probate_Records_Class_Handout. A series of links to state-specific handling of probate was found on the same date at https://www.familysearch.org/wiki/en/United_States_Probate_Records. Also, some estates never pass through probate. The author is not an attorney and claims no expertise in these matters, so the reader should not attach great significance to the specifics of any of the descriptions here or elsewhere in the book. Dramatic license has been employed where necessary to advance the story.

83   "the default distribution of assets"—For a summary of current Kansas law on intestate succession see https://www.nolo.com/legal-encyclopedia/intestate-succession-kansas.html, found online February 1, 2021.

86 "the most deadly cluster of such storms"—For details of the 1985 tornado outbreak in Pennsylvania prepared by the University of Chicago and the National Weather Service, including satellite photography of the aftermath, see https://www.weather.gov/media/cle/Wx_Events/85outbreak/storm_data.pdf, found online, November 17, 2022.

90 "It's an adage as old"—As it turns out, not quite. According to one source, the earliest usage of an equivalent phrase came in Philadelphia in 1809. Found online February 1, 2021, at https://literarydevices.net/a-man-who-is-his-own-lawyer-has-a-fool-for-a-client/.

93 "The only wrinkle he could see"—On the consolidation of the leagues into Major League Baseball, see McCue, p. 138.

93 "Andy knew that two separate franchises"—For a thorough historical examination of expansion and team movements in the American League, including the industry politics of the various moves involving Kansas City, see McCue, especially pages 25–26, 75–88, et passim. For insights into the operations of the Athletics franchise after it had moved to Oakland, see Lewis.

101 "I think you need to study"—The asymmetrical tactics Sajak is referencing are summarized in Manheim, passim. For an example of the conceptual development of such strategies in a military context, see Arquilla and Ronfeldt, eds. Jacobsen's study of the history of the Defense Advanced Research Projects Agency (DARPA) provides still broader historical context, tracing the challenge forward from the period of the Vietnam War.

109 The most recent *Forbes* listing of such values was found online November 17, 2022, at https://www.forbes.com/sites/mikeozanian/2022/03/24/baseballs-most-valuable-teams-2022-yankees-hit-6-billion-as-new-cba-creates-new-revenue-streams/

130 "his good friend"—Veeck, p. 25.

177 "He had cited what he said"—For a summary of this rule and its applications, see https://lawshelf.com/coursewarecontentview/rule-against-perpetuities/, found online February 21, 2021.

177 "He cited a 1998 case"—The case in question is *Jesperson v. Minnesota Mining and Manufacturing Company*, 700 NE 2d 1014, Illinois Supreme Court 1998. A summary of the case was found online, February 21, 2021, at https://scholar.google.com/scholar_case?case=8163416033162334075&q=rico+industries+tlc&hl=en&as_sdt=4,14.

179 "If the facts are against you"—This turn of phrase and others like it have been attributed to a variety of sources over the years. For a summary of these attributions, see https://quoteinvestigator.com/2010/07/04/legal-adage/, found online February 21, 2021.

186 "Andy arrived at the Federal Correctional Institute"—For a photo of the FCI Otisville campus and information about the facility, see https://www.inmateaid.com/prisons/federal-correctional-institution-fci-otisville, found online November 18, 2022.

Sources Consulted

Adler, Eric. "A coronavirus lesson? How KC's response to 1918 flu pandemic caused needless death," *The Kansas City Star*, March 15, 2020, found online, January 10, 2021, at https://www.kansascity.com/news/business/health-care/article241058181.html.

Akerman, James R. and Robert W. Karrow, Jr., eds. *Maps: Finding Our Place in the World*. Chicago: University of Chicago Press, 2007.

Arquilla, John, and David Ronfeldt, eds. *Networks and Netwars: The Future of Terror, Crime, and Militancy*. Santa Monica, CA: RAND, 2001.

Barry, John M. "The site of origin of the 1918 influenza pandemic and its public health implications," *Journal of Translational Medicine* 2(1):3. 20 Jan 2004, doi:10.1186/1479-5876-2-3, found online at https://www.ncbi.nlm.nih.gov/pmc/articles/PMC340389/, January 10, 2021.

Berry, Susan Debra Sykes. *Politics and Pandemic in 1918 Kansas City*. Masters Thesis, University of Missouri-Kansas City, 2010. Found online, January 10, 2021, at https://mospace.umsystem.edu/xmlui/bitstream/handle/10355/7521/SykesBerryThesisPolPan.pdf?sequence=1.

Bradbury, J.C. *The Baseball Economist: The Real Game Exposed*. New York: Penguin, 2007.

Brickell, Francesca Cartier. *The Cartiers: The Untold Story of the Family Behind the Jewelry Empire*. New York: Ballantine, 2019.

Edmonds, Ed and Frank G. Houdek. *Baseball Meets the Law: A Chronology of Decisions, Statutes and Other Legal Events*. Jefferson, NC: McFarland & Company, 2017.

Gilbert, Thomas W. *How Baseball Happened: Outrageous Lies Exposed! The True Story Revealed*. Boston: David R. Godine, Publisher, 2020.

Grow, Nathaniel. "Insolvent Professional Sports Teams: A Historical Case Study," *Lewis & Clark Law Review*, 18:2 (August 2014), pp. 345-384, found online, January 15, 2021, at https://law.lclark.edu/live/files/17804-lcb182art2growfinalpdf.

Harris, Robert L. *Information Graphics: A Comprehensive Illustrated reference*. New York: Oxford University Press, 1999.

Jacobsen, Annie. *The Pentagon's Brain: An Uncensored History of DARPA, America's Top Secret Military Research Agency*. New York: Little Brown, 2015.

Levitt, Daniel R. *The Battle That Forged Modern Baseball: The Federal League Challenge and Its Legacy*. Lanham, MD: Ivan R. Dee, 2012.

Lewis, Michael. *Moneyball: The Art of Winning an Unfair Game*. New York: W.W. Norton, 2004.

Lind, Carla. *The Wright Style: Recreating the Spirit of Frank Lloyd Wright*. New York: Simon & Schuster, 1992.

Manheim, Jarol B. *Strategy in Information and Influence Campaigns: How Policy Advocates, Social Movements, Insurgent Groups, Corporations, Governments and Others Get What They Want*. New York: Routledge, 2011.

McCue, Andy. *Stumbling Around the Bases: The American League's Mismanagement in the Expansion Eras*. Lincoln: University of Nebraska Press, 2022.

Pessah, Jon. *The Game: Inside the Secret World of Major League Baseball's Power Brokers*. New York: Little Brown, 2015.

Pietrusza, David. *Judge and Jury: The Life and Times of Judge Kenesaw Mountain Landis*. South Bend, IN: Diamond Communications, Inc., 1998.

Ross, Robert B. *The Great Baseball Revolt: The Rise and Fall of the 1890 Players League*. Lincoln: University of Nebraska Press, 2016.

Sun Tzu. *The Art of War: The New Translation by J.H. Huang*. New York: William Morrow, 1993.

Tufte, Edward R. *The Visual Display of Quantitative Information*. Cheshire, CT: Graphics Press, 1983.

———. *Envisioning Information*. Cheshire, CT: Graphics Press, 1990.

———. *Visual Explanations: Images and Quantities, Evidence and Narrative*. Cheshire, CT: Graphics Press, 1997.

———. *Beautiful Evidence*. Cheshire, CT: Graphics Press, 2006.

Veeck, Bill, with Ed Linn. *Veeck—as in Wreck*. Chicago: University of Chicago Press, 2001.

Wiggins, Robert Peyton. *The Federal League of Base Ball Clubs: The History of an Outlaw Major League, 1914–1915*. Jefferson, NC: McFarland & Company, 2009.

About the Author

J.B. Manheim is Professor Emeritus at The George Washington University, where he developed the world's first degree-granting program in political communication and was later founding director of the School of Media & Public Affairs. In 1995 he was named Professor of the Year for the District of Columbia. He learned his love of baseball watching Dizzy Dean on the Game of the Week and huddling with his grandfather for warmth on July nights at The Mistake By The Lake, AKA, Cleveland Municipal Stadium, and renewed it when the National Pastime finally returned to the Nation's Capital. Manheim brings to life his expertise in propaganda and strategic communication through his fictional stories of baseball behind the scenes. His writing will lead you to question whether what you think you know about the history of the game and about the powers who control it is real, or whether it's just a carefully nurtured product of lies, deceptions, misdirection, and propaganda. JB Manheim is a member of the Society for American Baseball Research and the Internet Baseball Writers Association of America.

Printed in the USA
CPSIA information can be obtained
at www.ICGtesting.com
CBHW020958210524
8878CB00009B/69